Books by John Triptych

Wrath of the Old Gods series (in chronological order)

The Glooming

Pagan Apocalypse

Canticum Tenebris

The Fomorians

A World Darkly

Eye of Balor

Mortuorum Luctum

Expatriate Underworld series

The Opener

The Loader

Dying World series

Seas of Dust

City of Delusions

The Amoralist series

A Man of Leisure

Savage Wanderings

The Loader

Expatriate Underworld Book II

John Triptych

ISBN (soft cover) 978-621-95332-6-3

J Triptych Publishing

To the memories of JC and DG.
Remembering the good times, and leaving out all the
rest.

Author's note:

Dear reader, I would like to thank you for purchasing this book. As a self-published author, I incur all the costs of producing this novel so your feedback means a lot to me. If you wouldn't mind, could you please take a few minutes and post a review of this online and let others know what you think of it?

As I'm sure you're aware, the more reviews I get, the better my future sales would be and therefore my financial incentive to produce more books for your enjoyment increases. I am very happy to read any comments and questions and I am willing to respond to you personally as quickly as I can. My email is jtriptych@gmail.com if you wish to contact me directly. Again, thank you and I hope you enjoy reading this book as much as I enjoyed writing it!

Please join my exclusive mailing list! You will get the latest news on my upcoming works and special discounts. Subscription is FREE and you get lots of FREE books! Just copy and paste this link to your browser: http://eepurl.com/bK-xGn

Oh, what a wicked world it is that

drives a man to sin.

— Mario Puzo

1.

It was early afternoon when we made the turn into the driveway of the Thai Regency Hotel in downtown Bangkok. There were already five cars ahead of us, so I leaned back and relaxed for a bit. We were still pretty early, but when it came to meeting local big shots, especially the biggest one of them all, I wanted to make sure we wouldn't keep them waiting. I could see at least three uniformed security guards checking the car trunks and using a mirror attached to a metal pole to check underneath the vehicles ahead of us. There had been rumors of terror attacks by separatists from the south, so the whole city was somewhat tense.

Elliot Cohen was sitting on the front passenger seat. At twenty-seven, he was the youngest loader I had on the team, and he was also the best. "We could have just walked over here, the office isn't that far," he said as he looked out past the windshield.

I tapped my fingers on the steering wheel of the Ford SUV. In Thailand, the driver's side was on the right of the car's interior, even though the country had never been part of the British Empire. It was something that always made me wonder about this strange land. "You want to walk around in this humidity? We'd be sweating like pigs by the time we got over here."

Elliot laughed. "You're right, Don. I guess I still have to get used to the nuances of this place."

I shook my head slightly as I smiled at him. "You've been here, what? Just a few months and already you might have just landed the biggest whale in the history of this industry. You're a winner, kid."

He grinned as he looked away. "Nah, I just got lucky."

"That reminds me, did you talk to him today?"

"I talked to him just yesterday, so no need to call him again for another couple of days, at least," he said. "Everything's good so far. If this plan of yours works, then I might just decide to retire out here."

I slapped the top of his right knee. "That's the spirit, kid. You've only worked with my crew for a short while, but you've already surpassed your quota for the year. You keep this up, you'll be opening your own office soon."

"I don't know why you're always calling me a 'kid', Don," he said. "You're not even thirty yet and only a couple years older than me, but you're making yourself out like an old man already. What's up with that?"

I noticed that the driver of the silver Jaguar in front of us seemed pretty agitated. He was arguing with the hotel guards. It seemed that he was in a hurry, but the guards were pretty slow with regards to checking out his vehicle. "Every day in this business is like a year working in another industry, Elliot. So much shit just happens and it happens so quickly. It's unreal."

As a gap opened up in front of the Jaguar, it suddenly accelerated and drove down towards the underground parking entrance at the side of the hotel. One of the guards, who had been holding the mirrored pole underneath the car, wasn't able to react in time as the Jaguar's rear right wheel smashed the mirror into bits. Another car behind us honked their horn so I drove into the spot where the Jaguar had once been, making sure the wheels of my own vehicle didn't drive over the broken glass.

The group of guards looked at each other as they realized they were unable to check underneath my car. They started arguing for about a minute before the car behind us let out another angry blast of its horn. Either they didn't have a spare mirror, or whoever was in the car behind me was a big kahuna, so they just waved me to go ahead and drive on to the side of the lobby entrance.

Elliot was in stitches as he could barely control his laughter. "Holy shit, this country is something else!"

I gave my car keys to the valet as we walked through the entrance and into the cool, air conditioned reception area. It had been a few months since I had been back here and they definitely changed the décor of the place. Gone were the multi-colored Chinese paper lanterns that once adorned the high ceiling of the hotel lobby. Two gigantic post-modern chandeliers were situated at both ends of the massive hall, their candelabras shaped like glass shards. Black Italian leather sofas and clear glass tables had replaced the traditional Chinese embroidered couches and chairs. Even the staff now had different uniforms as they had switched to wearing business suits. The whole place looked like the entrance to a corporation. What didn't change were the massive thirty foot tall glass walls along the side of the ground floor that brought in much needed illumination. The outside gardens and the Olympic sized swimming pool could be observed from where we were.

Elliot followed my lead as we walked past the reception desk and made our way to the middle of the lobby area. Businessmen and tourists were lounging around while having their afternoon tea. A few foreign idiots were waving their stick mounted cameras around as they took selfies with each other as a testament to their shallow, empty narcissism. We found a vacant set of couches and chairs in the middle of the place facing each other, and sat down side by side. I was wearing a buttoned long-sleeved shirt and casual slacks while Elliot had his full office attire on.

A smiling waitress a dark blue blazer approached us. Like all hotel workers, her English was better than average. "Would you like to order anything, sir?"

I glanced around and noticed a cardboard menu that was sitting on a table beside the couch and picked it up. "Could you give us a minute, please?"

Elliot looked up at her and smiled back. "Do you have the drinks menu by any chance?"

The waitress nodded as she started to walk away. "Of course, sir. I'll be right back."

I looked at him and shook my head while giving him the

menu I was holding. "Don't order any drinks. Not unless the guy we're meeting orders it first and offers you one."

Elliot's eyebrows shot up. "Oh, sorry about that," he said to me as the waitress came back with the drinks menu. "Can I just have a cappuccino instead, please."

I looked up at her. "Just a bottled water for me, thanks."

The waitress nodded and then walked away to fetch our drinks.

"Sorry, I just keep forgetting," Elliot said as he rubbed his hands together. "I still feel like I'm a tourist here sometimes."

"Was this your first time out of the country?"

"Yeah," he said. "Born and bred in Boston."

"How did you get into this crazy business of ours, anyway?"

"Oh, Saul Silver is my uncle," he said. "I didn't want to stay in college because my debts were piling up and he just happened to drop by for a family visit. When I told him that, he suggested I go over and work here."

I nodded as the waitress came back and placed our beverages on the glass table in front of us. Saul Silver was a legend in the industry. He was a guy who would stay on the phone all day, not even getting up to go to the bathroom. "You're a natural. You were barely a few months in as an opener and then now you're a loader. I've listened to your phone conversations and you can convince the clients to do anything. I guess the sales talent runs in your family," I said. "Your uncle is successful because he works harder than anybody else, but you seem to do it without any kind of effort. You just make it look so easy."

Elliot smiled again as he stirred his cappuccino. "Thanks, but you seem to be buttering me up for something. Is that why you asked me to join you in this meeting? I thought my job was just to stay on the phone and load up the paid clients?"

"You think I pirated you away from that Singaporean just to make you a loader? I got plans for you, kid," I said as I sipped on the water bottle. "Loading is the easiest job in the world. Our openers tell lies to get the client to send us some money. Once the sucker bites, we know we got him so we send them over to the loader. When the loader steps in, he tells an even bigger lie, and gets the client to come in for even more money. But it's all so freaking easy because the client has already paid- he's proven that he trusts us. Once the fish bites on the hook the first time, it's trapped. Now all the loader has to do is to take him for everything he's got, every single penny. Keep taking it as long as the client pays, and he will keep on paying since he's now in the loop. Keep on going until we get it all."

"Don, I know all that already," he said. "So what's your point exactly?"

I winked at him. "You haven't been listening. Loading is easy. Anybody can do it, that's why owners usually just give the position over to their friends, not to the top openers. The best openers stay in their position, that's why your uncle Saul will never be a loader, because everybody knows he's better off as an opener- he is simply too valuable to be promoted. Now in your case, I've been looking for someone to take over my position as head of Doc Bull's loading office. That's where you come in."

Elliot tilted his head back and laughed. "You want me to take over your position?"

I nodded. "That's why I brought you along with me. You'll be meeting the guy who runs all the banking for us in this country. His name is Mr. Panupong. All the owners pay him a percentage to make sure the money goes through the bank accounts he controls and nothing gets traced back to us. He's the reason why nobody in this industry ever gets caught unless they cross him."

His thick eyebrows furrowed. "Wait a minute, I thought all our banking goes through Malaysia? That's what we tell all of our clients."

"Doc's people has been handling our banking so far," I said. "But I don't want him to get involved with this whale of yours."

Elliot grinned from ear to ear. "Oh, I get it now! You don't want Doc to know about this deal even though he's our boss. But ...uh, aren't you married to his daughter though?"

Paul "Doc" Bull was the man behind our entire operation. I was running the whole business for him since I happened to be his daughter's, Jessica, husband. Everybody called him Doc because he had a doctorate in education. He was also the most ruthless man I ever met. Doc was the one person I didn't want involved in this potential deal. This was going to be my money, and I didn't want his grubby hands in any part of it. "You let me deal with Doc," I said. "And

I'll promise you that your commission on this will be bigger than your usual share."

He started tapping his feet on the floor. "This is getting me excited, Don. Leopardi said he would go in for at least four million. How much will my percentage be then?"

"We normally give out ten," I said. "How does fifteen percent suit you?"

His eyes lit up. "Six hundred grand? Holy shit! If I can get him for more, can I have a higher percentage?"

I smirked. "I'll take it under advisement. I'm pretty sure we could work something out."

Elliot could barely contain himself. He was fidgeting with excitement. "Okay, I'll see what I can do. I won't let you down on this. I feel like calling him right now and getting this deal done."

"See that you don't let me down," I said. "We both got a lot riding on this. I want to be free from Doc's influence once and for all. The moment this load is done, I'll be my own boss. Bob Duffy- the manager who runs our opener team, is loyal to me. Once I got a dependable loader by my side, then the sky's the limit for all of us."

"I appreciate your faith in me," Elliot said. "So if all is said and done, are you sure there won't be any fallout between you and Doc? I don't want to get caught in the crossfire, if you know what I mean."

"Once I get Panupong to agree, there's nothing Doc can do about it," I said. "I'm also married to his daughter, so he can't take it out on me personally either. My wife is loyal to me."

"How sure are you that this banking guy is gonna take this offer? Didn't he try to have you killed the last time you tried to do business with him?"

I looked down at the shiny marble flooring. "The last time, I kinda screwed up when I tried to deal with him. That was my fault. But now we're on the level- and in the end, Panupong is a businessman. No way is he going to turn down a multi-million dollar opportunity like this."

From the corner of my eye, I noticed a fleet of black Mercedes-Benz sedans pulling up beside the lobby entrance. Four very fit Thai men wearing black business suits and sunglasses came out and walked through the glass doors. Standing in between them was a squat, brown skinned man with a bowl cut. His thick, steel-rimmed glasses drooped over his flat nose and he had to continually adjust the temples in order to keep them from falling off. He was smiling as he slowly made his way into the lobby area while he constantly adjusted his dark blue, pin-striped three piece suit to hide away any wrinkles. A very beautiful young Thai woman dressed in business attire walked beside him. Yup, it was Panupong and his entourage alright.

There was a pair of tourists sitting by a sofa directly beside us as they sipped their thick iced coffees. Panupong's bodyguards hovered over them like a pack of hyenas as they gestured at them to leave. It was an old couple, the man wore a golf shirt and shorts that exposed his pale, skinny legs, while the woman wore a red sleeveless blouse with a hat full of fake flowers on her head. The old man got up and tried to protest, but the grinning hotel manager immediately ran over, clasped his hands in a prayer-like fashion and bowed, using the universal Thai greeting of wai as he tried his best to calm everybody down. The old woman realized her hubby was out of his league as she took him by the elbow, and they nervously made their way towards the reception area, the manager right behind them as he continued to apologize profusely.

Elliot and I both stood up as Panupong and the woman greeted us with the wai. All of us clasped our hands together and bowed to each other. Panupong's bodyguards stood in a semi-circle around him as they kept their eyes focused at the other people in the lobby.

Panupong flashed a perfect smile with his unnaturally white teeth. "Mr. Don, it is nice to see you again."

"Likewise, Mr. Panupong," I said as I smiled back before gesturing over to my colleague. "This is my top loader, Elliot Cohen."

Elliot clasped his hands together and did the Thai greeting for the second time. "Hello, sir."

Panupong gestured at the young lady. "This is my personal secretary, Sanoh."

I smiled, giving her a slight bow. "Ms. Sanoh."

"Mr. Rouse, we talked over the phone a few times before," Sanoh said in perfect English, as opposed to her boss. "It is an honor to finally meet you."

I nodded. "Likewise."

Panupong gestured at the couches. "Let us sit, please."

So we did. Less than a minute later, a waiter approached us carrying a tray of four tall glasses with a dark green liquid in them. I remembered being served these flowery drinks when I first met Panupong over at his karaoke club. They were thick, syrupy fruit juices that tasted like a combination of flowers and aloe. Sanoh gestured at the menu as she made a short conversation to the waiter in Thai. From my limited knowledge of the language, it seemed like she was ordering some snacks to go with the drinks.

Sanoh smiled slightly at us as the waiter left with her order. "Please forgive us, for Mr. Panupong hasn't eaten his lunch yet and he wanted to order something right away. Can we get you gentlemen something to eat as well?"

Elliot was about to say something before he noticed my glance. Instead he just smiled and shook his head. "We're good, thanks."

"So, Mr. Don," Panupong said. His broken English was typical for locals who only needed to use it sporadically. "We are here for a big meeting, yes? You have good proposal for me?"

I smiled as I nodded my head. "Yes, Mr. Panupong. The reason why I wanted to meet with you in person is because Elliot here is about to close a very large transaction, and we need your banking expertise to make sure that the money flows smoothly, and without any problems."

"I do recall, as per your standard business arrangement with the other bankers," Sanoh said. "All of your monetary transactions actually goes through Malaysia and the Philippines, does it not?"

"Yes," I said as I placed my hands on the sofa. "Our current arrangement is through Malaysia and our expenses here does go through your own networks as well."

"I take only small percentage of your money coming here because it is already cleaned by Malaysia," Panupong said.

"Exactly," I said. "That's why I want to make a slight change. We have a very big deal going through and I do not want it to go through Malaysia this time. If we can come to an agreement, I would like the funds to be transferred over here and converted into cash, at which time it will be delivered to me personally. I would also request we keep this confidential so that only the four of us knows about it."

Panupong looked into my eyes. His interest was piqued. "How much is payment?"

Elliot realized it was now his turn to speak. "The minimum is going to be four million, but I think I can probably double it to eight. In dollars, of course."

Panupong's eyes began to gleam. This would be the largest transaction ever if they pulled it off. "One payment only?"

Elliot looked at me. The banking was my responsibility. "The client says he can make a single transfer," I said. "But it can be two bank transfers, if that's okay with you. Will that be a problem?"

Panupong turned his head to look at his secretary. Sanoh was lost in thought for a brief moment, then she looked at me and smirked. "I think we can handle that transaction. How sure are you that this deal will go through?"

"We're almost there," Elliot said. "Just a few things to iron out, but I'm pretty sure he's on board for a few million, at least."

Two waiters wearing blue sport coats walked over to us carrying several trays of covered food. The bodyguards glanced at them briefly before turning away to look at the people across the room. Panupong looked up and smiled. "Very fast food today," he said as he unbuttoned his top coat.

I smiled as well while I looked up at the waiters while they began to place their trays on the glass table between us. It was the moment when I noticed that one of the attendants serving us had a familiar face. He was clearly a local Thai man with deep brown skin, but he had a pale scar that ran from his forehead all the way down to his chin. A jumble of memories started coming back at me. This guy was awfully familiar, but I just couldn't remember the exact circumstances as to...

Then it hit me. The waiter hovering above me was the same guy who had pursued me a year ago. He was some sort of hit man and he had killed an enemy of mine right in front of me. There was no mistaking it, it was definitely him. I immediately tensed up as I partially raised myself up from the sofa.

The man with the scar sensed my alertness as he reached into his sport coat and pulled out a stubby black Glock pistol. In less than two seconds, he pivoted as he fired two shots each at the bodyguards standing behind him. The sounds of gunfire at this range was deafening as my ears immediately reverberated from the extremely loud, firecracker-like noises. The other waiter also pulled out his own handgun, then he fired at the two other bodyguards near the opposite side of the couches. I was already halfway up so by the time I stood fully upright, all four bodyguards were down.

Panupong's smile disappeared as he too began to stand up. It seemed that he recognized the assassin as well while raising his hands. The man with the scar fired two quick shots into his chest and then a third shot right between his eyes. Panupong slumped back into the sofa. The second shooter was in less than two feet from me and I had to get away from him. I twisted to my side and tried to hurdle over the sofa behind me. Elliot started pushing his legs up and the entire sofa inched backwards while he too tried to get up. The second waiter reacted, he turned and fired at our direction and Elliot took a shot in his neck. My protégé finally stood up with both his hands clutched at the gaping wound in his throat, blood pouring down to his trousers. Elliot was trying to say something, but all he could muster was a loud gurgle. I was already trying to leap over the couch I had been sitting on when I saw the man with the scar shoot Sanoh in her forehead.

I must have lost my footing as I tried to get away. I tripped over the top of the couch and fell backwards, landing on my back on the marble floor behind it. The second hit man loomed over me as he stood up on the sofa and aimed the pistol directly at my face. An icy chill poured down my body. My whole life began to flash before my eyes. This was it. I held out my hand, palm forward, hoping that the bullet would magically stop in the air somehow.

Just as he was about to pull the trigger, the second

waiter's face jerked sideways when a bullet tore into his right cheek. My luck held since the first shooter was looking the other way. I twisted my body and got on my knees as I noticed that one of the fallen bodyguards had pulled out his own gun and had fired it at the assailant. I immediately sprinted towards the double doorways leading towards the kitchen, all the while trying to stay low. As I made a backwards glance while swinging the doors open, the last thing I saw was the man with the scar firing several shots to finish off the wounded bodyguard before aiming his gun at me.

A bullet struck the side of the door just as I dove into the kitchen. The place was a stainless steel factory of burners, ovens and ventilation ducts. Apron wearing chefs were running back and forth as they screamed at each other in panic. I noticed a few other waiters fearfully crouching down as they took cover behind cabinets and tub-like kitchen sinks. I quickly got back on my feet and started sprinting to what I figured was the back door. As I kept glancing behind me, the double doors swung open and the man with the scar entered, pistol in hand.

I managed to drop down behind a deep fryer just as he fired. The bullet hit the top part of the cooker and ricocheted away, the sound was akin to being inside of a bell tower as the slug bounced around the steel pots and pans. More screams could be heard within the kitchen as the staff reacted to the terror of what was going on in the lobby. I could see the exit just ahead so I stayed low while I ran to it and opened the door. Then another bullet smashed into the wooden paneling of the doorway, just inches from the top of my head as I ran through and started moving quickly along a narrow, half-lit corridor. There was a plump Thai woman sitting on the ground ahead of me, she had her hands over her ears and was screaming hysterically. I didn't lose a single step as I jumped over her and kept on going. At the end of the corridor was a red metal door that said FIRE EXIT. I twisted the steel knob and ran out into the garden area. The crowds of fat tourists and their bawling children continued to hang out near the hotel swimming pool, their moronic obliviousness a stark contrast to the massacre that just happened in the lobby.

2.

My ears were still hearing nothing but a constant ringing noise as I ran across the street before ducking into a narrow alleyway. While I put on my sunglasses to keep a low profile, I kept looking over my shoulder, but it didn't look like the man with the scar was pursuing me. Perhaps he never made it past the kitchen area. The street was narrow and largely deserted as I walked rapidly on the bare concrete. There was an occasional dog turd piled along the sides, and the overhanging roofs above cast long shadows. The air was humid, Bangkok in the summertime was like a giant steam bath and I was already sweating. Thoughts began to swirl in my head as to what had just happened. What I needed to do was to make sure no one was pursuing me, so I kept on moving while I rounded a number of streets until I got to the more touristy spots. From there, I could blend in with the crowd of foreigners so I wouldn't stick out like a sore thumb in an oriental city.

There were a number of shopping malls close by, so I walked inside their air-conditioned interiors for an instant respite from the humidity. As the cool air started to evaporate my sweat, I tried to clear my head in order to think. I walked into a coffee shop, ordered some iced tea and sat down at a corner table so I could see everyone coming through the mall entrance. I took out a handkerchief from my front pants pocket and wiped the sweat off my forehead. The events that happened less than half an hour ago kept replaying itself in my head. Was I in the wrong place at the wrong time back there, or was I one of the targets? Losing my top loader didn't help much either, but I was sure I could find a replacement.

Either way, I needed to act just in case and assume the worst. I took out my smartphone from my shirt pocket and dialed up Lee Hammond's number. Lee was the other loader who worked for us in the office. He had been with me for about six months to the day. The number rang for about ten times before he answered.

Lee's hollow sounding voice was on the other line. It was obvious he had been sleeping when I called him. "Hullo, mate," he said groggily.

"Don't come into the office, Lee," I said tersely.

His tone of voice instantly changed to one of alertness. "Am I being let go?"

I sighed. "No, dude, you ain't fired. It's an emergency. I'll be calling you from a different number in a few hours' time."

"Oh, is it the heat?"

"Something like that," I said. "Either way, do not come in—it might be good for you to take a little holiday, like out of Thailand for awhile."

"Oh, so it's that kind of trouble is it? Right, mate. Let's stay in touch by email, yeah? Might be better."

"Good idea, talk to you later, bye," I said as I cut the line off. Then I started dialing Bob Duffy's number. I always looked at Bob as my mentor, since he showed me how to close deals over the phone when I first started in the business. Old Bob was a laid back hippy from California, and I had rewarded his friendship by making him the manager of my opener room.

"What's up, Don," Bob said as he answered almost immediately. I could hear the sounds of his crew pitching the clients on the other line. "We got two confirmed closes just this minute and I think I was able to turn around one guy who wanted to cancel an order for ten grand. It's shaping up to be a damned fine day, dude."

"Bob, listen to me carefully," I said. "I need you to close the office right now. Get everybody out."

Bob's easygoing demeanor instantly became serious. "Is it a raid?"

"It could be," I said. Anything was possible at this point. "I can't talk to you over this line, I'll be buying a prepaid sim card very soon and I'll call you from that number. I'll send a text first with the words 'black flag', so you'll know it's from me. Have you got enough money to pay all the openers a draw for this week?"

"I do. You'll pay me back, right?"

I nodded, even though he couldn't see me. "Of course. Just get everybody out now and meet them somewhere out in public tonight. Pay them ten thousand each and tell them we will contact them once a new office is up and running."

"What about the office assistants?"

"Give them their salary too. Email me the total amount using my personal email, and I'll wire the money to you by tonight."

"Okay, you got it. I'll talk to you later then. Bye for now, Don."

"Bye bye," I said as I cut off the line. I wasn't sure if I was one of the targets in this hit but I needed to make sure that the business was secure. I quickly went through my contact list and dialed Doc's number.

No answer, just a busy signal. I tried calling him a few more times and still nothing. Something stirred at the back of my head. Doc was my father in law, but I sure as hell didn't trust him. Anyone who was cold blooded enough to have his own office raided just to get rid of a potential rival couldn't be loyal to anything. I nearly got killed trying to find out what had happened to him the last time, when all the while he had orchestrated the entire thing behind the scenes. So it looked like I would have to pay for the office expenses out of my own pocket for now. I still had considerable funds under my control, but I couldn't keep this up for long. At least until I got in touch with him again.

I nearly threw my phone up in the air as it suddenly started ringing. My nerves were still frayed and anything unexpected would jolt me like an electrical surge. I looked at the caller ID on the phone and sighed in relief as I activated it. I was my wife.

"Hi Don," Jessica said. "Mom and I will be taking the fast ferry over to Macao and we're probably gonna stay overnight. If you're coming over by tomorrow, I think it's just better to meet us here rather than in Hong Kong, unless you already bought the ticket, of course."

"Uh, I'm actually not sure if I can make it tomorrow, Jess. Something's come up."

"What? Oh, come on! You want me to carry all the shopping bags all day long? It can't really be that important, can it?"

"I'm afraid it is, Jess," I said. She knew the general gist of the business I was in, but not the nitty-gritty details. "I'll be using another number when I call you again. Best way to contact me in the meantime will be through email or leave me a message using your internet chat app."

Just like the others, the tone of her voice changed, but only slightly. "What kind of trouble are you in, Don?"

"I can't really talk about it right now," I said. "I'll tell you about it later."

"Do you need me to go back there and bail you out or something?"

I laughed a little, if only to reassure her. "No, no, it's nothing like that, Jess. Let's talk again soon, okay?"

"Okay, but if I don't hear from you by tomorrow, I'm going back there."

"Don't worry, you will get a call or email from me," I said. "I'll talk to you later. Love you, babe."

"Love you too, Don, bye bye."

I put the phone back in my pocket as I stood up. At least

my wife was safe in Hong Kong. I went to a nearby phone store and bought two prepaid sim chips with cash. Then I tried Doc's number again but got the same busy tone. A suspicious thought started to grow itself at the back of my mind. Ever since I married his daughter, Doc was always just a phone call away. Now all of a sudden his number was silent, and it was right after the hit on Panupong. Could Doc have had something to do with this? I closed my eyes and absentmindedly shook my head. No. It can't be. I took precautions to make sure that nobody knew about this meeting other than myself, Elliot and Panupong. But even if he knew, why would I be targeted as well? I was his son in law for chrissakes. Did he just try and have me killed for trying to sneak a huge deal past him? This whole thing was crazy.

Dark thoughts continued to etch themselves in my mind as I started walking to the mall exit. As far as I knew, Doc had never had anyone killed before. Then again, this deal I was about to do had the potential to fund my own business and it would make me completely independent from him. Would he go that far just to get his hands on this particular load? Then I remembered Doc telling me a story once, it was back in the time when he started out as an opener. He had called up an old woman because her son, who had made a deal to buy some stocks from him, was killed in an auto accident. Doc called her up every single day and kept badgering her until she sold her house to pay for the stock purchases her son made. But Doc wasn't done. Not long after that, he kept on calling her until she sold all of her possessions, even her late husband's car.

When I asked him about it, he just shrugged. "She was old and she was going to die soon anyway", he had said to me then. "Better to let me have the money since her son and heir was dead too."

I stood along the street corner, my eyes darting around to see if there was anyone suspicious nearby. So far, there was nothing out of the ordinary. A small group of tourists were there by the taxi stand, so I walked over and waited for my turn on the line. I sensed that I couldn't go back to my condominium up in nearby Bangrak, just in case there was someone waiting for me there. A couple of taxis pulled up. The group of tourists got in the first one and I took the other.

I got in the rear passenger seat and closed the door. "Soi Krung Thonburi one."

The driver nodded and we drove off. The cab made a few turns as we got on the ramp and moved across the Phra Pokklao Bridge. There was a sense of déjà vu which hung over me while I looked out of the taxi window. I remembered the time when Jessica and I were making a furious getaway in her dad's car while being chased by the very man with the scar on his face. We had gotten on the wrong side of the road and ended up in the bottom of the Chao Phraya River. It was an incident that still gave me nightmares every now and then.

While I took the prepaid sim chips out from the small plastic bag, my phone was immediately inundated by a stream of texts from the people who worked for me as well as other shop owners that I knew of. A few of them even tried calling, but I just let the phone ring out. It meant that the hit finally made it on the local news. Once Panupong's death hit the airwaves, it was only a matter of time until everybody in the country closed up their shops and moved them to other places, usually to the Philippines or over to Malaysia. I checked all the messages to make sure there wasn't anything important before turning the phone off and replacing the sim chip with the new prepaid number I had with me.

By this time, the taxi made it onto the street that I wanted to go to, so I told the driver to stop, paid him the fare and got out of the car. I walked around a few blocks and kept turning into alleyways to make sure no one was following me. My paranoia satisfied, I crossed a street and walked into the lobby of a nearby condominium. The guard near the reception desk was familiar with who I was, as I gave him a friendly wave on my way to the elevator. Once I was in, I pushed the button to the fourteenth floor while taking off my sunglasses, then folded and placed them in my front shirt pocket as I stared at my own reflection in the mirrored glass. My eyes had a blank, faraway look, no doubt caused by what had happened just a few hours ago. The sudden chime that signified my arrival and the slight whoosh of air as the elevator doors opened snapped me back into reality. I turned around and moved out into the corridor.

I walked down the bare passageway until I stood in front of a white painted door. I knocked three times and waited. A few minutes later, the door opened and a young Thai woman briefly took a look at me before she moved out of the way. She gave a slight smile and gave me the wai greeting as I walked inside.

"Hello, Don," Dang said. She was my girlfriend's older sister. Like all Thais, her full name was convoluted and I gave up trying to remember hers along with the others, but since most of them went by nicknames anyway, that was the name they usually went by. Despite her courteous greeting, I knew she didn't like me. She never did. It was a fact that even though they would always act pleasant when they met up with white foreigners, or farangs as they called them, the Thai people secretly hated anyone outside of their ethnicity. In Dang's case, it was even more personal since she had always thought of me as a lowlife, but in the end, she couldn't do anything since it was my money paying for the rent of this place. I tolerated her since she was the one keeping Ti on the level. When it came to sex, Jessica was great, but I would sometimes got bored with doing just her. Ti gave me an added bit of variety.

I looked around as I took off my shoes and placed them by the door. It was a Thai custom to always leave your shoes by the entrance and walk around either barefoot or in socks. "Is Ti here?"

"She coming back later," Dang said. "You want drink?"

"No thank you," I said. "I'd just like to rest for a bit."

Dang didn't respond as she just turned and went back to her room. The condominium was furnished in the typical way a pair of young sisters would decorate it with. There were posters of Thai movie stars taped along the walls and Hello

Kitty throw pillows on the sofa, along with traditional Thai motifs that consisted of octagonal Chinese mirrors, a portrait of the Thai king and the ever ubiquitous small bronze statues of Buddha that were on every table. The living room smelled of lemongrass, ginger and incense.

I went into Ti's room and opened her closet. At the far end of the cabinet was a pair of slacks and a short sleeve button shirt suspended on a pair of wire hangers. I left them behind the last time I had visited her. I took them out and placed them on the queen sized bed before going into the bathroom and taking a shower. As I dried my hair with a still damp towel that had the smell of her shampoo on it, I tossed my used clothes into the laundry bin. There was a painting of Buddha beside the mirrored dresser, so I walked up to it and took it down from the wall. Behind the painting was a wall safe and I started to turn the dial clockwise first, then counter clockwise and back again until I got it open. Inside were wads of cash and a Canadian passport with a fake name on it. I took the passport and placed it in my back pocket. Then I took out two hundred thousand baht in crisp bills that were tied down with rubber bands and placed them in the front pockets of my trousers. Ti knew about this safe, but only I knew the right combination to open it. Either way, I trusted her enough to know that she wouldn't try to steal from me, especially since I was fully financing her life now. I heard the outer door of the condominium being unlocked as I closed the safe up and placed the painting back to cover it.

As I walked out into the living room, I saw Ti glance at

me and smile as she took her shoes off and rushed over to give me a hug. "Don, is been long time since I see you," she said as she threw a half dozen kisses to my lips.

I gave her another long kiss. "Yeah, I missed you too. But you know, when my wife is around, we have to be careful."

"Why you have to marry her? Why you not marry me?"

I laughed a little. "You know why."

"Because she daughter of your boss? That not good reason to marry."

"Oh? So tell me, Ti, what would be a good reason to marry someone then?"

"Love."

"Love? I love you both."

She turned away with a sour look on her face. "You love her more than you love me."

I sighed. Jessica was important to me because I loved her and she served as an insurance policy to my father in law, but I wanted Ti as well. "Oh come on, Ti, you're not being fair."

"You the one not fair," she said as she pulled away and walked into her room.

I followed her inside and closed the door behind me. "Ti, you know that this is the best arrangement I can do for you."

She sat on the bed and looked down at the tile floor. "You know we cannot do this forever. My parents want me to marry. Start family."

I sat down beside her. "I understand. So what do you want to do?"

"I don't know," she said before looking into my eyes.

"You want we go out, like old times, huh?"

I bit my lip as I shook my head. "I can't. There's some trouble going on in my business. It's best for me to stay low until I know what's going on."

She looked away again. "You always like this now. Just want money now."

I chuckled as my hand slid underneath her blouse and cupped her right breast. Asian women have smaller boobs than the other ethnicities, but I've always found them to be cute. Ti was a little reluctant at first, but she soon warmed up. It wasn't long before our clothes were off and I was on top of her. I had been seeing Ti off and on for the past several years, ever since I had met her when she was a bar girl at one of the clubs in Soi Cowboy. We had a relationship long before I even met Jessica. Even though I had made a vow on my wedding day, I soon realized I couldn't just stick with one woman, I needed variety, so I kept up my secret relationship with Ti, even paying for all her expenses so she wouldn't have to work as a bar girl any longer. In the end though, I knew she would eventually drift away from me, so she could fulfill her parent's wishes to marry a respectable Thai and start a family. For now, however, I knew I needed her as I took off the blouse she was wearing and we slid into the bed. I needed to get rid of the stress that was boiling inside of me and she was the perfect antidote to that kind of poison.

After a couple hours of fun, Ti was too tired to go on so I let her sleep. I went out into the living room, sat in the sofa and turned on the TV. The local news was in Thai so I kept on flipping channels until I got to the news segment about the hotel hit. I didn't speak a lot of the local language so I could barely keep up with it. The report was very short, just a mention by the news anchor of a hotel shooting and some footage of the bloody sofa were Panupong was killed. There weren't any interviews on the air, other than a police spokesman saying that everything was still under investigation. Elliot wasn't named, they merely mentioned that a foreigner was killed along with two Thai nationals.

As I turned the TV off, I realized that Dang was standing in the middle of the room and was staring at me. The expression on her face was unintelligible, but she was giving me the evil eye.

I looked up at her in confusion. "Yes, what is it?"

"When I clean her room, I found this," she said as she threw a small, clear plastic bag at me.

I caught it in the air and took a look. Inside the clear plastic wrapper were about two dozen little pink pills. I immediately recognized them as yaba tablets. Yaba means "crazy medicine" in the Thai language—these little pills held a mixture of methamphetamine and caffeine. It was the drug of choice for young people and the working class to keep them going all night and day. Yaba tablets have been around since the 1960's and were outlawed almost fifty years ago. I used these pills back when I was working as an opener, but I was able to wean myself away from them years ago. "Where did she get it?" I said.

Dang's face was a mask of stone but her eyes were like daggers being thrown at me. "You can get yaba anywhere."

"So how is this my fault? I don't give her any drugs."

"You give her money," she hissed. "You give her lots of money and you keep her here."

I took a deep breath. This stupid bitch was giving me a guilt trip. Not going to work. "I don't keep her locked up in here, she is free to come and go whenever she pleases."

Dang pointed a crooker finger at me. "She become addict because of you. She bored and she have money."

"Fuck off," I said. "So what do you want me to do? Stop giving her money?"

"You make her wait for you," she said. "She suppose to start family now. She supposed to get married."

"So you want me to stop paying the rent here? You want to live back in that shit hole where I found you?"

"We poor back then," Dang said. "But we live better. No drugs."

I stood up as I threw the bag of yaba pills onto the sofa. "Hey, you know where your sister worked when I first met her? She was a bar girl. Just like you were, before you got old and ugly. I got her out of that job and now you both have a nice place to live, and she doesn't even have to work. This is the kind of thanks I get from you? You stupid, ungrateful bitch."

"We don't want your money."

"I'd like to hear it from her."

"She not tell you that because she a drug addict," Dang said.

I walked over to where the door was and started putting on my shoes. I wasn't going to stay here for one minute longer. "Dang, if you want to fucking leave, then go! If Ti wants to stay, then it's her choice, goddamn it."

"You not care she a drug addict?"

"Of course I fucking care!" I said as I pointed a finger at her. "Don't you ever put the blame on me for this. Ti is an adult, just like you. She makes her choice, and I make mine! Go to hell, bitch!"

Dang switched to Thai as I opened the door. I could tell she was cussing me out in every which way as I walked through the entryway and closed the door behind me.

3.

Every foreigner living in a strange land ultimately suffers a bout of homesickness at least once during their life abroad. A good way to alleviate the sense of alienation and displacement would be to experience something that reminds them of home. For American expatriates, it usually means going to the nearest McDonald's. Since everything but the bread is shipped in from the United States, every hamburger served within the confines of the golden arches tastes the same. For expatriates of the former British Empire on the other hand, it's the pub. All over Asia, one can always find either an authentic English or Irish pub to pass the hours after work. From the dark lacquered wood paneling, to the slightly dim interiors, the pints of beer and a game of darts or billiards, the concept of the pub is probably the most glaring aspect of British culture other than the English language itself.

Timmy O'Toole's Irish Pub was located in the city's Riverside district. Unlike the grittier, closed-in urban areas of Silom or Sukhumvit, Riverside was more sophisticated.

The area was a showcase of both the glitziest and the more traditional venues that the country had to offer. O'Toole's was a better meeting place since it was away from where the people in my line of work would usually hang out at. The place was new and more upscale. While the higher prices obviously made it a tourist trap, the constant gaggle of unfamiliar faces helped to shield my anonymity. For anyone looking in, I was just another stupid farang who was willing to pay top money for the usual swill that could be found in cheaper places elsewhere in the city.

I sat by myself in a booth close to the rear area. Most of the tourists would usually hang out by the bar or near the entrance, right at the outside tables so they could both see and be seen. Just beyond the corridor to my side was the office and it was already closed by this time, so it was a lot quieter than usual. I hadn't expected to come over this early, but my bitter fight with Ti's sister made me decide to spend an extra hour or two by myself. I was already on my third pint of Guinness and I decided to slow down, lest I become too drunk to think properly.

Dang was an ungrateful bitch, but she was right. I was too much of a bad influence on her younger sister. Deep inside, a part of me wished I could divorce Jessica to marry Ti. To live that simple life which so many farangs in this part of the world craved and could only dream about. I knew I already had enough money to live comfortably in the Third World for the rest of my days if I chose to quit right this minute. But there was another side of me, it was another part of my jumble of memories and consciousness that propelled me to keep on going, to prove to everyone, most of all myself, I could hang with the big guns. After all, I was in a prime position to finally become a power to be reckoned with. I was a year away from turning thirty. I didn't want to quit while I was just slightly ahead, I wanted to leave the party when everybody else would be looking in awe at me, wishing they could be in my shoes.

Bob Duffy's familiar face soon appeared amongst the crowd at the pub's entrance. We made eye contact with each other and he made his way over to my booth. After all these years, he still looked the same with his long, grizzled hair tied up in a pony tail. His lanky, Southern California surfer's frame with its tanned wrinkles were obvious as he got closer. Bob was wearing his usual blue and white pinstriped shirt and dark slacks. He shook my hand and sat down beside me with a smile.

I asked a passing waiter for another pint of stout before turning my attention back to my manager. "How did everything go?"

Bob shook his head slightly as he let out a short giggle. "You should have seen the look on everyone's faces when I had my assistant shut the phones down. The moment I told them to pack their stuff and go, they all looked at me as if they couldn't believe it. Scotty though, he knew what was up, so he was first out the door."

I leaned back on the padded booth sofa and laughed. "Good old Scotty. I miss talking to him. How's his production going?"

"He's okay. Hanging in there. That load that he got in last

week really helped him out. At least now he isn't behind on his rent."

"That's good," I said. Scott Wellman was an addict, but he saved me from getting caught by the cops during the raid on Doc's office over a year ago and I figured I owed him. "As long as he's doing okay, I want to keep him with us."

"I guess I can give him an allowance," Bob said. "If that's okay with you."

I pulled out a wad of cash from my pants pocket and doled out a small stack. "Yeah, that's fine. Here's thirty thousand baht. Don't give it to him all at once, or he'll go on a heroin binge. That's the last thing we want."

Bob took the money and stowed it in his pants. "This is fine, but we can't keep Scotty on ice forever. If he gets bored for too long, he's gonna turn back to drugs."

"It ought to be enough to keep him afloat for the next few weeks or so," I said. "I just want to get to the bottom of this latest mess I'm in."

Bob was silent as the waiter came over with my pint of stout. He ordered a light beer and didn't say anything until the waiter came back and placed his beer on the table. Then his eyes locked onto mine. "What the hell happened today?"

I took a sip of the dark beer since the foam had largely dissipated. "A total fuckup, that's what. Elliot's dead."

Bob briefly looked away. "Jesus H Christ. He was just a kid."

"Tell me about it," I said softly. "He was a fucking good loader too. One of the best I'd ever seen."

"Don, I know you prefer to keep me out of the loop

when it comes to the loading aspect of the business, but what in the hell where you doing bringing Elliot along for a banker's meeting?"

I sighed. "This was going to be the biggest deal in the history of the industry, that's why. I wanted Elliot in there so he could learn about the banking side of things. I had plans for that kid. He was the one who set the client up for it. It was his deal."

Bob nodded. "The whale, then?"

I frowned. A whale was the term for big time clients. "You heard about it?"

"Just rumblings," he said. "Everybody thinks you've got something big coming in. All the openers are hoping it's one of their deals."

I exhaled deeply. "Fuck. This means that if the whole crew knows about it, then so do a lot of other owners. It could also mean Doc knows too."

Bob had a surprised look on his face. "You didn't want him to know?"

"No," I said. "This was strictly between Elliot, myself and now you."

Bob put his palms up. "Hey, you know me, Don. I can keep a secret."

"I know, that's why I'm telling you now. Were you able to pay everyone off today?"

"Yup," Bob said. "We met over at the coffee shop on a one on one basis a few hours back. A few of the openers have got commissions due though, and they were asking what the status was. So what do I tell them?"

"These openers that have got money coming, you okay with bringing them back once we reopen the office? I only want the best ones back in."

Bob thought about it for a few seconds. "Let's see, I've got four guys with commissions. One of them is that jerk asshole. The Canadian named Boyle. You remember him, right?"

"Not really. What did he do?"

"I think he might be funneling some of our leads to another office. I want to get rid of him and I was going to meet you about it."

I took another sip of the beer. "Then do so. We split whatever's coming to him."

Bob nodded. "Alright. I can follow up on the client's payments from my house anyway. I've refurbished one of the bedrooms as my personal office, so I can make calls from there, using your phone server, of course."

"Fine. Just email me the copies of the bank transfer receipts so I can follow it up with the bankers. I'll advise you when the payments clear, then I'll send the money over for the commissions and your usual override fee."

"Sounds good," Bob said. "I've been getting calls from Saul Silver all day today. What do I tell him?"

"There's not much to tell," I said. "His nephew is in the morgue, but it might be better if he stays away for now. It would be best for him not to get mixed up in this mess."

Bob adjusted his glasses before looking at me again. "Don, how old are you now?"

"Going on thirty, why?"

Bob's voice turned into an insightful whisper as he placed his hand on my forearm. "You've got money stashed away, don't you?"

I nodded. There was slightly less than two million in a joint bank account I had with Jessica, along with another cool million I had in my own private account under another name. All in dollars, of course. "I do, and I know what you're about to say, but it's not enough to quit on just yet."

"I hear you," he said. "But this whole business with Panupong getting wacked like that. Plus Elliot's dead too. Are you sure you want to keep going with this? Why don't you lie low as in go somewhere safe and take a breather for a few months. Why can't you do that at least?"

I smirked. "This is what I like about you, Bob. You're always the voice of reason and sanity. But I can't sit on my ass right now. Elliot's deal is still on and it's big money. If I let it go then this once in a blue moon opportunity will be gone too. Once I got that cash in the bag, I can think about retiring."

Bob withdrew his hand, then shook his head. "Don, I've known you since you were a rookie in this business. You've gone far, kid. You were a damned good opener and then became a damned good loader. Now you've become my boss. I don't want to lose you, dude. This whole affair stinks. And I have a feeling a few more people are gonna die before it's all over."

The image of the second hit man with his gun pointed at me flashed before my eyes. "I know what you're saying, Bob," I said. "But I gotta do this."

"Why though? You've got a damned beautiful wife, who happens to be the daughter of the guy who runs our little enterprise. You've got money and you're almost half my age, son. Why would you want to risk all of that?"

I downed half of the pint before answering him. "It's something I gotta prove, not just to the others, but to myself too. You remember what I told you about my life before I got in this business, right?"

"You did," Bob said. "You came from a broken home, worked your way through college and your rich Bostonian girlfriend's father rejected you. So what? You ought to be past all that now. You're a legend in this industry already, Don. What else is there?"

I grimaced while the flood of memories from my past came to the forefront of my mind. It was like a fire burning inside of me. "I wanna show them. I want to go back to America in a private jet and show them all. I want to go to my ex-girlfriend's father and spit in his fucking face. I want to go see my mom and her fucking lesbian girlfriend, or whoever she's living with now, and show them just how much money I got. I want to see them all come crawling at my feet and apologize for rejecting me."

Bob had an exasperated look on his face. "Seriously, Don? Come on, man. Let it go. You don't need any of them. You've got Jessica for chrissakes, she's better than that New England snob you used to go out with. Your existence is good here. You can't go through life with a chip on your shoulder every day of the week, dude."

"I have to get this deal done, Bob. It's almost there

anyway. Just a few more things to do and the money's mine."

Bob took a sip of his own beer. "I've done what I could to dissuade you. Okay then, it's your life. Just how close were you to Elliot when he got killed?"

"Closer than where you are right now," I said. "I was sitting right beside him."

Bob nearly choked as he tried to take another sip. "Jesus! How in the hell did you manage to survive that?"

"The gunman had me dead to rights," I said. "But one of Panupong's bodyguards was just wounded after their initial attack and he took out the assassin who was about to shoot me. I ran into the kitchen and got away."

"So you got lucky then. Just like you got lucky last year. You're using up your nine lives pretty quick there, Don."

"Speaking of last year," I said. "It was Doc who orchestrated the raid on his own office to get rid of Petru and his Romanians. I'm beginning to think that it might be Doc who had Panupong killed …and tried to have me killed as well."

Bob's eyebrows shot up. "Are you serious? Doc? B-but he's your father in law for chrissakes!"

"I know it sounds nuts," I said. "But you know just how ruthless he is. I tried calling him up all day today and there was no answer. I sent him an email, still no reply."

"What did Jessica say?"

"I haven't told her my suspicions as of yet," I said as I pulled out my smartphone. "Come to think of it, you just gave me a good idea." I sent my wife a text message, asking if she had any contact with her father today. The reply came back in less than a minute later. She said no.

Bob leaned forward. "Well, what did she say?"

"She has had no contact with him either," I said. "It was always easy to call him before. But after today's incident, I can't reach him."

"You could be right," Bob said softly. "But I've never known him putting out a contract on anybody, it's just not his style. Yes, I know he's a pathological liar and all, but he's more conman than killer."

"It wasn't him who was doing the killing, Bob. You can hire hitmen easy out here if you've got the dinero."

Bob ran his hand over his forehead. This was heavy stuff. "Okay, let's assume he wanted you dead to get that whale's deal. But taking out Panupong too? Aren't they both allied with each other?"

"The whale that Elliot got is a very big whale. He's probably gonna fork over the biggest load in the history of this industry, Bob. This kind of cash is something to kill for," I said.

"I get it," Bob said. "This could be the biggest whale ever, I know that. But taking out Panupong is ...something that just isn't supposed to be done. The guy controlled all the banking in Thailand. Everything goes through him and now that he's dead, the whole industry this side of Asia will be at a standstill."

"Unless somebody wanted both the whale's deal and Panupong's banking network," I said. "You're right about all the money in the country going through to him, but now that he's dead, there will be a successor because there needs to be."

"You're saying that Doc will take over the banking network for the whole of Thailand? No way, the Thais would never accept a farang over one of their own," Bob said.

"And if that farang had a very powerful Thai ally?"

Bob gave me a blank look. "Doc is setting up a competing banking network here? Are you serious?"

I downed the last of my beer. "A few months back, Doc was telling me about a guy named General Sangsorn, who happens to be a bigshot in the military and has got a big stake in several banks here. He had a few meetings with him and Doc thought he could give better rates than what Panupong was charging us. Apparently this general is doing the banking for a lot of the drug cartels in this country. Doc was telling me that Sangsorn didn't know about the kind of industry we do, but if he could show him the kind of money we make with very low risk, it might entice him to come onboard as a partner on the banking side of things."

Bob looked up at the ceiling. "Holy shit. You're telling me there's a powerplay happening right now and Doc and this Thai general will be taking over?"

"I'm just putting two and two together," I said. "Doc has got the expertise and any Thai general worth his salt has got the muscle to take any competitor out of the game. I didn't really think about the connection until just now. Doc doesn't have what it takes to try a hit on Panupong, but General Sangsorn certainly does. The fact that Doc knew who he was can't be a coincidence."

"Assuming your theory is right," Bob said. "This all just

sounds …so crazy. You seriously want to mess with these guys?"

"I'm not going to mess with them," I said. "I just want to get that whale's load in my pocket and slip away quietly into the night."

"How are you gonna do that? Elliot was the loader and he's dead, right?"

"I'll take over the loading," I said. "I've loaded before so it won't be a problem. My only issue right now is to find a banker that can take the kind of money the whale's got and stash it away without any fuss."

Bob nodded. "With Panupong out of the game, why don't you use our bankers in Malaysia?"

"My contact in Malaysia is good," I said. "But he reports to Doc and I don't want him to find out. I need another alternative."

"I could ask around," Bob said.

"I'm open to anybody, as long as they're trustworthy and we keep things quiet."

"Okay, I can do that," Bob said. "I'll keep in touch with you and let you know if there's any potential prospects. You staying in Bangkok?"

"Probably not, Jess wants me to meet her and her mom in Macao so I guess I'll be flying out in a day or two," I said. "It might be good if you lie low too."

"I'll go take my wife and the kids up north to Chiang Mai," Bob said. "Lamai's parents have a big house up there I helped purchase. I guess it's time to take that vacation I wanted."

I took the valet token from my pocket and gave it to him. "My car is still in the hotel parking lot. Can you have somebody pick it up?"

Bob examined the plastic token. "I can have Lamai's brother go get it. Nothing incriminating in the car?"

"Nope, the car's clean," I said. "It's even registered to an old trading company so it's not in my name. Your brother in law can have fun riding it, but he pays for any damages if he gets into an accident, okay?"

Bob laughed. "Sure, I'll keep your car safe. It's that new Ford, right?"

"You got it."

Bob slid out of the booth sofa and held out his hand. "Okay, I'm gonna head back home and start driving those accounts that we still have coming in. Stay in touch, dude. Please keep me abreast of what's happening. Now, how much do I owe you for the beer?"

I shook his hand. "I will, Bob. Thanks for understanding. Don't worry about the tab, I got it."

"Alright, dude, stay safe."

"Bye, Bob."

After he left I ordered a shot of bourbon, then asked for the bill. Bob was right in a way. I was ahead of the game and I could have easily called it quits. Tempting fate a third time after escaping death twice already was bucking the laws of average. Then again I figured this would be a calculated risk. The monster deal was there: all I had to do was play my cards right, get a banker and all would be well. Once the money was in my possession, I could kick back, relax and be just like my father in law, only this time, I would have achieved it all while still being half his age.

I left a generous tip and got out of the bar. There were a ton of tourists and locals walking back and forth along the concrete wharf that bordered the dark waters of the Chao Phraya. The night was less humid than usual so I took a little stroll, being careful to stay clear of the moronic hipsters and their constant demands of taking selfies whenever they felt like there was a slightest chance of a new scenery behind their empty smiles and egomaniacal gestures. If they only knew what kind of life I was leading, they would be down on their knees in awe.

A couple of hours passed and I decided to head over to a nearby mid-range hotel for a night's rest. I could have easily gone to one of the swankier, more expensive hotels, but I figured that if anyone was looking for me, they would have a harder time in finding out where I was. My plan was to just blend in with the hordes of foreign tourists that flocked around Bangkok at this time of the season. When I got to the front desk I gave the receptionist the Canadian passport with my fake name on it and paid for the night in cash. As I expected, she didn't even look to see if the immigration stamps were recent.

"No luggage?" she asked.

I merely smiled. "Nope, I just flew in from Hong Kong. No need for a porter, I've stayed here before."

After taking the keycard from her I took the elevator up to the third floor and went into my room. There were some stains on the carpet and the aircon was noisy when I turned it on, but at least they gave me a single large bed. I still felt horny after my tryst with Ti, but the last thing I wanted to do was to go back to her place and put up with her queen bitch of a sister. I sat on the foot of the bed, the whole day's exertions suddenly started to pound in my head. I flopped down on the mattress with my clothes still on as I closed my eyes for a brief respite. I must have been more exhausted than I thought because I fell asleep almost immediately.

I must have slept for most of the night since the moment I opened my eyes I could see a slit of sunlight bearing down behind the drawn curtains. The room was bathed in a twilit shadow. Although the aircon was still going, for some reason the lights were out and I didn't even remember having turned them off the moment I laid down on the bed. When I sat up I sensed something wasn't right. The corner of my eye detected some sort of movement behind me, near the wall parallel to the headrest. When I turned my head, I realized there was a man dressed in a very dark business suit standing by the wall. I tried to get up but another intruder came out of the bathroom and pushed me down onto the carpeted floor. As I tried to roll away, I felt multiple people grabbing my arms and pinning them behind my back. I was still pretty groggy from sleep so I tried to fight back, but I wasn't doing a very good job at it. When they twisted my arms and applied pressure on my spine I cried out as a black hood was placed over my head.

"Be quiet or you die," a heavily accented voice whispered in my ear. Then I felt the cold steel barrel of a gun being pressed to my neck. I stopped struggling as I was forced up on my feet and I heard the door open.

4.

Even though they placed a hood over me, I could still hear
and feel what was going on. There must have been at least
three of them as they led me by my elbows into what felt like
a service elevator. The next thing I sensed was the smell of
cooking and the metallic clangs of pots and pans while I was
dragged along in what seemed to be the hotel's kitchen area,
until the rush of warm air which signified that we were
finally outside. At that point I heard the sound of a car door
being opened as somebody held my head down and I was
pushed into the vehicle's backseat. There was plenty of
talking in Thai, but since I couldn't understand too much
of the language, most of it was incomprehensible.

Once the car got rolling, I could tell I was sitting in the
middle of the rear passenger seat in between two people. The
car's air-conditioning system was at full blast so it was quite
chilly inside, but I was still sweating heavily. What made the
whole thing surreal was the fresh scent of jasmine and car
leather that wafted up to my nostril. This meant the car was
either new or was very well-maintained. If these guys were

planning to kill me and dump my body somewhere, then they were obviously doing it in style.

The next thing I knew, the hood was lifted from my head by a guy sitting beside me. He folded the black cloth neatly and placed it on top of the rear dashboard behind him. There were five of us in the car: the driver, a man in the front seat and the two other men in sitting beside me. All of them were locals and they all wore identical black suits. Their shirt collars ranged from neon green to red with assorted ties, and they all wore sunglasses. While the two men beside me stared straight ahead, I could tell that they both were on guard for any sudden moves in case I was stupid enough to try and make a break for it.

I made eye contact with the man in the front seat when he glanced back at me. "Are you all with Mr. Panupong?" I said softly.

The man didn't say anything as he simply stared at me for an uncomfortably long minute. His eyes were obscured by his sunglasses so I couldn't get a bead on what he was thinking about. The man merely placed his index finger over his mouth, silently telling me to shut the hell up before turning back to face the front of the vehicle once more.

There really wasn't much else to do but twiddle my thumbs, so I sat back and tried to relax. Within half an hour we had made it on a three lane highway. The sedan sped up since it was no longer being held back by the downtown traffic. As I glanced at the road signs while we passed them by, it was obvious we were heading north out of the city. The once tight urban sprawl became less apparent as we passed by more greenery on our way to the district of Nonthaburi. Although it was officially designated as a separate province, Nonthaburi was still considered as part of the greater Bangkok Metropolitan Area.

Another fifteen minutes passed when the car made a turn and drove into an adjoining road. We passed by several strip malls and suburban houses before the land changed into nothing but green rice fields around us. This went on for awhile until we soon turned into a road marked PRIVATE in both Thai and English. There was a guardhouse near the edge of the road with two uniformed sentries, but they waved us through as soon as they saw the vehicle we were riding in. The next thing I knew we were driving past a bridge that overlooked a small stream before we stopped in front of a massive, walled compound.

The grey concrete walls must have been at least fifteen feet high so anyone on the outside wouldn't be able to see whatever was going on in there. The steel gate was opened by two uniformed guards and they once more waved us through. I looked around in amazement as we drove through a lush garden landscape that must have been several acres of converted farmland. To my right stood a small hill that was the centerpiece of a carefully manicured golf course with artificial lakes and sand traps. As the car made another turn, we quickly made it into a cobbled stone driveway that overlooked a huge mansion on top of another hill. I could see at least half a dozen gardeners tending the carefully arranged tropical scenery all around me. A couple of them looked at me briefly as I was led out of the car, before they went back to their pruning and landscaping toils. A couple of smaller villas were within walking distance, overlooking an unnaturally calm river.

As my handlers led me up the white stone steps leading to the entrance of the large house, the front doors suddenly opened and a young Thai man wearing a red polo shirt and khaki pants came out. As he walked down the steps, he glanced at me briefly before making his way to a golf cart. Unlike the other locals, he had much lighter skin and wore expensive jewelry. The man who was in the front seat of the car I was in nodded to the man with the golf shirt as soon as they saw each other, but the younger man merely acknowledged him with a slight tilt of his head as he put on his white golfing gloves. I didn't have time to figure out what it all meant, since the two men behind me used their elbows to give my back a slight push so I kept going until I was inside.

The interior of the mansion was a mix of traditional oriental influences mixed it with the modern. The walls and marbled flooring were gleaming white. I could see a couple of uniformed maids doing their daily cleaning routines to make sure that the place was spic and span. White leather sofas, lacquered wood cabinets and dark teak paneling were commonplace. Free standing plants grew from giant ceramic pots which were conveniently placed near the large windows. Large ceiling fans were in constant rotation as they circulated air from the twenty-foot tall high ceilings. Along every wall was a painting that depicted either the Buddha or scenes from the lifestyles of the ancient Thai. I couldn't do much but glance briefly at all this opulence since the men behind me continued to prod me along. One thing was obviously apparent, Panupong sure made a lot of money from all the banking he did for us.

My handlers soon led me along a side corridor. To my left were large sliding glass doors that led out into a gargantuan swimming pool, its turquoise waters reflecting the sunlight, casting undulating waves of bright, wavy lines along the walls of the house. We soon passed by another set of rooms, one of them had a large, life-sized stone statue of Buddha sitting in a lotus position. The smell of tropical flowers and incense permeated the place.

We soon turned into an interior corridor that fronted a large entryway. The antique wooden double doors that faced us were closed. One of my handlers knocked a few times before he opened it slightly and slipped through before closing it.

The man from the front seat turned and looked at me as he gestured at another door at the far end of the corridor. "You want to use toilet?"

"Yes, thank you," I said as I started walking towards where the bathroom obviously was. The two men behind me quickly followed. I opened the door but didn't close it as I took a piss in the toilet and washed my face, while the two of them stared at me from the open doorway.

Just as I started walking back, the two double doors were suddenly flung wide open. The man who offered me to use the bathroom quickly took me by my elbow and led me past through the large entryway. Within seconds, I was now standing in a large hall that was obviously the main room of this floor. The rear part of the hall was open to the outside, with thirty foot tall marble pillars supporting its outer façade. It seemed that the swimming pool extended all the way to the edge of the elevated hill, creating an infinity effect, which made it look like the water was emptying into the air. I could see a billiard table fronting a library at the far end of the hall, along with a dining area at the opposite side. Although the furnishing in this room was in the same style as the others, what made it striking were the two people in front of me.

They were both Thais. The first was a middle-aged woman sitting on a wheelchair, wearing a purple dress. Her skin was pale and her dark hair was combed back in the traditional Thai way, but her eyes were bearing down on me with a determined intensity. The second was a young man wearing white slacks and a black buttoned down shirt. With his bowl cut, flat nose and thick glasses, the young man looked like a slightly paler version of his father.

The last thing I wanted to do was start trouble, so I broke the icy silence as I clasped my hands together and bowed slightly using the wai greeting. "Sawadee kap," I said, using the Thai way of saying hello.

"Mai ko sabai ka," the woman said as she shifted slightly in her wheelchair. I knew a little bit of Thai to realize she had just said she wasn't too happy. About what she was pissed off about I wasn't too sure, though I had a suspicion it would have something to do with her husband. Then the woman turned and started speaking in rapid Thai to the young man as the three men in suits continued to keep a watchful eye while they stood just behind me.

The young man listened intently to her for a few minutes before looking up at me. "Greetings to you," he said in perfect English. "My name is Thinnakorn Panupong. I am the eldest son, but you can call me Ek. It means 'important' in my language."

I nodded. "Alright, Ek. I'm Don, by the way."

The woman talked in Thai once more as Ek listened patiently. Then we locked eyes together again."I'm sorry, but my mother does not speak much English, so you will allow me to translate. Her name is Pim and her late husband is my father, Thaksin Panupong. I am sure that you are familiar with him and who he is," he said.

"Yes," I said softly. "My condolences to you and your mother for such a tragic loss. I'm so sorry this has happened. But I have to say that I had nothing to do with your esteemed father's death. I was there and was nearly killed myself."

Ek smiled slightly. "Oh, if we knew you had something to do with it, you wouldn't be standing here in front of us right now."

Mrs. Panupong started talking to her son in Thai once more as I shifted uneasily. The young man was right, they could have simply killed me by now if they wanted to. It was clear they were going to question me as to what had happened and to try and find some clues as to who was behind the hit. My first suspect was Doc, but I couldn't just tell them about him without compromising my relationship with Jessica. Besides, I didn't have any proof, just a mere set of circumstantial hunches. At the same time, I didn't want it to look like I was hiding anything from them so I had to play this game very carefully. One mistake and I could end up as fish food in some muddy pond somewhere out here. I kept my composure as I looked out into the nearby golf course and saw thunderclouds forming in the skies above.

As she finished talking with him, Ek turned to face me once more. "My husband …I-I mean, my father …was meeting with you when he was killed." He was obviously translating for her verbatim and clearly bumbling it. "Please tell me what it was that you two were discussing."

I breathed in deeply before I answered. I needed to choose my words carefully. "Just a routine business arrangement, sir. Your honorable father and I were coming to an agreement regarding a payment I wanted his bankers to receive. This was to be a large payment and I wanted it to be handled very discreetly. We had agreed that it be known only between the two of us."

Ek's eyes narrowed. "We have done research on you, Mr. Don Rouse. From what the sources tell us, your business already has an arrangement with two bankers in Malaysia. Why did you want my father involved in your affairs?"

I pursed my lips. Better to tell the truth on this. "Yes, it's true that I already have bankers in Malaysia. But this deal was to be kept secret from them and from the rest of my company. This upcoming payment was to be handled by me personally."

Ek's mother grabbed his elbow and started talking to him

in Thai again. After a few minutes, the eldest son glanced up at me. "We know you are overseeing Doc Bull's businesses for him. Did he know about your meeting with my husb …er, my father?"

"No."

"May I ask if your father in law found out about your dealings with my father," Ek said, "would he try to have you killed too?"

I shook my head. I was defending Doc even though I felt I shouldn't be. My father in law was my primary suspect as the mastermind behind all this, but I needed to be sure. "No, my father in law is not a killer. I don't think he could ever order anyone to be killed, it's just not in his personality."

Ek adjusted his glasses. He had the same gestures and mannerisms as his father did. "We know that, but what about his allies?"

"Your father was one of his allies," I said. "There is no reason for Doc to do that to one of his friends."

Ek gestured at the man standing behind me. "Ah, but your father in law has made many friends here, including enemies of my late father."

One of the men behind me pulled out a photograph from his coat pocket and handed it to me. It showed Doc, along with me, Jessica and her mother, sitting at a large table during a party last year. Sitting and laughing beside Doc was none other than General Sangsorn. Although he was in civilian clothes, Sangsorn's broad, barrel-shaped chest and military crew cut clearly stood out in the picture.

I gave the printed photograph back to the man standing

behind me. "So what? It's just a picture. My father in law is always being invited to many parties here and he tries his best to attend them all. As I remember, all four of us went to your father's birthday party as well."

Ek nodded as his mother said something to him. "Can you tell me how you were able to get away from the shooting that killed my father?"

"One of your father's bodyguards survived the initial attack," I said. "Just as one of the hitmen was about to shoot me, the bodyguard shot him. It gave me enough time to run out the back door."

Mrs. Panupong said something in Thai before Ek made his reply. "Who was the other foreigner with you in that meeting?" he said.

"Just a colleague of mine, it was his deal. I can assure you he was completely innocent."

Ek tilted his head as his mother whispered in his ear. Then he looked back at me. "Why do you think my father was killed in that attack?"

I shrugged. "I have no idea. Maybe it's a rival trying to take over? I really don't know."

"Do you have any enemies, Mr. Don?"

I thought about it for a minute before answering him. "A few, but I don't think any of them would want to kill me along with your father. All my enemies are other farangs-foreigners, and they don't have the kind of power to arrange a hit like that, not in this country anyway."

Ek and his mother spent the next few minutes whispering to each other before they turned their attention back to me.

Once again, it was the son who asked the questions. "I see, Mr. Don. My mother has one more question for you. Those two assassins, did you recognize either of them?"

The image of the Thai man with the scar on his face loomed before me. I knew him. Last year, an enemy of mine- a Brit named Finny, was about to execute me after he abducted both Jessica and myself, but that very man who tried to kill me just the day before saved my life by killing Finny with a shot to the back of his head. It was last year that I tried to play a game of deception against Mr. Panupong, and I was pretty sure the man with the scar was one of his own men. It meant only one thing: an inside job.

I shook my head. "I'm sorry, I didn't recognize either of them."

Mrs. Panupong had a disappointed look on her face, it was as if she was expecting a different answer from me, but I couldn't really tell for sure. She whispered something else to her son before gesturing at the men standing behind me. A side door opened and a uniformed nurse walked towards the woman. The nurse got behind Mrs. Panupong and began wheeling her out of the room.

Ek just stood there for a few minutes in silence. It was as if he had somehow lost his sense of initiative the moment his mother left. Then he turned his attention back to me. "I would like to thank you for answering my mother's ...I mean, our questions, Mr. Don. I must apologize if we surprised you by bringing you here, but you see my mother told my father's men to make sure you arrived here by any means possible."

I smirked to break the tension between us. Without his mother around, this kid seemed more pliable. It was something I could work on. "It's okay. Your men just gave me a bit of a scare, that's all. I thought they were going to bring me somewhere remote and kill me."

Ek tilted his head up and laughed. "Once again, so sorry! My mother you see, she is still very upset by my father's death. It was her orders to take you from your hotel, not mine."

I kept up my smile. "It's alright, if I were in her shoes, I'd feel the same way. Will your esteemed father's funeral be a public one or a private ceremony?"

"My father's body will be brought here this afternoon for the bathing ritual," he said. "That ceremony is private, but his body will be on display over at his villa, near the golf course for one week starting tomorrow so that all our relatives and his friends can visit and pay their respects." Ek pointed to a cottage at the other side of the golf course as a light rain had begun outside. "Then he shall be cremated according to Buddhist custom afterwards. If you wish, you may return anytime starting tomorrow. I can have my mother's people pick you up if you wish."

"Thank you for allowing me to participate. Your father was a trusted friend. No need to have me picked up, I have a car," I said. "Oh, by the way, do you know if the police needs to question me about what happened?"

Ek shook his head. "No, we took care of the police. Your friend will need a family member to claim his body though, it is still in the morgue. The police have reported his cause of death as an accident."

"I'll take care of that, thanks again," I said. The question about the banking was still in the center of my mind. "Oh, if I could ask one other thing, what will happen to your father's business deals?"

"My mother and I will honor the present arrangements," he said after a pause. "If I am to understand, you had a very big potential deal that you were about to discuss with my father, yes?"

"I do indeed," I said. "Would you be willing to meet in regards to it?"

"Yes, give us a few days to sort everything out first, and we will contact you to set up a meeting," Ek said as he looked over to the men behind me. "They will take you back to your hotel now for I will be very busy today. So much things to sort out. Goodbye for now, Mr. Don, I hope we see each other again."

I did a quick wai gesture before turning around and making my way out. This time it was only the man who was in the front seat that accompanied me as we made our way back towards the front entrance of the mansion. The bodyguard pulled out my phone and my faked Canadian passport from beneath his coat pocket and handed them to me before gesturing we move on. As we made our way into the marbled foyer, the young Thai man with the golf outfit came through the door. A short, brown-skinned servant followed right behind him, carrying a golf bag full of clubs. The shorter man stumbled a little bit as his wet shoes slid on the smooth stone flooring, as he staggered while trying to balance the bag slung uneasily over his shoulder, one of the golf clubs slid out and clanged noisily as it fell to the floor.

The young man turned and delivered a hard slap to the servant's face that nearly toppled him, but the caddie was able to compensate by bowing down in meek submission before hurriedly picking up the fallen golf club and sticking it back in the bag. The golfer then made a fleeting gesture which sent the servant on his way to an adjacent corridor.

As the young man glanced in my direction, I made the wai greeting as a form of politeness, just to be on the safe side. "Sawadee kap," I said.

The young man returned the greeting. Unlike Ek, who was pretty short, this guy was taller than the average Thais I met in my time here. His nose was sharp and it looked like he had dyed his hair orange. "Ah, so you're the one who was with my father when he died, yes?" he said. Just like Ek, his English was perfect as well, but it carried more of a British accent to it as opposed to Ek's neutral, American–like accent.

"Yes, it was a terrible experience," I said. "I'm Don Rouse, and you are?"

"I am Jettrin Panupong," the young man said. "But my friends call me Jet, for short. I am sure you met my brother Ek …and my mother."

I nodded to him. "I did indeed. It looks like your brother will be taking over the family business then?"

Jet snorted as he looked away. "My brother is a baby who can't even change his own diapers without my mother. And to think he is now running things because he happens to be the older one, my mother's number one son. What kind of bullshit is that?"

"I can sympathize with your view," I said. "I'm also a second son. But I never knew my father, and my mother ...well, let's just say she didn't have any money at all. So you're way better off than I ever was."

"Don, you're an American," he said. "You do not understand our culture here. It is always the older one who gets more respect. It doesn't even matter if the eldest son is an idiot, he gets it all no matter what. This is what makes me wish I was born an American instead. Over there, you are rewarded by how competent you are, not by your date of birth."

I smiled. He was not a typical Thai. "Not all the time though. In many cases the next in line is usually the eldest child, it happens in America too. Though I wouldn't feel too badly if I was in your shoes, you seem to be doing pretty good."

Jet looked out at the light rain falling outside through the open front door. "Perhaps you are right, perhaps I should just continue to sit in my second chair, and support my older brother instead. But mark my words, he will be bad for business, he doesn't know what he is doing."

"Maybe you could talk to your mother about it? She might listen to your reasons once you prove you're better than your brother."

Jet hissed. "My mother is too traditional. She already knows I'm the smarter one, but she still won't allow me to be the head of my father's business!"

I kept on smiling. "Well, just keep on trying. You never know, maybe one day she will realize what you can do. In the meantime, keep your head up because you're in a good position to succeed in case your brother stumbles."

Jet was quiet for a bit as he pondered on what I said to him. Then he held out his hand. "Thank you, Don. At least you made me feel better today."

I shook his hand. "No problem. Maybe we can do some business in the future."

Jet leaned over as he whispered in my ear. "That may come sooner than you think. Leave your details with my man and I will be in touch with you very soon."

I nodded. "Okay."

As soon as he let go of my hand, Jet rapidly walked away towards the living room area. "Just remember who will be running things here soon, Don," he said, his voice trailing into the near empty room.

When we walked down the front steps, the sedan was already there, waiting for us. The bodyguard who was with me quickened his pace. He made it to the rear passenger door ahead of me and opened it while he gestured for me to climb aboard.

Just as I was about to duck into the car, he whispered in my ear. "It is good you do not say who you saw in hotel."

I paused for a bit before sitting down at the back seat of the vehicle. The door beside me slammed shut and the driver sped off. As I turned my head and glanced back from the rear windshield, I could see the Thai bodyguard just staring at me as he gradually faded away into the distance.

5.

Since I wasn't in any immediate danger, I had the driver drop me off at my own condominium. When I reached the top floor and opened the door to the penthouse, I could see that the whole place was ransacked. Every cabinet had been opened, all the drawers had been searched through. Even the safe in the master bedroom had been broken into, most probably with a crowbar and hammer. I figured it must have been Panupong's wife who ordered everything to be checked in her crazed attempt to find out who had her husband killed. As I checked the contents of the broken safe, I was astonished to find the cash I had left in it hadn't been taken. Even Jessica's gold earrings and her diamond ring collection were still there. So it looked like they were just after information and not valuables. I had to admire Panupong's men. They were so disciplined, they didn't take anything for themselves.

What was really curious to me were the three laptops that were still lying around untouched. If they were truly looking for information then why didn't they take the computers too? Sitting down on the living room sofa, I turned on each and every laptop as I checked to see if they were vandalized in any way. I activated the anti-virus software and searched through the files, looking for any signs of intrusion, but there were none. As soon as I got the internet up and running, I used my phone to dial Doc's number and checked to see if he emailed me back. The call didn't go through and there was no reply in my mail inbox.

I dialed Jessica's number on my smartphone. After a few rings her voice was on the other line. "Don, how are you?"

"I'm fine, Jess," I said as I started going through international flight reservations on my laptop. "I'll fly out of Bangkok tonight and meet up with you. Are you still in Macao?"

"Yeah, we're staying at the Grand Orient. Text me your flight schedule and I'll pick you up at the airport. We've got the presidential suite so they have a limo service available at any time for us."

I was digging into my savings to keep everything afloat while they were enjoying themselves on my account. "You're just a big spender, aren't you?"

She laughed. "Hey, we're doing okay, right? Anyway, Mom and I haven't met since our wedding, so I figured it's okay to splurge a little."

"Alright," I said. "A five grand a night suite isn't too bad, I guess. Especially since it's been awhile since your mom's last visit."

"You ought to see her gambling tab."

"What?"

Jessica continued to giggle. "Just kidding, she only lost a few hundred dollars so far. She's not doing that badly to be honest."

"Hey, she's your mom."

Her voice became serious all of a sudden. "My mom's name is Crystal, Don. Please remember it because you forgot the last time. That was downright embarrassing- for both of us."

What a time for her to rub that in! "Look, I said I was sorry already. Do you always have to keep bringing this up? I must have apologized a million times to you about that."

"It happened during our wedding, Don."

Now it was my turn to get irritated. "Yeah, yeah, yeah! It's Crystal, alright? Your mom's name. Crystal. I got it. I got it!"

"Alright, Don. I'll see you in a few hours then."

"One more thing," I said. "Did your dad contact you at all since we last talked?"

"No. But then, he always goes off to do whatever it is he does for weeks on end, so I'm not worried. Should I be worried, Don?"

No sense in stressing her out necessarily. "No, don't worry about it. I was just checking, that's all," I said.

"Okay, I'll see you in awhile then." She hung up.

I placed the phone down on the coffee table as I logged into the load server. Popularly known as the load box, it was nothing more than a spreadsheet that contained the complete contact information on all of the paid clients I had in the business. Once a client paid the first time, all of their details would then be passed onto the loaders using the database so they could keep track of all the things that were said, in order to keep the stories consistent. It was important that I familiarize myself with all of Elliot's accounts since I would be the one taking over as loader until I found a replacement.

Based on all of his records, Elliot was maintaining close to fifty clients. Most of them were small fry, no more than five figure punters, but there were a few big guns I would need to make some calls to, just to keep them happy about their supposed investments. I kept scrolling through the spreadsheet until I found the details on Elliot's whale. What I needed to do was to familiarize myself with what Elliot had been saying about the new investment scheme. The last thing I didn't want was to get the client's suspicions up. If the story we were telling them didn't match, then the deal would go down the drain. It was important that I got every detail right before I would call him up.

His name finally came up in the server. Antonio Leopardi. Goes by Tony to his friends. Ethnic Italian, but a dual citizen of South Africa and based over there. He was a senior director of one the largest diamond mining conglomerates in the world. It was a huge, multinational corporation with exclusive mineral rights from Canada to Africa. Being in that business meant he was practically swimming in dough. Elliot got his details through a load referral, of which one of our paid clients gave away Leopardi's details as another potential investor right to us. I always loved referrals, because these kinds of people were the ones you just couldn't find using a corporate directory, therefore our openers never touched them, nor even knew about the trade. What made it even better was that these people were filthy rich and practically untouched by the other swindlers in my industry. It was like a rock star seducing a horny, virginal groupie. Easy money, if you covered all the bases right.

I got up, went over to the kitchen and made myself some lunch while I thought things over. I needed to convince the client that I would be taking over the handling of his account. The transition needed to be smooth, and I would have to set up the banking fairly soon. The moment Leopardi would commit, I needed the fund transfer details and it would have to be clean. The only problem was, I had to find a new banker, now that Panupong was out of the picture. His family might go with the deal, but I sensed there would be a bloody civil war between the two sons before anything could be hashed out. II figured it might be better to try and find another banker outside of Thailand.

After taking out the coffee pot from the cupboard, I poured some filtered water into it and started up the percolator. All that was left in the fridge were some leftover ham from the deli and tomatoes in the crisper, so I slapped them in between two pieces of stale bread along with mayonnaise and the cheap yellow mustard that Jessica always seemed to buy. By this time the coffee was ready, so I poured a steaming cup and started to sip. There wasn't any sugar around but it didn't matter, I always preferred my coffee to be black and bitter. As I thought of alternatives, the names of my old friends like Otis Schnorkel came up. Otis was the first ever boss I worked for in the industry. He was retired, but still kept in contact with everybody, so when it came to getting things done and finding out information, he was the one to talk to. If there was somebody who could point me in the right direction it would be him. It was a long time since I spoke with Otis, simply because I didn't approve of his choice of lifestyle. Now I had to swallow my disgust and ask him for help once more.

With a bellyful of coffee and a ham sandwich, I walked back over to the sofa as I picked up the headset and plugged it into the side of the laptop. I had a special internet phone server set up so that I could choose the caller identification numbers. When the clients checked to see where the call originated from, I could either patch it through our fictitious offices in Hong Kong or in New York City, depending on who we were, and what the deal was. As I did a voice check using the Hong Kong line, I mentally rehearsed what I was going to say in order to make it sound as smoothly as possible. Grabbing a yellow pad and a pen, I even wrote down a few things to make sure I could easily remember the salient parts of the deal.

I double checked the time with my watch. It was noontime here in Bangkok, which meant that the time in South Africa was very early in the morning. Looking at Elliot's notes, the client was usually in his office before eight o'clock, which meant that he would be personally answering his direct phone line, instead of a pesky secretary who generally asked too many questions. I hated having to go through these personal assistants, but the big bosses we called usually had one or two of these gatekeepers to keep people like me away. It was now or never, so I went ahead and punched in the numbers on the soft phone application. Within two rings, the call was answered.

"Antonio Leopardi," the voice on the other line said. The heavily-accented English had a fusion of Afrikaner and Italian filters to go with it.

"Mr. Leopardi, good morning to you, sir," I said. "My name is Richard Marietta, and I'm calling you from MAM's Hong Kong offices. I'm terribly sorry for bothering you so early in the morning, but I have some news for you. Is this a good time for a short chat?"

"Oh yes, Mr. Marietta. This is the best time to speak to me, actually. A call from your company is always welcome. I have a representative who works for your firm, his name is David Johnson. He's based in your New York office, yes?"

"Exactly, sir," I said as I looked at the notes and made sure I got Elliot's phone identity right. "That is actually the reason why I'm calling. You see, Mr. Johnson's wife had an emergency and she's in the hospital right now. David sent me your details and gave me specific instructions to make sure that any questions that you have are to be taken care of. This means I will be handling your account for the time being."

Leopardi's voice dropped. "Oh dear, what happened? Is his wife alright?"

"We're not quite sure, Mr. Leopardi. His wife is undergoing some tests, so David will be by her side for the next few days, at least."

"Oh my goodness! Please send his wife and David my regards. Is there any way I could help at all? Perhaps I can fly over there and help?"

"No need, Mr. Leopardi. Our firm has a pretty robust healthcare plan, so the financial aspects are all taken care of," I said. "You don't need to worry, but I will definitely pass on your good wishes over to David."

"Well, it seems you really jolted me this morning, Mr. Marietta," he said. "Thank you for being so kind as to have informed me about Mr. Johnson's situation. Since I am assuming that you are in charge of my account, how is the pending offering with our little project going?"

"Please call me Rick," I said. Typical idiot, he believes every word I say. Might as well try the casual approach to put him even more at ease. "All my friends call me that."

Leopardi started laughing. "And you can call me Tony. I understand it is somewhat of an informal nature, but I feel you are a sincere person, just as David was. We called each other on our Christian name basis as well."

"I'm honored, Tony. As for the Apgen Pharmaceuticals initial public offering, everything is a go. I wanted to be the first to tell you that we are expecting the announcement of the formal listing price to be around twenty dollars a share when it opens for the first time on NASDAQ in the next couple of weeks."

The fool's excitement began to intensify as his voice took a higher pitch. These morons were so predictable. "Twenty? Wow, that is amazing! David was telling me the listing price was expected to be only seventeen dollars per share. Why the sudden jump?"

"The stock underwriters readjusted their numbers because of the still secret news of one of their drugs, Tony," I said. "This is privileged information I am about to tell you, so please keep it to yourself for now. The FDA approval for their anti-viral drug has been confirmed. It will be announced a week after the company goes public."

His tone of voice became agitated. "Well, thank you, Rick! I am honored to be getting such information. But, is this legal?"

I laughed a little to put him at ease. When the conversation turned too serious, the negativity also increases. Best to ease off every now and then. "Tony, we both know that when two businessmen talk and somebody mentions a rumor, it's all just that- a rumor. There is so much information out there and one never knows which one of them has any kind of importance. I am only passing this along to a few select clients, and since David considers you not just as a client but as a friend, he insisted you be notified about this new development. It's all just a matter of timing."

There was a brief pause on the other line before he answered me. "This …is very significant news then. I was planning to place an order for about eight million dollars worth of shares when I spoke with David, but if you are sure this is information is correct, then I was thinking I might place around twenty million. Would you be able to accommodate that size of a purchase for me?"

I was ready to jump up and explode with joy, but I

needed to temper my enthusiasm and concentrate. I've always believed in keeping it cool, never betray your emotions to the client. Make him work for it. "Well it's funny you mentioned that since I have several Chinese clients that are planning to put in similar amounts. This definitely puts me over the limit with the number of shares I can allocate, even with David's own limit added to mine."

"So you can't allocate twenty million dollars worth of shares for me? Come on, Rick, I have been a client with your firm for several months now! I will be a safer investor than those Chinese ones!"

He was getting hot. I could sense it. Time to close him. I paused for a bit to pretend that I was thinking. "Okay, here's what I can do for you, Tony," I said. "I don't normally do this, but I think I can transfer some of the allocated shares from my other clients over to you so you can place your full twenty million in, but you have to give me a commitment, in writing as well as some proof that you have the funds ready for transfer. Remember, it's me on the line here if you suddenly change your mind, and refuse to proceed with the payment once the shares have been allocated in your name, Tony."

"Alright, I will do that for you, Rick," Leopardi said. "I'll have my accountant prepare an official, certified bank statement in my name, and it will state that I have the funds available. In addition, I will prepare a personal letter that says I am committed to buying these shares in writing. To whom should I address it to?"

Oh shit. His accountant? I think my plan just backfired.

The last thing I wanted to do was to get a third party to be in on the deal. The best way to close a sale was to keep the client in your exclusive control, with myself being the only one who could influence him. "No need for your accountant to be involved with this, Tony. Just your letter on its own should be sufficient enough evidence for me to get approval for the share allocation. You can address that to me."

"I'm sorry, Rick," he said. "But my accountant has to be involved. For a transfer this size, I have to check off with him. Don't worry, he usually approves every one of my decisions, so this deal is as good as gold."

Despite his reassuring words, my worry meter just broke. I hated accountants and wives because they were deal killers and this moron was going to tell! "Oh, I understand your relationship with him, Tony. But remember that I have given you privileged information, so it means that it was for your ears only."

The fucker laughed. "Don't worry, Rick! I won't tell him about that part. If you could give me a few days, say …call me at this time around Monday so we could finalize this. I am eager to invest in this recommendation of yours."

I silently let out a deep breath. There really was nothing I could do to stop him from telling others. If I insisted, then it might just make him suspicious and the whole thing could unravel. "Alright, but is it possible for me to contact you sooner in case something comes up?"

"Of course, Rick. Do you have my mobile number?"

I double checked Elliot's notes. "Yes, I have it."

"Good, call me anytime on it. Now that I have your

number, I will be sure to answer it. Send me your email too so that I can forward my personal letter over."

"Alright, but don't forget that I need an answer, or otherwise my other clients will end up with the stocks I allocated for you," I said.

Leopardi laughed again. "Don't worry, Rick! It's in the bag. I have a morning meeting so I have to go. Bye for now."

"Take care, Tony. Enjoy your day. Bye bye." I said just before I ended the call.

I took the headset off as I slumped on the sofa. Goddamn it. Now he was going to talk to his scum sucking accountant. I knew I had him, but any sort of adviser just complicated things. There was no point in moping around and being negative, so I got up, took my clothes off and had a long hot shower. Oh well, if it happens it happens, if not, then it's back to square one. Even though I've had deals bomb out on me before, this one would hurt.

It was around late afternoon when I took a cab to Suvarnabhumi Airport. While I waited in the departure area, I sent an email to Otis, asking for a meeting in a public place. Although I wanted a private conversation with him, I didn't want him to bring his boys over so it was better out in the open. Otis was intelligent enough to be discreet about his sexual orientation, so I figured it would be best for both of us. Once more I tried calling Doc, but his phone was still off. This whole affair was getting stranger by the hour. Just as I sent off a text message to Jessica telling her I would be boarding soon, an incoming call came through from Bob Duffy.

I pressed the answer button. "Yeah, Bob. What's up?"

"Good news," he said on the other line. "Your car is safely in my garage. You can pick it up anytime. I left the keys with my housekeeper."

"Great, thanks Bob," I said. "I'm at the airport, I'll be going to Macao to meet with Jessica and her mom in a bit."

"Oh, will you be coming back anytime soon?"

I nodded, even though he couldn't see me. "Yeah, I will be. I had a talk with Panupong's widow and children, by the way."

"Really, how did it go?"

"I can't give you the details over the phone, but something's definitely up," I said. "I'll talk to you about it the next time we meet in person."

"Okay dude, you got it," he said. "So you're not in any danger I assume?"

"At this point, probably not," I said. "But I don't have the whole picture yet. It's one hell of a Chinese puzzle. The good news is I talked to the whale, the bad news is that the deal is fifty-fifty."

"Oh? I thought it was done and dusted."

"It was, then he decided to talk it over with his accountant. You know how third parties are," I said.

"Oh shit, yeah, they're fucking deal busters. But I prefer to deal with accountants than their wives, if you know what I mean."

"I hear you," I said. At least there was a silver lining in all of this. If the client's wife said no, it would be a hundred times harder to turn him around. "I'll keep you updated on it. Have you found any alternate banking we could use?"

"Well I talked to Erich in Manila. He might be able to do something, but I'm not sure about his rates and whether he can handle the amount yet."

"Oh no, no," I said. "Fuck Erich. I hate dealing with that asshole."

"He's trustworthy though."

Erich Bierly was an American who used to run his own office, but he had eventually retired to become a go-between to office owners and bankers. When it came to business, he was alright, but he had a terrible, abrasive personality and would always start rumors behind everyone's back. He was the guy who'd say shit about you when you weren't around, but would treat you like a king when face to face with him. Erich was a misanthrope, and he secretly despised everyone. A dickless, backstabbing coward and braggart. I nearly put my fist through his face once.

The more I thought about Erich, the angrier I got. "No, not him," I said. "I'll only go through him as a last resort."

"I totally understand, dude," Bob said. "You and him do not get along."

"That's an understatement. He doesn't get along with anyone."

"Do you want me to contact the Singaporean? He might have some bankers."

"Herbert the options guy? He's another dick," I said. "And that little oriental Napoleon will probably steal the money right from under me. No way. I would rather deal with Erich the asshole than him."

Bob sighed. "Okay, that pretty much is all the bankers that I know of."

"No problems, Bob. I'll keep asking around," I said.

"One more thing," he said. "You remember Roderik Navarro?"

"It kinda rings a bell," I said. "But not really."

"He was a Filipino opener who worked in the office a few months ago. He closed a few deals for us," Bob said. "He was doing pretty well actually. Then he disappeared without telling me. I assumed he ended up working for somebody else."

"Okay, and?"

"Well, I was going through his old accounts and when I called up one of his clients, the guy said that Rod called him up again using the phone name he used with us, but he told the client he moved to another firm and loaded him there," Bob said.

"The bastard," I said. It was not uncommon for one of the people who worked under you to go ahead and steal your customers so that they could bring it to another office. There were no hard and fast rules about doing it, but it pretty much pissed off every owner out there. Whenever somebody did it, they would usually be blacklisted from the industry as a lead stealer. But there was usually at least one owner desperate enough to take those scoundrels in. Money talks.

"The client told me the name of the firm he was dealing from," Bob said. "An outfit called Brinton and Dukes Securities."

I stood up as the flight to Macao was announced. "Okay, try to find out about who owns it. My flight is now boarding. I'll talk to you later. Bye."

6.

As expected, the flight was packed full of tourists. Since the travel time was around two and a half hours, there was no need to buy a business class seat, so I just reserved the aisle seat nearest to the exit. There was a large family standing in front of me as they looked back and forth and had to find their proper seats with the assistance of a flight attendant. It was the one thing I hated about traveling in planes, one was usually hemmed in like cattle with a bunch of idiots who didn't know left from right. I had this theory about people losing half their IQs when they went on vacation, it sure looked this was a textbook example. The other thing I hated was when planes didn't take off on time because of some idiot coming in late at the last minute. While airlines nowadays would usually just take off if someone was too late, what made it worse was when a dolt already checked in their luggage, so we all would have to wait while it got removed from the cargo hold. This particular flight was no exception as we were already running thirty minutes late from our scheduled departure time.

There was no point in getting angry about it, so I took out an in-flight magazine from the rear pouch of the seat in front of me and started reading it. The bawling noises from a screaming toddler a few rows behind me was getting unbearable. I took out my smart phone so that I could drown out the brat's incessant crying with some music, but I quickly realized that I had forgotten my earphones back in my condo. I closed my eyes as I tried to calm myself down.

"Really small children shouldn't be allowed on flights," a slightly-accented voice beside me said.

I opened my eyes and turned my head. Sitting beside me was a, smiling middle-aged woman with silvery blonde hair. "I completely agree with you," I said softly.

"I just came back from spending a week in Pattaya," she said. "My first time in the orient. Everyone has the same colored hair here. All black. Unlike in Europe, where you see all different colors!"

So I would be spending the next few hours with a chatty tourist. Great. "Yeah, it takes some getting used to," I said. At least it was taking my attention away from the terrible two year old behind us.

She pulled out a tourist map and started writing notes on it. "Have you ever been to Macao before?"

"A few times."

She giggled. "It will be my first. Is it anything like Hong Kong? I'll be going there after I tour Macao."

"Nope," I said. "Very different. Macao is a part of China but it was a former Portuguese colony since the Sixteenth Century. Hong Kong was under British rule and that only started in the Nineteenth Century. So Macao had been under European influence for a much longer time."

The woman took out some cash from her handbag as she counted them. "That's good to know. They use the same currency, right?"

"No, they don't. Hong Kong uses the HK dollar," I said. "While Macao uses the pataca. Don't worry though, most places will take Hong Kong dollars."

"Oh wow, I didn't know all this."

"That's quite alright."

"It must have been pretty chaotic when the Portuguese handed Macao back to the Chinese," she said.

I smirked. "Actually, the Portuguese wanted to hand Macao back to China back during the seventies, but China refused."

Her eyebrows shot up. "They refused? Why would they want to do that?"

I shrugged. "I guess they just weren't ready."

The cabin doors were finally shut and the plane started moving, but the baby behind me kept on crying. I felt like getting up and screaming at the parents to shut their bratty kid up, but the last thing I wanted to do was spark trouble all over again.

"It's a good thing that I have music on my phone," she said. "I think I'm just going to listen to it so I won't have to hear that horrible child."

"Lucky you," I said. "I forgot my earphones back in Bangkok."

The woman beside me took out an old pair of earphones

from her handbag and handed them to me. "I have an extra pair," she said as she pulled out a second, newer headset as well. "You can borrow it for a few hours."

I grinned. "Thank you very much."

A few minutes later, we were airborne as I sat back in the chair while listening to rock music from my smartphone's playlist. This made the flight somewhat more bearable.

After we landed on the airport, I bid the woman goodbye as I made my way through the arrivals gate. I didn't have any luggage other than a small bag for hand carry, so I breezed through customs and immigration pretty quickly. Unlike Hong Kong's own gargantuan airport, Macao International had a rather small terminal. There were colorful goldfish and dragon decorations hung up with wires up on the ceiling, but other than that the airport was pretty subdued. As soon as I got outside, I noticed a black Mercedes pulling up alongside the sidewalk.

The rear passenger door opened and Jessica came out. "Don, over here!"

I walked up to her and gave a big hug as I kissed her luscious lips. I was horny and she was already giving me a hard on. "I missed you, Jess."

"Likewise," she said. "Come on, we're late and my mom's waiting."

I got in the backseat with her and we soon sped off. Within minutes we were soon crossing the Amizade Bridge towards the main peninsula. At night the bridge looked like a gigantic, golden glowing harp as its support piers were illuminated with blazing yellow lights. The tension of the past few days slowly began to drain away from my body as Jessica's presence alone started to sooth me, while we held each other's hands in silence.

Macao has a pretty small land area and the limo service dropped us off in front of the hotel. There was a gigantic golden statue of a Chinese dragon sitting on a stone platform beside the driveway, red and green lasers emanating from its plastic, lifeless eyes. At the opposite end of the entrance was a gigantic water fountain throwing multicolored lights up into the sky. Electronic billboards alongside the hotel showing unearthly models lit up the neon night. The whole place seemed to be made of glass, steel, gold and ambient waves of light. I waved the porter away as I casually carried my gym bag over my shoulder while we strode through the VIP lobby. Apparently, Jessica picked out the most expensive hotel she could find. The one thing about Macao was that there was a casino located in every hotel, the whole city generated at least five times more gambling revenue than Las Vegas did, so this was literally the gambling capital of the world. In this particular hotel, the casino must have covered the entire lower ground floor and then some. Ultra rich Asians and foreigners from all over were dressed in tuxedos and evening dresses as they made their way along the concourse leading to the casino area. Ferraris, Porches and Lamborghinis were parked out in front, their new, shiny paint jobs glistening beneath the glare of the spotlights.

Jessica took me by the elbow as she led me towards the VIP elevators. "I figured you might want a change of clothes and freshen up first."

"Good idea," I said. "I'm not exactly in a gambling mood anyway." I just wanted to relax and maybe screw her later.

There was a subdued chime as the elevator doors opened. Jessica stepped inside first. The frame of the lift was decked out in gold. With the side panels as mirrors, it felt like we were in some shining, auric crystal cage as she used the touch screen to bring us to the penthouse. "Well, Mom is over at the casino so I figure we can meet her there and then just go to dinner afterwards, what do you think?"

I shrugged. When it came to anything outside of business, I always let her make the decisions. "Whatever you want to do, Jess."

Her eyes scanned me from head to toe. "Something's really bothering you, Don. Are you going to tell me what?"

"What makes you think anything's bothering me?"

"We've been married for close to a year now," Jessica said as the doors opened. "I can read you like a book."

I stepped out first. "Am I that obvious?"

She smiled as she stood beside me. "No, you're pretty good at hiding your feelings from others."

"But not from you."

"Bingo."

She led me down to the door as she took out a keycard and placed it near the door knob. The double entryway opened up and we walked into the suite's living room. Marble coffee tables, beige padded chairs and sofas, a small dining table that could fit eight with a chandelier above it. The walls along the side were glass and a sliding door led out into a balcony that overlooked the South China Sea. There were a few boats traversing the waters, their navigation lights glowing like fireflies in a sea of undulating darkness.

I walked over to where a padded massage bed had been laid out. "Impressive."

Jessica giggled as she stood beside me. "Yeah, Mom had the full spa treatment this afternoon after we did a bit of sightseeing in the morning."

"Where did you go?"

"Oh, the usual places: the Maritime Museum, St. Paul's Ruins, Fortaleza do Monte, the usual stuff. She didn't like the egg tarts, but she sure as hell liked the pork buns."

I shrugged. "Who doesn't like a pork chop sandwich?"

"Devout Muslims and kosher Jews?"

"Good," I said. "More for us."

She wrapped her arms around my neck as our foreheads touched. "Now, are you going to tell me what's bothering you?"

The tip of my tongue touched her nose. "Can I change to some better clothes first?"

She pulled away from me and rolled her eyes. "Fine. But you will end up talking to me sooner or later, Don."

"I know." Better it be later since I wasn't in the mood right then and there.

Thirty minutes later I showered again and put on a black tuxedo. The casino had a strict dress code and Jessica insisted we looked as snobbish as possible. She apparently thought we had an image to maintain. As I walked out into the living room while putting my jacket on, Jessica stood up from the couch and walked on over to me as she started to adjust my collar.

"Sorry," I said. "This is like, only the second time I ever wore this."

"Sorry ain't good enough," she hissed as she started to set my bow tie. "I already told you how to make a knot for a bow tie when we rehearsed our wedding, remember?"

I shrugged. "I forgot."

"You forgot? How could you forget? You did wear a bow tie when we got married, so how did you get that on your collar back then?"

I grinned sheepishly. "I forgot how to put it on so I got a snap-on tie at the last minute."

For a minute she paused. Jessica looked up into my eyes as if she was ready to slap me. "You didn't. Did you?"

I pursed my lips. She was going to find out sooner or later anyway. "I did. I'm sorry."

Jessica grimaced as she suddenly tightened the knot she made around my neck. It felt like a hangman's noose as I groaned and backed away. She fumed for a minute or two, then gestured at me to move closer so she could finish the knot. We both started laughing afterwards.

When we got to the casino floor it seems that I had underestimated the size of the whole place. The establishment was spread out over two floors and there were over two hundred gaming tables in the main hall alone. Not one, but four full service bars where you could get your drinks from as well as hundreds of slot machines lined the walls. There were private rooms near the far end of the casino, where high rollers in baccarat and high stakes poker could have some measure of peace and quiet while gambling a typical man's annual wages on a single hand.

Jessica kept looking down at the elaborately designed carpets on the floor as we made our way silently through the main hall. Within ten minutes, Jessica squeezed my elbow and pointed to a table near the center aisle. We made our way over to the table that hosted a game of Texas hold'em. Jessica's mom noticed us with a curt nod as she continued to play a hand while sitting near the center, facing the dealer. There were two other players beside her on the table. One was barrel-chested man with blond hair and a cowboy hat. The other was a bespectacled Asian man wearing an oversized pinstriped suit. A waitress approached us to see if we wanted any drinks but we waved her off. Although our suite room entitled us to an unlimited bar tab at the casino, the last thing I wanted to do was to get drunk over here.

Crystal Bull was exactly how I remembered her from last time. Aside from her yellowish blond hair and the wrinkles around the sides of her mouth, she looked like a carbon copy of Jessica. I knew Doc was in his mid-fifties so he must have found Crystal while she was still young. Both mother and daughter had hazel eyes, but Crystal's peepers had a different sort of intensity. While Jessica's eyes projected a sense of eager playfulness, her mother's eyes seemed to indicate a sort of deception. It was as if Crystal could see into another person's inner soul and the hues of her eyes would change as a means to gain an advantage over those she wanted to dominate, like the way a praying mantis would change their skin color before closing in on their prey.

The man with the hat kept checking his cards as he looked at the flop of three community cards on the green felt table. "I think this is gonna be my lucky day, yessiree."

The Asian said nothing as his hands kept rubbing at the edges of his own playing cards. Chinese gamblers had a tendency to massage their cards, dealers would run through a whole bunch of new stacks every night because they had to throw away lots of bent and mangled cards at the end of every evening. This man was obviously a baccarat player, because one didn't do that when playing poker.

Crystal didn't say anything at first, then she placed two chips into the pile. "Raise you two thousand." Her words were short and direct. She had a much deeper voice than Jessica.

The man with the hat laughed a little as he called her raise by adding two of his own chips into the pot. "Ooh, the lovely lady's making a move."

Crystal didn't answer him as she just kept looking at the pile of chips in the center of the table. The Asian man was clearly in a worried mood as his hands kept fidgeting with his cards. From looking at the pot, there must have been at least twenty thousand dollars in chips on the line. Jessica was about to say something, but I clasped her hand and made a silent gesture at her not to interfere. The Asian man finally relented since nobody backed off by adding two chips into the pot.

The dealer nodded as he took out another card from the

deck and flipped it onto the table. Jack of diamonds. All three players said nothing. The Asian man's lower lips trembled, exposing his crooked teeth. The man with the hat stole a glance at Crystal with a smile on his face. He clearly had gold dental work embedded in his two front teeth. Jessica's mother stared off into the distance with a bored look on her face.

"This'll all be mine," the man with the hat said confidently as he added a small stack of chips to the pot. "Raise y'all five thousand. Let's see y'all beat that."

The Asian stared at Crystal to see if she would counter. For a long minute nobody did anything. Finally the Asian man moved his slightly mangled cards into the used pile. "I'm out," he said softly.

All eyes were on Jessica's mom. Crystal's body movement seemed to indicate that her hand wasn't the best, but her pride kept her in the game. She silently added her own chips into the pile, matching the man with the hat.

The dealer nodded as he took the final card out and flipped it onto the table. Jack of clubs. With two jacks, a king of spades, a ten of clubs and a seven of hearts in the five community cards, the final showdown between the cowboy and Jessica's mom promised to be a good one.

"Sorry, beautiful lady," the man with the hat said as he grabbed a handful of his own chips and started wriggling them in his hand. "I got this one, be best if you just fold 'em up now, ya hear?"

Crystal shifted her gaze at the man as her eye color suddenly took on a golden sheen. She used both hands to push her entire pile of chips into the pot. "All in."

The cowboy started laughing. "You must have a real hot hand in there, lady. Real, real hot. Let's up the ante. I'll buy you a drink if I lose- but if I win, I take you out to dinner, huh?"

Crystal's visage was a mixture of calculating menace and cold contempt. "Either call it or fold your hand, you hick son of a bitch."

The man with the hat suddenly tensed up. For a moment I thought he was going to get up and slap Jessica's mom in the face, forcing me to intervene, but he calmed down to the point where he countered with his own full stack of chips. He was about to say something until he noticed me and Jessica, and immediately sensed we were with Crystal. The man glared at her with wanton hate but stayed silent as both sides were now all in.

"Ladies and gentlemen," the dealer said. "Please reveal your cards."

With a sneer, the cowboy flipped his two cards over and revealed a pair of kings. Along with the king and two jacks in the community cards, it meant he had a full house: three kings and a pair of jacks overall. A very tough hand to beat.

Crystal stared at him blankly for a few seconds before turning over her own cards. A pair of jacks. She had four of a kind. As the two men started at her with open mouths, Jessica and I helped her gather up the pile of chips as we left the table and headed off to dinner.

7.

There was not one, but two fine dining establishments located within the hotel. Since Crystal volunteered to buy us dinner, we let her decide as to which one we would eat at. The three of us ended up taking a table at a Michelin starred restaurant, presided over by a world famous celebrity chef. We all sat by the large window overlooking the sea from the fortieth floor. The tables were made of green colored, volcanic obsidian. The cutlery was pure silver and gold. From my own experience, every dish in these tasting menus were great for a couple of bites, but left your stomach feeling empty by the end of the meal. As I dug into the small plate of frozen durian and dragon fruit compote with pomegranate and truffle syrup, I thought about going out in the middle of the night and grabbing a couple of Macanese pork buns. Hopefully there would still be some places open, I figured.

Crystal stared at me as a half-filled wine glass hovered near her face. "Enjoying yourself, Don?"

"I am indeed," I said. "Thanks for this wonderful dinner."

Jessica put her spoon down and stared at me. "So can you now tell us what happened in Bangkok?"

I sighed. "Do we have to go through this now, Jess? Can we just let it go? It's been a long day for me."

She had been bugging me about what was happening the whole time I arrived. Now I sensed her impatience was at the boiling point. "What kind of a relationship is this, Don? You nearly got killed the last time something happened, and now you don't even want to discuss it? I thought we were partners?"

"We are partners, Jess," I said softly. Jesus. I can't believe she was bringing this out right then and there. And with her mom in attendance. "I never lied to you ever since we got married."

Jessica looked away. "You don't tell me anything, so why would you even need to lie?"

I looked down at my half empty plate. "Look, let's not start this again."

"Start what? We've barely said anything to each other ever since you flew in."

Here we go again. I was exasperated. "You know what I do and you know what your dad does. You even know all my passwords to all my business emails and server access. Do I need to explain it any further?"

Jessica grimaced. "You've been asking me nonstop if I heard from my father, and now you don't want to tell me anything? I was with you all the way when we got the load box and the money last year, remember? Is my dad in trouble or is it about something else?"

I tapped my fingers on the stone table. I really didn't want her involved in this. Not when I was still working the whole thing out myself. "It's just that you're going to end up lecturing me again about this morality shit and stuff. I don't want to argue tonight. I'm tired."

"But isn't that what you do? You swindle people, right?"

"I work for your dad," I said tersely. "Which means we all do it. Like I said, you're starting to lecture me all over again. We're sitting where we are right now because of what I do. We wouldn't be able to afford that lovely presidential suite up there in the penthouse if it wasn't for the kind of work I do. I'm doing all of this for you, Jess."

Jessica leaned over so her face was right next to mine. "Yet, you treat me like I'm some sort of idiot. You use me like you use the people who work for you. To you, I'm just a source of information. If my dad is in some kind of trouble then I deserve to know about it!"

"Look, I don't really know what's going on yet. I just need time to try and find out about things," I said.

"Then include me in it," Jessica said. "I can help."

"You've never made this kind of demand on me before, Jess. You've separated yourself from the day to day running of the business, but all of a sudden you now want to know everything?"

Jessica leaned back on her chair. There was a stunned expression on her face. "Are you accusing me of hiding something from you?"

I rolled my eyes. "No, I didn't say that."

"I can read it on your face," she hissed. "I already told

you I haven't heard from my daddy for the last few days, but that's normal because we don't see each other much. It's always been that way. So you need to tell me what's going on."

My fingers touched the base of the wine glass in front of me as I swished its liquid contents around. "I just can't tell you what I think until I've got some sort of confirmation, okay?"

Jessica was quiet for a whole minute. Then she suddenly stood up and threw her napkin on the table. "There is no point in talking to you," she said as she turned around and left.

I turned my head as I started to stand up. "Jess, I..."

It was too late, she was halfway across the room as she rounded a corridor which led to the elevators and was soon out of sight. I didn't want to leave her mother by herself- especially since she was paying for this expensive dinner- so I slumped back down on the chair. How could I tell my own wife that I suspected her father had tried to have me killed?

Crystal had been silent the whole time. I noticed that she had been observing me with her golden flecked hazel eyes. "There's still half a bottle of wine left, Don," she said without a trace of emotion. "Why don't you top up your glass? It's a Petrus, so it's best not to let it go to waste."

I leaned over as I took the bottle of Bordeaux and poured some more into my glass, then I gave her some as well. "Sorry about that."

Crystal gave a faint smile as she shrugged with a cool indifference. "Husband and wives, they always fight. Give her some time to cool off and she'll be okay. Jess is a lot like me, it doesn't take much to get our temperatures up."

"Oh? I've never really seen you lose your temper."

"You didn't see my flare up with the southern country bumpkin at the hold'em table a couple of hours ago?"

"You didn't lose your temper back there," I said. "You were just playing him so you were able to take all of his money."

Her smile became more pronounced. "You're an excellent judge of character, Don. It's a pity we haven't seen much of each other ever since we met at your wedding for the first time. I think I would like to make up for that right now."

"You think we can get to truly know each other just over a few glasses of wine?"

She giggled. "Let's try it, shall we? You were able to size me up at the poker table back there after just a few minutes, why not try to figure out the rest right now?"

"I'm not quite sure what it is that you want from me," I said.

"You're my son in law," she said. "I would like to get to know you more, that's all. Doesn't every mother have a right to do that?"

"Mothers, yes. Mother in laws- well, you know what they say about that."

Her left eyebrow arched. "You think I'm a stereotypical mother in law, out to defend her daughter at all cost?"

I laughed a little as I shook my head. "No, no. I'm sorry- I think that was an awkward thing to say on my part."

She looked directly into my eyes. The golden flecks in her pupils combined with the brown pigment made it seem like her soul was opaque. "There's no need for caution, Don. Even though I'm like my daughter, I think there's a lot more similarities between you and me."

What was she getting at? "Really?"

She took a sip of the wine. "Yes, really. I know you came from a hard luck past, and so did I. My daughter, well she was given everything when I gave birth to her. Paul made sure we had whatever we needed. Jessica went to the best schools, she got her first car the moment she passed her driving exam, and all that. When she told me that you worked your way to a college degree completely on your own, I sensed a sort of kinship between us."

"It was just a degree from a cheap city college. Didn't really help me much," I said.

"The fact that you did it speaks volumes about your determination," she said. "I like that. You did what needed to be done in order to get ahead. I heard about your escape from my husband's office when he had it raided too."

"I worked in a sporting goods store and lived on instant noodles and hotdogs to get by during my college days."

"Good for you," Crystal said. "Before I met Paul, I was a stripper. I used my earnings in that job to take a few college classes."

I sat back, stunned.

She gave me another faint smile as she poured more wine into her glass. "Paul was actually a lecturer in one of my classes. When we locked eyes, I knew he was smitten by me.

We got married not long afterwards. I was carrying his child when he got his first taste of this boiler room business you people are in. I didn't hear from him for months and I was ready to get an abortion. Then the money started coming in. First a trickle, then the next thing I knew he booked a hotel ballroom and the surrounding gardens for our wedding. I liked to think he did it for us."

I let out a deep breath. "I'm sorry, I never knew."

"I didn't tell anyone about it. The only ones who know are Paul... and now you."

"Y-you didn't tell Jess any of this?"

Crystal shook her head. "No, then again I doubt she was ever interested in knowing about this. When money no longer became an issue I decided to take more classes to finish my degree. Jessica ended up in boarding school, so I was pretty much free to do whatever I wanted. I got into the high society crowd, but then I got bored talking to women who grew up privileged, the ones who never had to scrape by and instead had everything handed to them on a silver platter. I despised them so I left that scene. Even though we've gotten divorced since then, I know what my ex is up to, and I'm fine with it. I also know that Paul has got mistresses, just like you- but that's okay. It's the nature of the beast."

How in the hell did she find out? "I-I don't have any mistresses."

Her face instantly became like a block of stone as she examined me, as if I was some sort of amoeba under a microscope. "Don't think of me as a fool, Don. I know you have one. People like you always have. But don't worry, I won't say anything to Jessica about it. Just make sure she either doesn't find out, or get her to the point she's willing to accept what kind of a man you are."

I could sense that she was telling me I could trust her in a number of matters. "What do you think? What kind of a man am I to you?"

She took another sip of wine. "I believe there's only two kinds of people in this world: spiders and flies. My own dad was a spider and I was his fly when I was growing up. This kept going until I found his gun, put it to his face and told him that if he ever did that thing to me again, I would kill him. That was when I became a spider. My husband, the one you guys call Doc, he's a big hairy spider."

"That doesn't answer my question."

"So you want to know what I think of you, Don? I think you're a spider trapped in a fly's body," she said.

I'm not sure what her intentions were in all of this, but she was making me feel quite uneasy. "What does that even mean?"

Crystal poured the remaining wine into my glass. "Figure it out."

When I got back into the suite's living room, I took off my jacket and threw it onto a nearby chair. I slumped down onto the sofa in the center of the room as I untangled the bow tie around my neck. My stomach started growling, so I leaned over and reached for the room service menu lying on the side table. As I started checking the list for the late night supper entrees, the door to the bedroom opened and Jessica stepped out. Her hair was a little bit tousled and she was wearing a silk bathrobe. She made her way over and sat down beside me.

I put the menu down and placed it on my lap. "I'm sorry for what happened earlier, Jess."

She moved closer until she was sitting right beside me and gave me a kiss on the cheek. "I'm sorry too. I shouldn't have snapped at you like that, Don. Will you forgive me?"

I gave her a long kiss as our lips joined for about two minutes. Might as well get this over with. Jessica was going to find out sooner or later, better she hear it from me. "Just yesterday there was a man who pointed a gun at my face and was about to pull the trigger. I got lucky."

Her hands were in my chin as she twisted my head until our eyes met. "You are in trouble. Why would someone try to kill you?"

I hesitated for a few seconds before answering her. "I know you're going to find this hard to believe, but I think your dad might be trying to kill me."

It was one shock too many for her. Jessica pulled away as she slumped backwards at the opposite end of the couch. "Are you insane? Why would Daddy want to try and kill you?"

I looked at the coffee table in front of me. "I'll start from the beginning. One of my loaders has gotten a potential monster deal that would probably set me up as an independent owner if it pushes through. I met up with Mr. Panupong in a hotel lobby to try and work out a banking deal. Two waiters were serving us drinks- until they pulled out guns from underneath their uniforms and started shooting. Panupong and my loader were killed. I was able to escape through the kitchen. I tried to call Doc but he wasn't answering and I haven't been able to contact him since then. It can't be a coincidence, Jess."

Her eyebrows connected. "This ...this is nuts. Why would my dad want to kill you if you've got a big deal coming in, that's great for all of us, right?"

"I was meeting Panupong in secret because I wanted my own banking to bring the money in," I said. "I was cutting your dad completely out of it. I think he found out, and that's why there were two hitmen in that hotel."

Jessica's eyes glazed over. I could tell she was having a hard time believing in it. "B-but why? Why would you want my daddy out of that deal? Don't you work for him?"

"I was doing it for us. I want to be independent."

"What for? My daddy has been pretty good in making you run things, hasn't he? You can independently access the bank accounts for the business right? Wasn't that one of the things you demanded when you started your partnership with him?"

"Yes," I said. "But you know how he is, Jess. I want to finally be out, on my own. This deal will enable me to have no more partners. It'll be just me, myself, and I."

Jessica was clearly uncomfortable with this conversation. She was doing her best to stay in composure. "But why though? What could my dad do to make you want to get out of this beneficial relationship with each other?"

"It's not what he could do, it's what he did, Jess," I said. "Remember the year before? He had his own office raided in order to get rid of a rival. I barely got away and that's how we met. If he was capable of that sort of thing, then how can you expect me to work with him for a long time? You can't trust a man that ruthless. There's no way I can keep working for anybody with that kind of potential for long. This deal that this whale is gonna do is my ticket to independence from him."

She exhaled deeply. "But you yourself said that he needed to get rid of that rival of his in order to stop his enemy from taking over. He had cause back then. You're his son in law, he can't betray you like that now."

"I can't take that chance, Jess," I said softly. "I've never trusted him since the very beginning. He's capable of anything."

Jessica's lips started to tremble. She was ready to cry. "And so are you! No, no. I can't believe he would try to have you killed like this, no way!"

"Look, just calm down, okay? I'm just suspecting he did it at this point," I said to try and reassure her. "I'm not sure about it yet, but I can't discount that possibility."

Jessica looked away and stayed silent for a minute before she answered. "It could be just a coincidence that you can't contact him. Maybe he's up to something that has nothing to do with what happened to you."

She was in denial mode. Okay, fine. I needed more evidence to convince her. "I admit, what I've got is purely circumstantial, but the odds of him disappearing like this, right after it all happened- is too good to be true," I said.

"Well until you find more evidence implicating him, then I'm just not convinced at this point," she said. "If other people got wind of your deal, then wouldn't they try to take it from you as well?"

I nodded. "You have a point, there. But if the others did get wind of the deal, then they would try to steal it from under me, not try to have me killed. Jess, the hit was a professional one. Panupong had four bodyguards and they were taken completely by surprise. And I recognized one of the hit men."

Her eyes widened. "Are you kidding me? Who?"

"It was the Thai man with the scar, Jess," I said. "Remember the time our car fell into the Chao Phraya? Do you remember when Finny ambushed us and he was about to kill me, then you? Finny was shot and killed by that very man. The man with the scar was the one who chased us into the river and then he saved us afterwards."

"But wait, isn't he the guy who works for Panupong? I mean, last year you pretended to be someone else to try and get the money, remember? You met with Panupong and he said his men will meet up with us to give us the cash, right?"

"You're totally right," I said. "He was one of Panupong's men. When I met his widow this morning, they asked me if I recognized any of the shooters, I told them I didn't."

"But why? You could have told her that one of her own husband's men killed him!"

I looked at her with tired eyes. "Because if I did tell them, then there's a good chance I would have never made it over here."

Jessica ran her hand over her hair. "Are you saying that someone from Panupong's own family had him killed?"

"It's a distinct possibility," I said. "Think about it, who else but your own men would know what your schedule is that day? Someone with knowledge of his exact itinerary would plan the perfect hit. If Panupong was in his house or office, he would be fully protected, there would have been no chance to take him out unless he was in a public place."

"You think his own wife had him killed?"

"Or his two grown sons," I said. "The eldest one seems timid, totally dominated by his mother. The second son is a bit of a playboy and a rebel. Neither of them seem to be the killer types, but you can never know for sure. I know for a fact that the second son is pretty resentful because the older one is now in charge. It could be one of them, or it could be the wife, since she favors the eldest son while the father favored the second one. I just don't have enough evidence on who the culprit is. But all three of them have the motive and the means."

Jessica nodded. "Do you think there's different factions in Panupong's family?"

"I'm sure there is," I said. "He's got an army of bodyguards, and one of them said something cryptic to me as I was leaving the mansion. He mentioned that it was good that I had kept my mouth shut when I told Panupong's wife that I didn't recognize the assassin."

"Oh my god," Jessica said. "For them to kill their own father, that's sick. But if one of them did do it, then it would mean my daddy is innocent of the suspicion of trying to have you killed."

I bit my lip. "Doc and Panupong are partners, remember? Panupong handled all of Doc's banking until I demanded that we use the Malaysians instead. It was also Panupong who orchestrated the raid on your dad's office last year, with his tacit approval, of course."

"I don't buy it, Don," she said. "You haven't proven my daddy's involvement in this at all."

"You remember the mayor's birthday party last year?"

"We went to a lot of parties last year."

"It was the party where all the Thai big shots attended. Crystal was there too. We were all there."

Jessica nodded. "Oh yeah, that was the party we attended just before our wedding. Now I remember it."

"Panupong's widow showed me a picture of it," I said. "In the picture was you and me, your dad and Crystal, and one other guy. A Thai general by the name of Sangsorn. He's considered to be a big player in banking and is one of the senior leaders of the ruling junta."

"What about him?"

"Panupong's widow seems to think that General Sangsorn might have had something to do with the shooting."

"What does my dad have to do with that?"

"He's friends with the general, isn't he?"

"My dad is friends with a lot of people," Jessica said with a slight irritation. "That doesn't automatically mean he's part of every conspiracy out there. I think you're just paranoid, Don."

"All I'm saying is he knows both sides," I said. "And then

he disappears. You don't think that's suspicious?"

Jessica snorted. "Look, you need to get your theories in order because they contradict each other. First, you accuse my daddy of siding with one of Panupong's family members to have him killed, then all of a sudden, you make a claim that my father is in league with a Thai general to have Panupong killed. Which is it?"

"I'm not accusing anybody, Jess. All I'm saying is your dad seems to be at the center of this," I said. "If I can get in touch with him, I will have a clearer picture of what's going on. Right now I can't reach him so I'm hoping you can help."

"Well, I tried calling him too but I've gotten no answer."

"Did you email him?"

"Yes," Jessica said. "No reply as of yet."

"Well, we need to find him."

"Duh," she said. "Thank you, Captain Obvious. You got any ideas since we can't reach him by phone or by email?"

"He could be doing like what he did the last time," I said. "He was holed up in one of his condos and didn't communicate with anybody. I found him just sitting by the pool in his Singapore pad the last time, remember?"

Jessica sighed. "Okay, there's his condo in Hong Kong, and he's also got places in Singapore, Kuala Lumpur, Bangkok and Manila. Do you propose we fly off and go look into each and every one of them?"

"We could do that," I said. "We can split up and cover more ground that way. Do you think your mom would be willing to help?"

"I could ask her. It'll give her something to do at the very least."

"Does she know about your dad being missing and all that?"

"I told her you were looking for him and it was important," she said. "But I don't think she cares one way or the other. She's got her own condo in Florida and she has substantial savings, all courtesy of my daddy. Then again, I don't think she's worried with what's happening right now. When I asked her about daddy's business, she just shrugged and said she didn't know the full details as to what he does, but as long as the money keeps coming in, she couldn't care less."

I licked my lips. I sensed that there was more to Crystal than she was letting on. "Okay, we'll go ahead and ask her tomorrow if she could go to one of your dad's places and see if she could find him."

"Okay, you want to split up like what we did last time?"

"No, let's stick together this time," I said. I would rather keep her with me than have her fly off with her mom.

"Where do we go from here?"

"Back to Bangkok," I said. "I need to meet up with an old friend because with Panupong dead, I need another banker for this whale I'm bringing in."

Jessica made a faint smile. "So you're going ahead with it then?"

"It's a huge opportunity and I see no reason to back out of it now," I said. "Once I get the banking in place, this will be one hell of a piece of cake. It's still a gamble though, because the deal could fall through at any time."

"Oh, I thought it was a done deal already?"

"There's an old saying in my line of work that says, 'it's never a done deal until the money is in your pocket,'" I said. "The client wants his accountant to take a look, so a third party always complicates matters."

Jessica blinked a few times. "The way you describe your business makes it seem almost legit."

"It is legit, up until a certain point," I said.

She took my hand and held it close to her cheek. "Don, you know I think you're a pretty intelligent guy, even Mom thinks you're smart. Why don't you just give all this up and go truly legit. I mean, why don't we just go back to America and live, you know, like normal people?"

I started to laugh. "Seriously? You want to give all this up?"

She kissed my hand and giggled. "Look, it might be hard for the first few years, but with your brains, I'm pretty sure you don't need to do what you're doing right now in order to be successful."

I get it. She was doing her guilt trip on me again, but this time it was more of a reverse psychology. "Look, Jess. This kind of business, it's not something you can just quit on."

"Why not?"

I rubbed her soft hands as I brought her closer. "It's the mentality of it all. I know for a fact that I can never do any kind of normal work ever again. Once you're in this business, you start to get a taste for it. I talked to your dad about this awhile ago. I asked him how much would be enough for him to just forget about it. He told me it wasn't about the money anymore, it was about closing the next deal. I know for a fact that I could never ever work a nine-to-five job ever, not after experiencing all this. Who needs that when all you have to do is to pick up a phone, dial a number, tell some idiot a story and have him wire ten grand over? I couldn't fathom what Doc was telling me then, but now it all makes sense. It's become part of my nature."

She sighed. "Alright, we've argued about this countless times already. In the end, we just start fighting, so forget I asked."

I turned as my lips were close to her ear. "I'll tell you what. Once this deal is done, then you can ask me this question again. And I think I might have a different answer for you."

She turned and kissed me. "Seriously? This one client is going to change everything? You've said this on every deal you do."

I grinned like a madman. "This is it. If I can get this done, it'll be the biggest in the history of the industry. It'll be our fuck you money if we play it right, Jess."

She started giggling again as I nibbled on her ear and slowly ran my hands down to her waist. Then I untied the cord around her bathrobe. Her own hands started unbuttoning my shirt before peeling it away from my back. As I slid her panties off, Jessica unbuttoned my trousers and pulled them down to my knees. My cock was rock solid by then and was ready to burst through my boxer shorts. She maneuvered her thighs until it was just right and then took off my underwear. Jessica let out a soft moan when I entered her.

We ordered some food from room service afterwards. Sadly, there were no pork buns available.

8.

We met up with Crystal over breakfast at the restaurant near the lobby. When Jessica made the suggestion to look for her father, Crystal didn't object and volunteered to go to the Hong Kong condo, and then to the house in Singapore, if she couldn't find him in the former. We spent the rest of the morning doing some shopping in Senado Square before bidding each other goodbye. Jessica and I proceeded to the airport while Crystal took the ferry to Hong Kong. It was mid afternoon when we made it back to Bangkok. I hailed a taxi from the arrivals terminal and we made it to Bob Duffy's house. Old Bob was still up north in Chiang Mai, but his housekeeper gave me the keys to my car and we took it as we headed over to Doc's condominium.

Jessica still had the keys to the place, so we went up to the penthouse suite and got inside. The furnishings were a combination of traditional Thai woodcraft and modern plastic and leather. Interestingly, the whole place looked largely untouched. I ran my hand along the dinner table that was made from hand carved teak as I stared at the numerous paintings of

Buddha that adorned the walls. Jessica opened the doors to the bedrooms but she didn't find anything peculiar. I used the intercom system and asked the receptionist in the ground floor if Doc had been around lately. She replied that she hadn't seen him for the past few days.

Jessica's phone made a chiming noise as she turned it on. "Mom just sent me a text message. She's in my dad's condo in Hong Kong, but there's nobody in it. She'll go ahead and book a flight to Singapore for tomorrow."

"Okay," I said while flopping down on the sofa. There was a laptop sitting on the nearby coffee table so I flipped up the monitor screen and turned it on. "Do you know your dad's password for his computer?"

"No," she said from the bedroom. "Try my name."

I tried it but it didn't work. "Nope."

Jessica's head poked out from the open doorway. "You remember Casper, the Filipino hacker? He came up with a solution to that, I think."

I nodded. "Yeah, I remembered he did a combination of yours and your dad's birthdays, am I right?"

Her reply was distant as she went back inside the bedroom again. "I think so."

I tried it, but it still didn't work. Jessica's mention of Casper's name was a great suggestion though, so I sent a text message over to him and told him what the problem was. Casper Villar was a computer expert based in Manila, and he served as an unofficial hacking consultant with many politicians over there. In less than fifteen minutes, he sent me an email that contained some sort of software program called a password and registry editor. I opened it up on my phone and installed it, then linked it up to the laptop using my charge cable. When I booted up the program, it immediately found an installation of Doc's operating system on his laptop. I followed the text prompts and reset the administrator password. Within minutes, I was going through all the files in the laptop as I tried looking for clues.

Jessica came out of the bedroom and sat down on the sofa beside me. "So, you were able to get in after all."

"Your suggestion to ask Casper was great," I said as I kept my eyes glued to the monitor screen. "He emailed a Linux based program to reset your dad's passwords."

"Glad I could help. Did you find anything?"

"Hang on, I just got into it," I said as I searched through his virtual documents. A second folder popped up that contained nude pictures of a Thai girl that seemed familiar to me, but I couldn't recall her identity right at that very minute, so I saved one picture on my smartphone before I closed the file. "There's a couple of receipts here for plane tickets to Manila. One of them is pretty recent, just a few days ago. Do you think that's where he is?"

"Maybe," she said. Jessica was checking her own phone so she didn't notice the nude pictures. "Should we book a flight over there right away?"

"Not just yet," I said. "I still need to meet up with Otis later. I got an email from him as we boarded the plane. He said I could meet him for dinner tonight."

"I remember Otis. Dinner sounds great. Could I come with you?"

I looked at her. "I think it's better if you don't. He said to just meet him alone."

Jessica gave me an angry stare. "Fine, then!"

"Hold on," I said as I pointed at some entries on the laptop. "There's a bank receipt here. It's a transfer of funds from a Bangkok account to a Manila account. It just says the account number and the bank, but not the name. It's not much, just around twenty thousand dollars, but it's got nothing to do with the Malaysian bankers."

"Well that's a start," Jessica said. "Doesn't Casper know a lot of bankers in Manila?"

"That's true. I guess a trip to the Philippines will be in order in the next few days. Is that okay with you?"

She nodded. "If I'm missing dinner tonight, you owe me a nice dinner in Manila."

"Deal."

"And a whole day's worth of shopping which you'll be paying for."

"Oh, come on!"

I arrived at the fine dining establishment somewhat earlier than usual, so I had a few cocktails at the bar while I waited for Otis. This place looked brand new, right along the Silom strip that was inundated with tons of expensive restaurants. From the outside the place looked like a solid block of black granite but once you got in, the walls of the dining area was composed of intricately carved wood paneling. It was like being part of a medieval woodcut. The lighting in the place was quite subdued, so every booth that lined the sides of the restaurant was covered in shadow. There was an overhead lamp that hung low over each table, casting a spotlight on what was to be eaten, but keeping the actual diners obscured. As I glanced back, I noticed that all I could see were people's hands as they used their utensils to consume the food, the ones who were eating just darkened silhouettes, like a roomful of ghosts.

The bartender hovered from across the counter. The back end of the bar was also in the dark so I couldn't see his face either. "Would you like another Manhattan, sir?"

I nodded. "Sure, one more."

"Very good, sir," he said as he turned around and started mixing rye whisky and a little vermouth in a cocktail glass. The bottles in front of him were like a tiered altar of shining crystals since the ultraviolet spotlights above focused on the liquor display. The servers in this place all spoke excellent English. It was the one characteristic of fine dining places, their staff were usually of top-notch quality.

As the bartender placed another Manhattan in front of me and took the second, empty glass away, there was a sudden barking noise that broke the subdued atmosphere of the whole place. It sounded like a small dog. I was sitting on a stool, so I swiveled it as I turned around and noticed Otis's bulky form standing beside one of the booths at the far end of the dining area. All I could see was his darkened outline, but there was no mistaking his bald head and the way he moved. It looked like he was cradling something moving in his arms.

A waitress wearing a white shirt and black tie walked over

to me. "Sir, your fellow diner has arrived, would you like to follow me, please? I'll have your cocktail sent over to your table."

I nodded while getting up from the stool. She turned around and led me over to the booth where Otis was sitting. It was evident that the bundle around his arms was a small dog and he had placed it on the couch that snaked around the table. As soon as I got close, he stood up and walked over.

Otis held out his hand. "Don, it's been a long time! How are you?"

"Good, thanks," I said as I shook his hand. "Did you just bring a dog over here?"

He laughed while we both sat down. "Oh, I know the owner. He allows me to indulge in my whims."

"As long as they don't throw us out," I said. Otis was one hell of an eccentric. There was another uniformed waiter making his way towards us. The server placed my cocktail on the table and handed out a couple of menus. I had to lean forward so I could see the selections using the spotlight just above the table.

"Don't worry about that," Otis said as he gestured at the waiter to come closer. "We'll have the special tasting menu, please. Tell the chef that Otis is here tonight."

"Of course, Mr. Otis," the waiter said as he took our menus away and walked back towards the kitchen.

My hand was on the couch as I immediately noticed a growling noise just inches away from my fingers, so I brought it up on the table. "Is your dog a biter?"

Otis turned as he looked down at the couch. "Quincy, bad dog! Come here and sit. Sit down. There you go." The dog had made its way back to where he was and sat beside him, its muzzle staring upwards towards his face. "You'll have to forgive Quincy. He's not fully trained as of yet, but the boys love him so!"

"I'm surprised you didn't just leave it in your house."

He laughed. "Oh no, this dog is not yet a year old and so I want to acclimate it with other people. And Quincy loves to travel. Having a little dog like this while you walk around the city is great, so many kids love to look and try pet it."

"I bet."

The waiter came back with a couple of wine glasses which he set down on the table beside each of us. A second waiter came by with a bottle of wine that he showed to Otis. The dog started growling again, but Otis was able to keep it quiet by stroking its neck. The second server poured a bit of the wine into our glasses so we could sample it. Since it was his treat, I didn't mind if he went with it or not. All wines tasted the same, the only difference to me was either red or white. Otis gave his nod of approval so they poured a full glass for each of us before leaving the bottle at the table.

Within minutes, the first course was placed down in front of us. As we started eating, Otis would occasionally pick out a tiny morsel to feed to his dog. "So, about this Panupong business. I'm so glad you weren't killed, Don."

"It was pretty close," I said softly. "I still have nightmares about it. Jess told me my body jerked in my sleep while I was lying beside her last night. The fucking thing just keeps replaying itself over and over when I'm catching zzz's. It's like I can't even choose what I want to dream about anymore."

"I understand. Just give it some time. How is Jessica doing, by the way?"

"She's got money and she's been shopping with her mom all over Southeast Asia. She's fine as can be."

"Good, good. Now, the situation here in Bangkok is still pretty fluid. My sources have told me that the Panupong family is deeply divided, all the way down to the bodyguards."

I nodded. "Yeah, I figured that when they abducted me from my hotel room and brought me over to their hacienda for questioning."

His bald head suddenly jerked up. "Really? I haven't heard of that. This is definitely news to my ears. It does make sense that they would want to question you though."

"I'll say," I said. "I thought they were going to bring me to a rice paddy somewhere and shoot me. It was the wife and her eldest son who did the interrogation."

"That would be Ek, the momma's boy. Have you met the younger son?"

"I did," I said. "Just as I was being led back to the car. We had a short conversation. It seems that he isn't too happy about being son number two. His name is Jet, I think."

"That's correct," Otis said. "Jet was actually the favorite of his father. Mrs. Panupong the widow is the one who favors Ek. So as you can see, there might be a bit of a power play that's going to happen very soon, I expect."

"That guy was the favorite of his father? He seemed more interested in having a good time than actually running any sort of business. Why would Panupong the elder had wanted him to succeed his empire?"

Otis took another bite of the roasted truffle and mushrooms with vinaigrette emulsion from his plate. "Because Jet is the son who has a backbone, so to speak. Ek is too demurred, too indecisive to be running all the banking for the shops in the country. He tends to be hesitant and would consult with his mother before making a decision on anything."

I shrugged with indifference. "Well, I don't know. I wouldn't have either of them running the business if I was the one making the decision. The whole thing looks like a surefire recipe for disaster."

"I would agree with you," Otis said. "But if their family business is to survive, then one of them has to take the reins."

"From my first impression with those two kids, I would have thought that it was Jet who had his father killed."

"But why though? Jet was the favored one."

"Isn't it the Asian way of always having the eldest child take over?"

"Yes, but Panupong could have easily rectified that. He could have chosen his own successor regardless of age," Otis said.

"Okay, well it's just my hunch anyway."

"Think about it, Don. If Jet did have his father killed, then he would be sabotaging his own way to the throne, since it would be Ek who would automatically be in line for succession. I don't buy it."

"So you're saying Ek would be your suspect then?"

Otis shook his head. "No, as I said before, Ek is too much of a wuss to even think about arranging his own father's murder. If I had my suspicions, I would place it on the wife."

"Mrs. Panupong? But she's in a wheelchair. Why would that lady want to kill her own husband?"

"I don't know. Like I said, the whole situation is in flux and if you forced me to think of a suspect with the family who had the means to do it, then it would be her."

I suddenly recalled last night's conversation with Crystal. "Wait a minute, didn't Panupong have mistresses?"

"He had many."

"How many?"

"I'm not really sure," Otis said. "Maybe three, maybe four. Why?"

"I remembered hanging out with my old Thai girlfriend Ti a few months back," I said. "We were in a club called the Catty Cat I think, near Soi Cowboy. Jessica was back in the East Coast at that time visiting her college buddies. Anyway, Ti pointed out one girl who was sitting at the other end of the bar counter with her friends. She told me that the woman at the bar was Panupong's mistress. Her name was Waen, I think."

"So your mistress knows one of his mistresses, so what?"

I took out a smartphone from my shirt pocket and cycled through my files until the picture of the woman that I had taken from Doc's laptop showed up. I showed it to Otis. "When Jess and I got back here, we searched through Doc's condo unit. I was able to hack through his laptop and found this in his files. It's the same girl. I couldn't place her name earlier today, but now I totally remembered it."

Otis stared at the nude picture in the phone. "That photo was on Doc's computer?"

"Yup. Did Doc and Panupong share girls?"

"Not as far as I know," Otis said. "But it's possible that the women have more than one suitor. They're professionals after all, so it would mean more money for them."

"Listen, I know this sounds crazy," I said. "But I think Doc tried to have me killed along with Panupong."

Otis's was about to place some food in his mouth, but his fork stayed in the air. "What?"

"I'm serious. Right after the hit came down, I tried calling him and I wasn't able to get through. I've been phoning him all this time since then as well as emailing him. No response. I work for him for chrissakes. The last time he disappeared was when?"

"Last year," Otis said. "When he had Panupong raid his own office. It was the time that you went on the run."

"Exactly. Now all of a sudden I can't reach him."

"But you're married to his daughter. Why would he try and have you killed?"

"Because I'm about to pull off a very big load and I think he found out about it," I said. "You were the one who arranged the meeting with me and Panupong. Who else knew besides you?"

Otis's body stiffened. "Now wait a minute, Don, if you think that I betrayed you—"

I held up my hand to interrupt him. "I didn't say that. I

just need to know who else knew about the meeting, that's all. I'm not accusing anyone, not yet anyway."

He let out a deep breath. "Don, you know for a fact that I never divulge anybody's secrets. I was the one that got you into this business, remember?"

"I know that, and I'm eternally grateful. But look at it from my point of view. Somebody tried to kill me. If someone's after me, then I need to find out."

"I can tell you it didn't come from me," he said softly. "I understand your viewpoint and that you can't trust anyone right now. On the other hand, I have a reputation to uphold. People come to me with all sorts of needs and I make it a point to never tell on anyone. Now it seems I owe you a favor- if for nothing else that will prove you can still trust in me. I will help you find Panupong's mistress and help in your search for Doc as well. This I promise you. My other promise is that if the time and place of the meeting didn't come from me, then it must have been relayed from one of Panupong's people."

"That's what I'm suspecting," I said. "Either from within Panupong's own family, or from one of his men. And I know who the hit man is."

"Oh? Who?"

"One of Panupong's own men. The man with the scar on his face. You remember I told you about him, don't you?"

He nodded. "Yeah, you told me about him. He was the one who shot Finny."

"Right," I said. "I need to know his name and who he really works for, plus I need you to find Waen for me too."

"Okay," he said as he started eating again. "You told me you needed some banking as well, right?"

"Yeah, that was the reason why I wanted to meet with Panupong in the first place. This load is gonna require substantial banking and someone I could trust. Do you have anyone in mind?"

"I can put you in touch with several options," Otis said. "The Panupongs are still active. Jet is doing the rounds and wooing all of his dad's bankers and contacts, right from under his mother's nose while she is still in mourning. I can get you a meeting with him if you wish."

"You think I can trust him?"

"That I'm not sure," he said. "Up until now, everybody has been working with his father. As to what his temperament and competence is, I can't really say. You need to feel him out. If Jet is ambitious enough to take over, and I think he is, having known him personally for years now, then he might actually give you a good percentage to start with."

"That's assuming he gives me the money afterwards, of course."

"Of course. Jet is young, and he's intelligent and well educated. The only thing he lacks is his father's experience."

"How come you know him so well?"

Otis took a sip of wine. "Oh, he sometimes supplies me with boys from the provinces."

"So he's a pedo as well then?"

"I hate that word," Otis said softly. "It feels so vulgar and undignified. Even the label of boy lover sounds quaint. I prefer to use the term Ganymedian. It's a word I created myself."

"Whatever," I said. "Okay, set me up with a meet. I've heard that General Sangsorn might be in the banking business as well. What about him?"

"General Sangsorn is definitely making inroads on what was once Panupong's turf. Like Jet, no one has done any business with him yet, but I can try to arrange a meet with him as well."

"Has anyone tried to do business with him yet?"

"A few have opened up accounts in his military controlled banks on a trial basis," he said. "The Singaporean is one. The Pakistani is another."

"How are they fairing?"

"No complaints so far," Otis said. "But then again, things just started with him and the money flow is small compared to what you're planning."

"Okay," I said. "Might as well set me up with a meet there as well. At least this way I can shop around."

"What about your bankers in Malaysia?"

"Too close to Doc," I said. "If he is behind all this, they are the last people I would be banking with. I need someone with a proven track record, someone who won't chisel me."

"The only other bankers I know who could handle big money is in Manila," Otis said. "One of them is a big time mayor over there. Her name is Nilda Cabrera."

"A mayor? They actually have politicians doing this kind of thing in the Philippines?"

"That place is a little strange," Otis said. "It's like a

banana republic in Asia. The country is mostly Christian, and many of their surnames are Spanish since they were under Spanish rule for several hundred years, before we Americans made them one of our colonies. In most other places the mob sort of pays off politicians, but in the Philippines, it's the politicians that run the organized crime syndicates over there."

"Well that is pretty weird," I said. "Okay, I'll let you know when I'm heading for Manila. Probably in the next few days. Might as well meet up with all of them."

"Okay, looks like I've got a full plate on my hands too," he said. "I've got a lot of information to gather up for you."

I smiled as I forked some more food into my mouth. As I started chewing, a pungent smell of something truly horrible assaulted my nostrils. I almost choked as I spat out the food back onto my plate. Did they just serve me a literal piece of crap?

Otis laughed as he snapped his fingers to get the waiters to come over. "Oh look, poor Quincy took a shit on the couch right beside you. Don't move, Don. You surely don't want that on your pants."

9.

Sure enough, Otis called me up the next day and said Jet Panupong would be meeting me at a coffee shop in the Bang Rak district. It was just before lunch when I got there, ordered an espresso and sat down by the window while I waited. Jessica had gone out to buy some groceries, and she mentioned that she needed to clean up the mess in our condo, so I was alone. The day was overcast, but I was grateful to be inside the air conditioned interior of the place. The whole country was pretty much a gigantic sauna all year around. The humid air was so thick that one could conceivably scoop handfuls of water droplets from the space around them, I imagined. It was the one thing I could never get used to while living in the entire region. I figured since the locals were born into it then they couldn't have known any better.

Half an hour later, I had already downed my third espresso which kept me totally alert. There was still no sign of him, so I went back to the counter and bought a plastic bottle of water. Just as I made my way back to where I was sitting, my mobile phone started ringing. I checked the number and it said UNKNOWN, though I could tell it was a local ID. It must have been Jet's since I didn't have his number, but Otis did mention to me that he would be forwarding mine.

"Hello," I said.

Jet's voice came through the line. "I'm outside. Come take a ride with me."

I looked out the store windows and there was a black tinted Mercedes sport utility vehicle beside the sidewalk. Since it was the only other vehicle that just appeared, then it had to be it. I had just met this guy a few days ago and it wasn't exactly under cordial circumstances, but either way, I needed to know if I could trust him. Getting the banking for Leopardi's deal took precedence over and above anything else.

Clamping my jaw, I walked out of the coffee shop and kept on moving until I was alongside the car. As I peered in closer, I could see a single outline on the driver's side of the vehicle. The car window by the front seat opened up, but only by a couple of inches.

"Get inside," Jet said. He was clearly the driver and there was nobody else in the car.

As I pulled the handle on the front passenger door it gave way, but the door barely moved towards me. "I can't get it to open, I think it's stuck," I said to him.

"Pull harder. Use your strength."

This time I used both hands and the door finally pulled open. It seemed a lot heavier than usual. I slid into the front seat of the vehicle and used both hands to close the door. Then I noticed what looked like a heavy bolt lock just above the interior door handle.

"Please lock it into place," Jet said to me.

I was a little confused by all this but I obeyed as I slid the bolt through. Jet was wearing an orange t-shirt, white slacks and sunglasses. There were a bunch of customized controls in the center console that I was unfamiliar with. Jet clicked on the switch that closed the window on my side as he shifted gears and we were immediately underway. There was a smartphone attached to the top of the dashboard which showed a GPS map of the city and an open line to another number. A strange feeling came over me as I sensed that the whole situation was somewhat out of the ordinary. Jet pushed another button on the dashboard as I heard clicks and other bolts being locked into place. It was as if this car was his personal tomb and he was sealing us both in it.

The Mercedes made its way along busy Silom Road as Jet maintained a leisurely speed. It seemed that he wasn't in a hurry, so I just leaned back into the comfortable leather seat and put on the seatbelt. He knew the reason why I wanted to see him, so I felt it might be better to just wait until he said something about it first.

Jet gave me a sideways glance, but he kept his eyes on the road. "Do you know how old I am, Don?"

I shrugged. "No, not really."

"I was twenty-four," he said. "My father promised me that I would be head of the business around my thirtieth birthday. That is six years from now."

I just kept quiet. What was the point he was trying to make?

As Jet drove, it seemed that he was continually scanning in all directions. He kept glancing at the rearview mirror as well as both side windows. It was as if he was looking for something. "My father told me that the day of my twenty-fifth birthday, he would teach me everything about his business for five years, then after that he would retire, and make the announcement that I would be the new head of the family. He only told me this in secret, you see. He made me promise never to tell the rest of the family until it was time."

"Your father was a very good businessman," I said. "I'm sorry for your loss."

"My father told me to enjoy my life until my twenty-fifth birthday. He gave me whatever I wanted and I went to many parties, had many friends, and try to have as much fun as possible, because I knew that he expected me to change my life when the time finally came. He told me that there would be no more fun after that- it would be all business from then on until it was time to choose my own successor," he said as we made a turn into another, narrower alleyway. There were street vendors along the sidewalk as well as numerous scooters and motorcycles darting back and forth. "Do you know what today is?"

Was this some sort of trick question? I thought about it for a few seconds. "Uh, Monday?"

Jet drove the car into a side street as he flipped another switch on the dashboard control panel. Within seconds, the window tints started to fade away as the glass became more transparent. "Today is my twenty-fifth birthday," he said softly.

I twisted my neck to look at him and smiled. Was all this talk just to get me to go party with him? "Well, happy birthday then! Perhaps we ought to go to a bar and have a drink. I'm buying."

Jet glanced at the rearview mirror again before he spotted something, then he spoke rapidly in Thai so that the open line on his phone could hear him. My curiosity finally overcame my caution as I glanced back. All I could see were other cars and a half dozen youths on motorbikes. A pair of riders on one motorcycle accelerated and was soon beside us on the right side as Jet started to gun the car's engine. I stared back at the two riders. The one driving the bike had a helmet on while the second one behind him had long, flowing black hair and a beard as he glared menacingly at me. A sudden feeling that something wasn't right came over me and I began to tense up. The last time I sensed this sort of danger was in the hotel lobby when the hit came down.

We soon turned into Sathorn Road, one of the main thoroughfares in the city. The elevated concrete track of the skytrain was in the center of the road, over twenty feet above us. Jet kept his eyes on the street but made occasional glances at the two men on the motorbike as they tried to keep pace with us. Suddenly, the helmeted motorcycle rider drove his bike slightly ahead of us as he accelerated with an ear piercing screech. The man sitting at the rear of the motorcycle quickly pulled out a black sub-machinegun and fired it directly at the front windshield.

I screamed while I ducked down sideways, just as the glass shattered but didn't break. Jet didn't seem fazed at all as he concentrated on his driving. The two assailants seemed shocked that the SUV was still going as they disappeared, driving into a side street. Jet twisted and turned the steering wheel as he narrowly avoided a number of stalled vehicles and shocked pedestrians. I soon realized that I was holding my breath for too long and my lungs were now burning, so I let out a big exhalation of air.

Jet glanced at me and smiled. "This is my father's special car. He had it sent to America for modifications. It's armored to level ten, which is the same level your president's limousine has."

I turned around and noticed the two assailants had gone back to the main street and were now behind us as they accelerated rapidly for another try. I pointed to where they are. "They're at our rear!"

Jet looked at the rearview mirror. "I see them."

The man sitting behind the front rider of the motorbike extended his arm over his partner's shoulder and fired again. The rear window glass shattered as a half dozen bullets impacted on it. But once again it didn't break. I ducked my head down behind my chair as soon as the bullets started flying. Grimacing, I jerked my head back up and tried to look for them, but the shattered glass obscured much of my vision.

"Let me know when you see them again." Jet said calmly.

I was breathing quite heavily now. "Are you sure they're coming back for more?"

He simply smiled as he continued to scan ahead. I've never seen anyone so calm during a time like this. "Yes."

Then I realized the truth. "You want them to come back, don't you? You've set yourself up as a target."

Jet nodded. "I figured that whoever wanted my father killed would like to do the same for me too. I needed to be sure as to who it was before I plan my own counterattack. This way, I draw them out in the open."

Right after he said those words, the two riders appeared behind us again, just two car lengths away. The motorbike accelerated once more as we were now on a sloping road that led up towards the King Thaksin Bridge. Now there would be no side streets in which the motorcycle could dart into, it would have to be a straight up chase from then on, until we got to the other side of the river. Traffic had lightened considerably behind us, since everybody all around was bewildered by the gun battle going on.

"They're closing," I said tersely while keeping my eyes at our rear. Even though I knew that the car was heavily armored, I was still pretty nervous as to whether the defensive systems would hold from such a sustained and determined attack. My worst fears were that they would keep shooting until all the windows in the car broke.

Jet glanced at the rearview mirror once more. "I see them."

The Mercedes slowed down as it got to the middle of the Thaksin Bridge because of the traffic up ahead. Jet kept his eyes on the rearview as the two riders bore down on us with no one behind them. While the gap was closed to less than fifty feet, Jet switched the gear shift to reverse and pushed the accelerator. The Mercedes lurched backwards and we were soon on a collision course. The motorcycle driver noticed and began to swerve to try and avoid the car, but Jet continued to make adjustments as he kept the reversing SUV to make sure that we would be smashing into them. The second rider fired again but most of his shots hit the body of the Mercedes and failed to penetrate. In the split second before the collision, the motorcycle suddenly tried to jump over the small concrete divider on the left of the bridge, but it was going far too fast. The two riders ended up colliding with the steel guardrail that sent the motorbike flying through the air and down towards the murky Chao Phraya River below. Sparks flew as the rear of the SUV scraped against the side divider, but Jet was able to stop the car in time. The helmeted rider had somersaulted along with the bike into the water, while his long haired passenger was lying down beside the guardrails, his body a bloody mess.

While Jet shifted the Mercedes back to forward drive, a dark green Toyota Land Cruiser drove up to where the injured gunman lay. Two men in suits came out of the Toyota's rear passenger seat, ran over to the fallen rider and took him back in the car. A few cars in front of us had stopped to look at what happened, but there was enough of a gap for Jet to squeeze through as he drove the Mercedes to the opposite bank of the river.

I fell back into my seat, my forehead moist with sweat. "Who where those other guys?"

"My bodyguards," Jet said. "They fell behind in the

chase, but at least now they got one of the men who tried to kill me. I think it turned out okay, no?"

"Jesus," I said. "We nearly got killed."

Jet laughed. "They would need more than a machine pistol to get through this car."

His phone on the dashboard started squawking as we heard some shouting and moaning in Thai. Jet spoke rapidly in his mother tongue for a few minutes while other voices joined in. I only knew a few conversational phrases and they were talking way too fast for me to get a bead on what was going on. Finally I heard a scream and then it went silent for a bit before calm voices could be listened to again. Jet said a few more things in Thai, then he finally cut the call for good.

We soon made it into a more residential district in Khlong San as a light rain had begun. A few passersby had noticed the shattered glass in the car windows, but most of them just turned and walked away. Jet kept on going until we made it into a mostly deserted side street, then he stopped the car beside a storefront.

He turned and looked at me. "My men have concluded that it was my brother Ek who paid those two men to try and kill me. Now that I know it was him I will now make my move to legitimize my right to be the head of my family. Just give me a few days to sort this out and I can promise you good rates for this deal that's coming to you. Is that okay?"

I let out a deep breath. "Are you sure you will be the one on top after all this is done?"

He nodded. "I am pretty sure. I know my father's police

contacts. I'll make it seem like I was indeed killed, but the shooters were caught. This way, my brother will think I am dead and I let his guard down. Once that happens he is a dead man."

I scratched my head. "Okay, I'll just wait until it's all clear then."

Jet nodded. "I would like you to be my first client for the banking. Since you are loyal and Otis vouches for you, I can give you a discounted rate of say, ten percent. Good enough for you?"

"Sounds great," I said. "You could have just told me this over the phone, you know."

He laughed. "Ah, but then you wouldn't have had the experience of this. Now we are blood brothers! We fought the enemy together, and now we are friends forever!"

I rolled my eyes. This guy was nuts. "If you say so."

"I need to ask one other thing, Don," he said. "Will you help me kill my brother?"

"I don't have any contacts that could help you with that," I said, taking a deep breath. "Why are you asking me?"

"You're the only one I could trust, Don! I can't rely on my men to do it because one of them might end up telling my mother. Otis told me he will help me out in anything but that. I need someone from the outside to do this. If you find someone, please let me know, okay? I'll make it worth your while," Jet said.

Best to give him a safe answer rather than to refuse outright. "I'll see what I can do. No promises though."

"Of course!"

We met up with his bodyguards and Jet drove away in another vehicle. When I got out of the car after his bodyguards dropped me off back in front of the coffee shop, my knees were still shaking. If Jet succeeded in his revenge, then my banking would be set. But there was a part of me that wasn't so sure about what just happened. The would-be killers on the motorcycle seemed like amateurs compared to the two men who killed the elder Panupong in the hotel. The whole thing was a mess that I was still trying to sort through. Were there actually two sets of killers from different sides out there, or was I just being too paranoid?

I got into my own car that was parked in a nearby garage and drove slowly towards my condominium. It took awhile because I couldn't stop thinking about what had just happened and I half expected another pair of shooters to drive up towards me and put a few bullets into my body. When a youth riding in a scooter veered in front of me, I hit the brakes and nearly got rear ended by an apoplectic truck driver who was behind me. Ignoring his curses in Thai, I rounded the corner and finally made it into the underground parking entrance of my place.

10.

When I got back to the penthouse condo, I just slumped down on the couch. Jessica was making some lunch in the kitchen when she spotted me and gave a wave. Then she gave me a quizzical look when I just stared back at her blankly. I needed to get my mind off of what happened, so I grabbed the remote control lying on the coffee table and turned on the TV. It was at that instant that the local news started showing a body being pulled out of the Chao Phraya, I was pretty certain it was the motorcycle driver. Getting up, I walked into the kitchen and started rummaging through the cabinets for the bottle of bourbon I placed in the cupboard few weeks ago.

Jessica walked over and stood behind me. "Are you okay?"

I sighed while placing both hands on the marble-top counter. "I nearly got killed just now."

"What?"

"Jet gave me a ride in his armored car. The next thing I knew, a couple of bargain basement hitmen riding on a scooter started shooting at us."

She hugged me from behind while burying her face in my shoulder blade. "Oh my god! It's a good thing you weren't hurt."

I let out a deep breath. "That car of his looked pretty damned ordinary. But it was bulletproofed like a tank. One of the shooters ended up in the river- he died. And Jet's men took the other one alive. The whole fucking meeting with him was like a trap he set up, Jess."

She leaned forward until she stood beside me. "You think it was the same people who had his father killed?"

I looked down and shook my head. "I don't know. This hit felt a little …different. The ones in the hotel were pros, but the two men on the motorbike, it was pretty tacky."

"What makes you say that the shooting in the hotel was done by professionals and this one wasn't?"

"It's the little things," I said. "The shooters in the hotel knew that Panupong senior was vulnerable since he was out in public, and they took out the bodyguards first. If this second one was an inside job, then they really screwed it up since Jet's car was armored and they just went straight at him. He was expecting it too."

"Maybe whoever wanted him dead didn't have time to set up a proper hit."

"That's possible," I said. "I'm beginning to wonder if there's more than two sides in this whole mess."

"So what are you going to do now?"

I finally found the bottle and poured myself a couple of jiggers worth of whisky into a glass tumbler. "Get ready to make a call to the whale, that's what. I need to get this out of my mind."

"I was over at the European deli and made some turkey with cheese on rye if you'd like to eat," she said. "That's assuming you still have some appetite for lunch."

The bourbon started to warm me up just as my stomach started growling. "Yeah, I'll take one."

An hour later, I was sitting in the couch by the living room as I looked over my notes. Jessica stayed in the bedroom to watch a movie so there wouldn't be any distractions for me. It was time to make a follow up call to Leopardi and find out if the deal was going to go down or not. I was feeling pretty agitated from the incident this morning and the potential fallout with the client speaking to his accountant. If his bookkeeper had the last word, then it would be very hard for me to try and turn him around. I closed my eyes and tried to clear my thoughts for a minute before firing up the phone server and making the call. I read in a book somewhere that if one thinks happy thoughts before a business meeting, then that positivity would somehow mystically transpose itself into the client and everything would turn out fine. I didn't believe in god but I recited a silent prayer anyway. Any kind of luck or divine intervention that fell my way would be gratefully appreciated.

Sure enough, Leopardi answered after a couple of rings. "Leopardi here."

I smiled, even though he couldn't see me. One thing I learned in all my years in the business was in being able to control one's feelings while on the phone with the client. If you smiled, then it would bring your enthusiasm level up and the client would actually feel it and possibly reciprocate based purely on your tone of voice. "Tony! Good morning to you! It's me, Rick, calling from MAM in Hong Kong, how is the morning over in Johannesburg?"

He laughed. At least my enthusiasm was putting him in a good mood. "It's a wonderful morning out here, Rick! The sun has just started to rise and it will be an awesome day. Anytime you want to come visit me in South Africa, you let me know, I'll take care of you once the plane touches down on the ground, brah."

I returned his laugh. The fucker was making things tough enough already. "Thanks, Tony. I might just take you up on that soon once this transaction is in place. All I ask is that if you make at least a twenty percent profit on this stock purchase that you buy me dinner, okay?"

"I can do more than that, my friend. If everything goes to plan, I'll buy you a house. How is David's wife by the way?"

I bit my lip. "She's still in the hospital, I'm afraid. They're waiting on the test results."

Leopardi's voice inflections changed from a high enthusiasm to a low seriousness. "Please give David and his wife my regards. I hope all goes well for them."

There was no sense of continuing the small talk, so I had to know. "I'll definitely do that- I'm sure David will be happy that you mentioned him. Now, as far as the share purchasing for the offering, are we all set to go with it?"

There was a slight pause. "I am all for it, but as I've told you before I did have a talk with my accountant."

Son of a bitch. I knew it. His fucking bookkeeper told him to say no. "Yes, and?"

"Well, he really didn't say no or yes to it, but he did give me some very good advice," the voice on the other line said.

"Which is?"

Leopardi sighed. I could tell from his vocal mannerisms he felt a slight discomfort. "Please understand that I will be committing a substantial amount for this investment, so it is only fair if I ask for a few things in return."

I rolled my eyes. Now what? "Look," I said. "While I do completely understand how you're feeling, we need to act quickly on this. I have already pulled a lot of strings and even had to make excuses for a couple of my established clients, just in order to get the allocation that you wanted sorted out. So whatever it is you need, you have to let me know what it is right now." I was putting him on the spot. It was a risky move, but I felt that I had to get this over and done with one way or the other. I needed to either close him or the whole thing would unravel.

"Alright," he said. "Now please don't be offended, but my accountant suggested that you provide me with a copy of your passport. I know we haven't met in person yet, so I just want to be doubly sure that this transaction will be on the level, if you know what I mean."

I placed my hand over the microphone while I sighed. This would be an inconvenience, but I felt it would be a minor one. I quickly took my hand off just before making my reply. "Okay, that sounds like a reasonable demand. I think I could do that. Would you like me to email it to you in a few day's time?"

"Actually, you can give me a photocopy when I visit Hong Kong next week," Leopardi said. "My accountant also suggested to me that it would be good to meet you in person, so I've booked a flight already and I'll email you my itinerary. I know you're busy, so even just a five minute meeting in your office would be okay with me."

Fuck. His accountant was one smart son of a bitch. Goddammit. This made everything doubly harder now. I needed some time to see if I could pull this off. "Alright, but it will have to be later in the week. Everything's at a pretty frenetic pace right now with the upcoming offering of this stock so I'm always in and out all the time."

Leopardi giggled. "Oh, the last thing I want to be is getting in your way, Rick. I have been looking forward to see you and your firm, so I think this will be perfect. I can always do some sightseeing around Hong Kong for a few days while you fit me into your busy schedule. Let me tell you what, I'll even buy you the dinner you've been demanding! The last time I was in Hong Kong was ten years ago so I am looking forward to some authentic Chinese food."

"Okay, I'll have my secretary or myself give you a call to schedule the meeting at the end of this week," I said softly. "But once we're done with all of that, then do I have your full commitment on the purchase of these pre-IPO shares?"

"Absolutely," he said as his enthusiasm came back with a vengeance. "I'm so glad you've been very understanding with me, Rick. But oh, I have one last request though."

Motherfucker. Beads of sweat began to form on my forehead. Now what? I couldn't refuse at this point, but if he kept on demanding things, it was a sure sign that he was stroking me. "Okay, but it will have to be quick, because I've got a meeting that I have to go to this very minute," I said.

"Oh, this won't even concern you directly, Rick," he said. "Since I read the prospectus on Apgen Pharmaceuticals, it says on it that they already have one factory in Thailand that's manufacturing Ophemerol. Now since I'm going to Hong Kong next week, I figured why not take a side trip to Thailand as well and take a look at this factory. My accountant suggested that it's always good to try and see an actual demonstration of whatever it is that you're investing in, and I think it's pretty sound advice, so why not a tour of the factory that produces this lifesaving medicine for HIV treatment? Now, you don't need to do anything other than just point me in the right direction as to where the factory is, and I'll hire a car to go over there. On the other hand, it would be even better if you could give me a name of an Apgen representative in Thailand so I could get a guide since I've never been to that country before. Is that okay with you?"

Goddamn this fucking asshole of an accountant! I hoped that fucking cunt gets attacked by a lion and gets his balls chewed alive! First I needed to set up a fake office, now I had to find a factory that produces pills? There was a short pause as I tried to think of the proper words. "Tony, you realize that I will be pulling some major strings if I can arrange a tour within weeks of an announcement for the FDA approval, right? Apgen has specifically told us to keep everything hushed up at this moment."

"I'm so sorry about this," he said. "My accountant said that this was to be the most important part of my trip, he said I had to see that one of the major milestones they declared in the prospectus was real. I don't even have to tour the whole factory, maybe just a word or two with a representative there in the factory would be good enough for me. I promise you this will be the last request I'm making."

Request? It's more like a demand, you fucking prick! My hands were balled up into fists by this point. "Alright, I'll see what I can do. But no promises at this point for I am very, very busy."

I could hear an audible sigh of relief on the other line. "Oh thank you, Rick! I know this must be hard for you to accede to my requests at such a short notice, but you see, my accountant is very strict about it. According to my company's bylaws, he has to sign off on large scale money transfers such as this, you see."

"Like I said, I'll see what I can do. Now I would like to ask one thing in return. I need a certified, written commitment that the funds are ready for transfer to our correspondence bank, and it would be completed within twenty-four hours after our meeting," I said. If he was demanding so much from me, I needed to return the favor.

"Since you're going out of your way just to accommodate me, then I'll have that letter sent over to you by this evening your time," he said. "How's that, Rick?"

"That will be fine, Tony. Now do you have any other questions?"

"Not at this stage, Rick! I am so excited about this. I can't wait to meet you in person!"

"I look forward to it, Mr. Leopardi."

"Alright," he said. "I need to go. Check your email in a few hours time for the certified letter of intent."

"I will do that. Have a great day," I said.

"You as well, Rick. Cheers! Bye for now."

I turned off the phone server while grabbing the headset out of my ears and threw it across the room. Fortunately, the headset had an attached wire so it didn't travel very far as it fell on top of the coffee table. I closed my eyes for a minute while trying to control the frustration that was overwhelming my very being. Of all the things that could go wrong, it had to be this! I just couldn't believe the set of demands that fucker made. There was going to be no way I would be able to set this up in a week! I balled my fists and felt like pounding the laptop into little pieces. For a long time I just stared into empty space, realizing that this deal had just about unraveled. My one chance to get out of Doc's shadow was now fading away in a sea of hopelessness and complications.

Half an hour later, the door to the bedroom opened and Jessica came out, carrying an empty bowl in one hand. She instantly saw me and walked over. "Are you okay, Don?"

I grimaced without making eye contact. "No."

Jessica sat down beside me on the sofa and placed the bowl down on the coffee table. She must have been eating some ice cream. "I know you've had a rough day and it's only early afternoon. Do you want to talk about it?"

"Not much to talk about," I whispered. "Looks like the monster deal is dead."

"What happened?"

"The client had an accountant," I said. "A real smart accountant. Now he wants to meet me in person."

Jessica looked away. "I see. How dangerous is it if a client makes that sort of demand?"

"Not too dangerous since I can get Otis and his contacts to make me a fake passport. But the clincher is that the client wants to meet me in person at our Hong Kong office."

"So what? So meet him then."

I locked eyes with her. "We don't have a Hong Kong office. The address on our website is fake."

Jessica pursed her lips. "I know someone in Hong Kong. My dad's real stockbroker, his name is David Chen. Maybe he could help us out."

"How is a real stockbroker going to help us out?"

"David dabbles in real estate," she said. "His wife handles office rentals. Maybe we can rent an office for one day."

"Holy shit," I said. This felt like old times, like when we solved her father's mystery together last year. "That's one hell of a great idea!"

Jessica grinned. "See, I told you I was a Harvard graduate and you said you didn't believe me."

I laughed as I drew her in my arms and kissed her deeply. Her mouth tasted like Cherry Garcia. "Okay, I believe you. But what about staffing the place?"

"I'm sure we can think of something, Don."

I nodded. "Actually, you're right. I've got a whole office of openers that aren't doing anything. An all expense paid day trip to Hong Kong, plus a few hundred bucks in their pocket might just do the trick."

She giggled. "Now you're thinking right. See, there is a solution after all!"

"One other problem though," I said. "He wants to go to Thailand as well."

Jessica gave me an inquisitive stare. "The client wants to go here too? For what?"

"It's a long story," I said. "Basically I told the client that my fictitious firm will be selling shares in a fictitious pharmaceutical company that has a fictitious factory making fictitious pills in Thailand. So his final request before he sends the money is to take a look at this factory."

Her mouth hung open for a bit before she said anything. "Oh my god."

I simply shrugged. Lies upon lies.

11.

By late afternoon we were both in the airport. I kissed Jessica goodbye as she went ahead and took a flight over to Hong Kong so she could try and make contact with Doc's stockbroker. Crystal had sent in another message to us, saying she made it to Singapore but still no sign of her ex-husband. I was going to take the flight to Manila and hook up with Casper Villar. Although Jet Panupong already offered me generous terms to fence the money through his banks, I still wasn't too sure if I could trust him well enough. Casper had told me that the Philippine politician was eager to meet up with me, so I felt it was best to listen to all the suitors and pick the best one out of the whole lot.

I waited for my turn while standing in line at the immigration counter. The flight was delayed somewhat and they had sent me an email about it, but I wanted to see Jessica off, so I didn't mind the extra waiting time. My wife had already boarded her plane half an hour ago so now it was my turn. The woman in front was finally allowed to go through and the immigration offer gestured at me to come forward. I walked past the yellow line and gave him my passport through the glass partition. The offer scanned my credentials and waited. Time passed and the seconds turned into minutes. All of a sudden, two airport security officers wearing black uniforms and berets came out of nowhere and walked up beside me.

"Come with us, please," one of the security officers said.

I bit my lip as I was escorted towards a set of rooms at the far side of the terminal. What the hell was going on? Over a dozen scenarios started playing in my head as to why they were detaining me. Did someone tag me as a person of interest during the shootout on the highway leading up to the bridge, or was it about something else? I was starting to get hot and bothered, and not in a good way either. A few people stared at me while others cupped their hands and whispered as I was guided past them.

They led me into a bare white room with only a folding table and a pair of plastic chairs as furniture. A large mirror lined the opposite wall and I was sure it was a two-way looking glass. Was this supposed to be some sort of interrogation? The two officers still stood beside me and one of them gestured at a nearby chair while the second one closed the door behind us.

I sat down and turned to look at the guard to my right. "I'm sorry, could I ask as to why I'm being detained?"

The officer beside me said nothing as he just stared out towards the mirror. This was always the worst part- of not knowing why you were apprehended. What made it even more excruciating was that I was a foreigner in a foreign land.

Thai prisons were pretty horrible places to be in. The heat and the insects would be the least of one's problems, especially to someone who hasn't quite adjusted to the very humid climate of the region. What exactly did I do this time to make them arrest me?

The door at the opposite side of the room opened and a local man entered. He looked to be in his thirties, with a shirt and tie. He was short, like most Thais were, but somewhat lighter skinned than average. He carried a thick folder with him and he placed it on the table in front of me before sitting down at the opposite side. The man opened the folder and started scanning the papers on it. One of them had my picture as well as my vital statistics.

He adjusted his thin, steel rimmed glasses a little before looking up at me. His English carried a mild accent, indicative of well-educated locals. "You are Mr. Don Rouse, yes?"

I nodded meekly. "Is there a problem?"

The man smiled as he gave me a wai gesture. He signaled at the men behind me and the officers immediately left the room, silently closing the door behind them. "My name is Kit. I am a personal assistant to General Sangsorn."

I let out a deep breath. "So I'm not under arrest then?"

He grinned at me. "No."

The relief was like an elephant had just stepped off my chest. "Jesus H Christ. Are you here to talk about the banking?"

Kit's smile continued. "Yes. Since General Sangsorn doesn't speak any English, he appointed me to be a liaison to you. We felt that this was the best way to have a meeting with you so as not to attract attention."

I rolled my eyes. "Are you kidding me? Your guards just pulled me out from immigration and gave me an escort in front of half the people in this airport. Now everyone boarding their flights will think I'm a drug dealer, wanted fugitive, or something even worse."

"My apologies," Kit said. "But we had a hard time trying to contact you for a meeting. General Sangsorn had the idea to flag your name on the airport computers in case you showed up here."

Damn, I forgot to give Otis my new number. We had been mostly communicating using emails and social media since I switched my old phone off. "I'm sorry about that. There must have been a mix up. Why didn't Otis forward my email address to you?"

"General Sangsorn doesn't do much internet, so he might have received your online details, but he was probably unable to act on it," Kit said. "Nevertheless, your flight has been delayed so we have some time with which to negotiate in regards to this banking deal."

I sighed. Okay, we might as well get this over with. "Well, Kit, I have been receiving a number of offers, and the latest one is ten percent. If you can give me something that's in that particular range, I'll be happy to take it under consideration."

"We have other offices in your field making offers to us," he said. "From what I recall in dealing with them, the standard rate is fifteen, right?"

"Yes, well I will be bringing in a substantial amount on my first deal, so shouldn't a bulk discount be in order?"

"How much are we talking about, Mr. Don?"

"Around eight figures," I said. "In dollars, of course."

"Coming from where?"

I rubbed the back of my neck. "I can't give you the details at this time, but it will be definitely coming in from the outside of the country. I need assurances that the money will be exempted from the local currency controls if I choose to bring it out of Thailand."

"General Sangsorn's group controls not just many banks here in Thailand, but outside of the country as well," Kit said. "We should be okay when it comes to transferring the money to foreign bank accounts, if necessary."

"Okay, that's good to know," I said. Now on to the nitty-gritty. "No offense, but the second concern is how do I know whether I can trust your banking? We've never done business before and this first transaction will be very big."

Kit leaned back and made a short laugh. I wasn't sure if he found my question funny or he was just trying to break the ice. "In a few weeks time, General Sangsorn will be controlling most, if not all of the banking in your industry. The competition is weak and soon, the General's group will require that any business in Thailand will have to be dealt through him. So all your colleagues that own their own offices will be working through our group if they want to stay here. It is up to you if you do not take our offer."

So it looked like all-out war between Panupong's family and the general. I had a feeling this was coming. The last place I wanted to be was right in the middle of it all. "Look, I'm just a businessman looking for someone to partner up with. Whatever goes on in your country is your concern, I don't want any part of it since I know I'm just a guest here. I'll certainly consider the offer of fifteen percent and I will give you an answer when I return to Bangkok in a few day's time, is that alright?"

Kit kept on smiling as he reached into his shirt pocket and handed me my passport. "Of course, Mr. Don. Take your time and please consider our offer to you. I left my business card inside your passport so now you know how to contact me. I will be expecting a reply from you soon. You may now go to your departure gate."

My hands were still trembling as I sat in the waiting area near the gate leading to the aircraft. If there was going to be a conflict, then the best course of action would be to move everything out. If I could get a good deal with that mayor in the Philippines, it would make perfect sense to transfer the entire operation to Manila. The one problem was Leopardi, he was set to go to Thailand in less than a week's time. If I wanted this deal, then I would have to pick a side, at least temporarily. The risk was in choosing who to back. While the Panupongs controlled the cops, I wasn't sure as to whether Jet would succeed in toppling his older brother. General Sangsorn's group was part of the military, and the fact that I was picked up by airport security was a sure sign that he was flexing his muscles as a show of force in order to intimidate me. This would be one hell of a decision to make.

If I guessed wrong it would be more than just losing some money.

I was startled as the phone in my shirt pocket started to ring. I picked it up and took the call. "Hello?"

"Hey, dude," Bob Duffy said on the other line. "I just got back from a vacation with the family in Chiang Mai. I heard from my housekeeper that you came by and took the car. How's it all going?"

"It's definitely going," I said. "How was Chiang Mai?"

"A little cooler than Bangkok, that's for sure. Spent most of the time just visiting the wat temples in the area and I'm raring to get back to work!"

"I'm at the airport again," I said. "I'm going to Manila."

"You're off again? But you just got back too. Ah well, that's a pity, dude. I wanted to meet up with you."

"I'll take a rain check on that, but I promise we'll definitely meet up in a few days when I get back," I said. "Are you still in touch with the crew?"

"I am. Quite a few have been trying to contact me asking what's up. They need work."

I licked my lips. I needed to staff a fake office and Bib's crew wanted work. Perfect timing. "How would you like an all-expense paid vacation to Hong Kong with your family next week? I'll throw in ten grand in cash too."

"That's freaking awesome, dude! Now what's the catch?"

"I'm going to need you and the crew to act like you're in an office," I said. "I'm going to rent an office suite in Central and just staff it with you guys. It's all make believe, I just want you and the others to pretend you're working. It's to impress a guest that's coming over for a visit."

Bob's laughter was audibly loud on the other line. "It's that whale of yours, isn't it? He wants to take a look at the office, right?"

"No comment, Bob. Will you take the offer?"

"Of course I will, dude," he said. "Paid vacation and ten grand in spending money is one hell of an offer. I hope I don't have to do any talking in front of the client though?"

"No, not at all. I will be personally escorting the client all the way on this. The most of what will happen is that he shakes a few hands and that's it," I said. "It will be a very quick, an in-and-out meeting at the office before I get him out of there. Ten minutes tops."

"He won't be taking any pictures? We won't have to show him any IDs?"

"None of that," I said. "I just need you guys to act as extras in a fucking movie set, that's all you gotta do."

"Alright, dude, you got a deal!"

"Okay," I said. "Now, don't tell the others any details. They all have to be in proper office attire, so no shorts and all that shit. I will pay for their round trip plane tickets and hotel rooms, and they get around three hundred bucks each. Do you think you can sell 'em on that?"

"I don't think that's going to be a problem, dude," Bob said.

"Okay, just bring the professional ones with you, none of the scruffy looking ones, or the ones who could make trouble."

"What about Scotty?"

I thought about it for a minute. "No, let's not bring Scotty over, he could get drunk and cause a mess like he always does when he has too much money. Is he doing okay so far?"

"Funny you should mention him," Bob said. "His girlfriend told me he nearly got arrested two days ago when he pulled his cock out at a bar in Soi Cowboy."

I shook my head. "Goddamn it, just keep him on ice, okay?"

"I will indeed," Bob said. "Oh, since you're off to the Philippines, there's something you might want to know."

"Go ahead."

"Remember the time I told you about that Filipino opener we had who stole some accounts? Roderik Navarro was his name."

"Yeah, I remember. What about him?"

"I heard from the grapevine that he's in Manila right now," Bob said. "He was recruiting a couple of guys and one of the guys he was wooing is a good friend of mine. Guess what's the name of his firm?"

"Tell me."

"Brinton and Dukes Securities," he said. "Looks like we got a confirmation on it. And the bastard is still using the same phone name he had when he was with us: Johnny Real. He made it really easy to find out about his doings."

Filipinos always had a habit of coming up with stupid phone names. "Johnny Real? What a stupid fucking name."

"Yeah," Bob said. "So it looks like we got a confirmation about my suspicions. All you got to do now is to find out who the owner is and have a talk with him."

"You really think the owner of that shop is gonna say sorry to me? If that Johnny Real Roderik dumbass is making money for him, then he wouldn't give two shits about how I feel," I said. "But what I am going to do is to shut down his banking, at least."

"The banking they got in the Philippines seems to be more decentralized than the situation here in Thailand is, do you think you can pull it off?"

"Well I'll be meeting a big time banker so that's why I'm going in the first place," I said. "If she is as good as her reputation proclaims, then maybe she could shut their banking off. And if this Filipino impresses me enough, then I'm thinking we could move the entire operation back over to Manila."

There was a pause on the other line. Bob's family were Thais, so it would be an effort for him to have to move. "Whatever you feel is best. Did you meet with any bankers here?"

"I did, and I think there's going to be blood before everything quiets down," I said. "That's all I can say on an open line, so I'll spill the beans with you later this week when we meet up."

"Okay, dude. Anything else?"

"That's it for now. I'll talk to you later, Bob. Bye bye."

I placed the phone back in my front pocket. So I got the Hong Kong office staffed, now all I had to do was to get an update from Jessica as to the location and we would be good to go. That left the problem of the pharmaceutical factory in

Thailand. I had a few ideas running through my head but they all involved a certain degree of risk. I decided to hold off on any planning for it until I made a decision as to which side to back. All that could wait until I returned from Manila.

12.

I took a taxi from the international airport in Manila and had it drop me off in my condo at Bonifacio Global City, otherwise known as the Fort. Before going up to the unit, I went down to the underground parking area and revved up the car instead. Since I already had wheels, I decided to make the short drive over to Doc's penthouse at a nearby condominium. Jessica had left extra keys for her father's place in the car's glove compartment, so I grabbed them before taking the elevator. The keys still worked. I unlocked the front door to Doc's place and went inside.

As expected, I didn't find anybody in the place. There was a slight musty smell since all the windows were closed and the air was stale. I turned on the centralized air conditioning unit as I started to have a look around. Nothing seemed out of place and judging from the rotten food in the fridge, the last time Doc had been here may have been weeks ago. The third bedroom served as an office. I went inside and fired up the desktop computer while sorting through some papers lying on a nearby office desk.

Since I didn't know the password to Doc's operating system, I used the same reset program that Casper had sent to me before and it worked like a charm. One of the first things I noticed inside the hard drive was hundreds of pictures of the same Thai girl I had found when I was going through his laptop in Bangkok. Most of the photographs showed Waen in casual poses, while about a third were nudes and a dozen of them showed Doc having sex with her. I scanned through them as quickly as I could, hoping to find something familiar until I zeroed in on one picture in particular. It showed a smiling Waen with three other girls hanging out by a table in what looked to be a nightclub. Sitting right beside her was Ti and her sister Dang. So they did know her. It was kind of obvious since they were in the same circles. I held up my smartphone and took a picture of the monitor screen for future reference. When I got back to Bangkok I would need to get the full story from Ti, maybe she would know where Waen was staying at.

There were a lot of documents saved in the drive, so I spent the whole night sorting through them. The most interesting were a couple of fund transfers to a local bank account and the recipient's name was Roderik Navarro. A rental agreement also pointed out to an office in nearby Makati City.

I leaned back on the high chair and sighed. A lot of things just fell into place the moment I saw the scanned transfer receipts. It seemed that Doc was the money and the brains behind Brinton and Dukes Securities. While I was running his business for him in Bangkok, he had apparently set up a shadow office run by this Navarro guy and he was in complete control over it. This proved that he was indeed doing things behind my back. Doc had the means to keep his cash flow going if he got rid of me. Since this was the case, then I would need to deal with him before he tried another attack on me again. All I had to do now was to find out where he was hiding.

Dark thoughts began to intrude into my mind as I wondered how I would deal with this. Doc was family, at least I sort of considered him as such the moment I married Jessica. If I was going to have him killed, then there was no way I would tell her. Plenty of what ifs started running through my thoughts as to how it would be done. The most pressing concern was whether I could live with myself and stay happily married to Jessica. I never killed anybody, nor did I ever had anyone murdered. This would be a first. Then a possible solution popped up in my head. Instead of having Doc killed, why not get him arrested and put away instead?

The only problem would be if I got him jailed was to make sure he stayed incarcerated, preferably for a long time. Doc had a lot of cash available and he could definitely pay his way out of prison if he was arrested in Thailand or in the Philippines. Both countries had corrupt justice systems and all it took to get anybody out was money to be paid to the right people. That was the reason why our whole industry was centered in the area- we could buy cops and judges off with impunity. If I did get Doc behind bars, then I also needed leverage on him to stay quiet about me- and Jessica would be the key.

I looked at my watch. It was getting late. I turned everything off after I copied all the relevant files from Doc's computer. I left my father in law's place and headed over to my own condominium for some sleep. There was a meeting with the mayor tomorrow and I wanted to make sure I was fully rested for it.

The city hall looked brand new when I drove over and parked my car at a nearby lot the next day. There was an old beggar hanging around the parking area, so I gave him some cash and told him to look after my car. Just as he gave me a bucktoothed grin, a security guard came over and chased him away. The neighborhood was pretty dirty and in poor shape, but the gleaming new buildings in the local government compound implied that at least one class of people were doing well. The whole country was a land of contrasts, where the poor and rich were hemmed in side by side with each other. A couple of blocks away were wooden shanties and open sewers, while the street beside me was paved and had glass-enclosed luxury shops and gleaming restaurants with centralized air conditioning. Black and white. Yin and Yang.

I walked into the main building as I passed through a metal detector. There was a reception desk below the massive stone stairs leading up to the second floor. I made my way over there. The place was moderately crowded as cops, local politicians, city employees and those that needed them were constantly milling about.

The receptionist seemed pretty young, but she smiled at

me when I stood in front of her. "Can I help you?"

I returned her happy expression. "I have an appointment with the mayor. My name is Don Rouse."

She turned and pointed to the floor above. "Just go on up, sir. It's the door at the end of the right corridor."

"Thank you," I said.

I moved away and headed up the stairs. As I walked up the concrete steps, I noticed that there was an impromptu news conference at the upper landing. A gaggle of cops in their grey blue uniforms were posing with three tall black guys as a swarm of photographers were snapping away with their cameras. One of the more senior cops were saying that they busted a major drug smuggling ring coming from Africa. After glancing at them, I quickly turned my head the other way so my face wouldn't end up on some local newspaper or an online tabloid.

Passing through the corridor, I finally made it while I stood in front of a large white colored door. The sign above loudly proclaimed OFFICE OF THE MAYOR in big bold letters. There was a call button near the side so I pushed it. A few seconds later, a brown-skinned man wearing the traditional barong shirt opened the door and led me inside.

The anteroom had a very tall ceiling and the interior was thankfully air conditioned. Several clerks were sitting on old wooden desks as they typed away on their computers, while huge stacks of folders and paperwork were overflowing on their workspaces. A number of old couches lined the nearby wall and about a dozen people, wearing nothing but t-shirts, shorts and rubber pads over their bare feet were sitting down on them, patiently waiting for their turn to meet with the head honcho that ran their city. The man wearing the barong was obviously a security guard as he stood beside the door.

One of the clerks looked up at me. She was a cream-skinned, pudgy woman with thick glasses and had a Betty Crocker hairstyle. "Can I help you, sir?"

"Yeah, I'm here for an appointment. My name is Don Rouse," I said.

She stood up and headed for the door at the other end of the room. "Have a seat, sir. I'll tell the mayor you are here."

I didn't want to appear impolite, so I sat in between two locals since there was a slight gap in the old leather sofa behind me. An old woman to my right gave me a glancing smile as she adjusted her old, wrinkled dress. The man sitting to my left was obviously selling something as he was wearing a long-sleeved shirt and tie while cradling a stack of catalogs in his arms. After acknowledging both of them with a slight smile, I stared straight ahead at the far wall, keeping my eyes on the brightly colored posters of the mayor and of her upcoming reelection campaign.

The secretary poked her head out from the inner doorway and gestured at me. "Mr. Rouse, you can come in now."

I stood up again and headed to where she was. The secretary stood aside as she ushered me in. The mayor's office had several tall windows that revealed the manicured grounds of the inner compound. There was a set of luxury couches nearby while the main office desk stood at the far end of the room, a small pole holding the Philippine flag stood next to it. All along the walls were portraits of the mayor, her family, as well as members of the Philippine Congress and those of the president. Sitting on the couch at the far end were two uniformed officers from the Philippine National Police. Mayor Nilda Cabrera was situated in an easy chair beside them while the couch closest to me had Casper Villar sitting on it. All four of them noticed me and stood up.

I shook the mayor's outstretched hand first. "Mayor Cabrera, thanks for meeting with me."

"Welcome to the Philippines, Don," she said. The mayor was wearing a brown colored office blouse and she had wire rimmed glasses on. She was barely five feet tall and overweight. Her legs seemed bloated, as if someone had inflated them with a bicycle pump. The only wrinkles were under her eyes as her fatty skin was stretched out along the rest of her body.

"Thank you, mayor," I said smiling. When it came to dealing with big shots, the polite way was the safest.

Cabrera gestured at Casper. "May I present your friend, the one who arranged for this meeting."

Casper grinned as he shook my hand. "Don."

I acknowledged him with a familiar nod. "Casper."

The mayor then pointed to the two cops. "This is Major Besa and Colonel de los Reyes, my contacts in law enforcement for the city."

I shook hands with each one of them. "Nice to meet you."

With the greetings over, I sat down beside Casper on the couch while the two high ranking cops sat in the opposite sofa. There was a glass coffee table in between with a plastic potted plant in its center. Mayor Cabrera instructed her secretary to bring over some coffee for us before sitting down on the easy chair while rubbing her swollen ankles.

"Since you're already here, Don," the mayor said. "I will just finish up my upcoming re-election meeting and then we'll discuss my offer to you. I hope you don't mind waiting with us here instead of outside with the others."

I grinned at all of them as I leaned back and crossed my legs. "Oh, I appreciate it very much. Thank you, ma'am."

She laughed before turning to look at Casper. "Now, what can you do about those voting machines, Villar?"

Casper nodded. "Oh, it won't be a problem. Those voting machines are issued with sim chips that are being used for our cell phones. All we have to do is to replace those chips with pre-programmed votes, and I can definitely guarantee a win for you."

The mayor nodded. "Okay, how do we do that?"

"It's easy," Casper said. "During the transporting of the voting machines from the venues back to the Commission of Elections headquarters, we can replace them en route- all we need is the names of the drivers who will transport the machines and their vehicle registrations. We can have them stop at a checkpoint, and switch the machines there."

Mayor Cabrera nodded. "That is good, but I want to make sure. What other things can we do to insure I win?"

"We can also alter some of the hash codes in the main

voting server," Casper said. "I know several of the IT managers in the company that produces the voter machines and if we give them a little gift, they can definitely boost up your votes as well. They have full administrator access and that means they can delete their own recorded entries from the server log in case of an audit."

The mayor crossed her arms as the secretary placed a silver tray with a coffee pot on the table. Her personal assistant immediately sensed the kind of meeting it was and she left the room without pouring the coffee. When the door finally closed, Mayor Cabrera leaned forward. "Okay, how much are we talking about here?"

"I'd say a million pesos each," Casper said. "Since there's three of them, then three million ought to do it."

The mayor puckered her thick lips. "How much for the voting machines?"

"Another ten million should secure all of them," Casper said.

There was a short pause as the mayor looked away. It was clear she was doing some mental calculations in her head. When she looked back at Casper, she had a blank look in her face. "Okay, let's do it. I want everything in place in the next couple of days."

Casper and the two cops nodded.

The mayor gestured at the coffee while looking at me. "Please, help yourself."

The two police officers took a cup each and started pouring. I didn't want to be the odd man out, so I picked up my own cup and waited until Casper handed me the coffee pot, then I poured myself a small draught. Casper placed two spoonfuls of sugar in his own cup and helped himself to a plate of biscuits lying nearby. Since I liked my coffee black and bitter, I just sat back and started sipping on it.

Mayor Cabrera soon turned her eyes to me. "Now, Mr. Don. Let's talk about your business. I understand that you are looking for a banker. Casper tells me you've worked together for a long time, is that true?"

I laughed a little. "Yes, Casper and I go way back."

"Good," she said. "I understand things are a little topsy-turvy in Thailand at the moment."

"That is an understatement," I said.

"I know a few bankers myself here," the mayor said. "The Philippines has certain advantages you won't find in Thailand. For example, we do not have any currency controls. This means that your money can travel freely without any restrictions. If you need funds transferred to another country, we can facilitate that and vice versa. The other advantage is our bank secrecy laws. If you have a large number of funds, we can split it up into different accounts under false names. This way your money will be safe and anonymous."

"It sounds like a very good deal," I said. Very good perks, but I would be under her thumb the whole time. "What's your percentages?"

The mayor smiled as she put down her coffee cup. "I will give you a very good rate. How does twenty percent suit you?"

I bit my lip. Double the amount Jet was offering me. "Well, it does sound a little high, to be honest."

"So you can get better rates elsewhere?"

I nodded. "I've been offered about half that back in Thailand."

"Of course, I understand. My offer may be higher than what you're used to, but you can have better leverage here with us. In addition to the two factors I mentioned, you will also have my protection," Mayor Cabrera said as she pointed at the two senior police officers beside her. "If you decide on relocating here, I can make sure your operations will be secure. Of course, I may have to raise the percentages a little bit, but you get the whole package. No one will interfere with what you're doing and if you need things done, well let's just say that they will be done, and there will be no questions asked later."

I thought about it for a minute. The mayor's offer was excellent. I would not only have dependable and safe banking, but my operations would also be protected against raids by cops and any rivals in the industry. On the other hand, if I went with her, I would be fully under her influence. I would have to be careful and watch my every step. I've had dealings with Philippine politicians before and some of them were downright untrustworthy. If I placed all my eggs into one basket, she had the power to pull the whole rug from under me with just a snap of her fingers. Even though Casper said she was dependable, this first deal was going to be a big one. If she ran off with the money, my loss would be total.

"Your offer is very, very tempting," I said. "Though I do have to think about it first."

There was a sparkle in her eyes. She sensed that I was close to coming over with her on it. "Look, I know we've never done business before. So let me tell you what. Do you need a favor done? I have a number of resources at my disposal that would be a big help to you. As mayor, I control the police in my own city and I have contacts in the national police too. If I can prove to you that you can trust me, will you go for it?"

On second thought, maybe there was something she could do for me. "Okay. There is someone here in the city that used to work for me. He stole some accounts and I would like to ask him questions about who is financing him."

The mayor nodded. "Do you have a name?"

"I do," I said as I pulled out my smartphone from my shirt pocket and retrieved the office address for Brinton and Dukes Securities. "He actually has an office here in Metro Manila. If there's a way you could shut it down, it would mean extra publicity for your re-election campaign."

The mayor giggled as she clapped her hands. "Oh, Mr. Don. You have made a very good suggestion! Would you mind if I let my media contacts accompany me when I make this raid in person?"

I smiled as I handed her my phone so she could see where it was located. "Not at all. Feel free to get some publicity for it. All I could ask is if you would allow me to question the manager of that office for a few minutes."

The mayor said a few things in Tagalog to the two senior cops before turning her attention back at me. "No problem at all. You can even accompany my men on the raid and be side by side with me. It would look good to have a foreigner helping the city out."

I shook my head as I kept on smiling. "I'm sorry, but I would rather not be in the news, if you don't mind."

One of the cops said something in their language and the mayor nodded. "This operation will cost a little money too," she said. "Would it be okay to give a small donation to help out our poor policemen?"

"Of course," I said. One of the first things I learned about this country was that nothing comes free. "Not a problem."

13.

It was early afternoon when I got the call from the mayor's police contacts about the pending raid on Brinton and Dukes. I hopped in my car and the drive took about half an hour through the horrendous Manila traffic. By the time I got over there, the arrests were pretty much done. The news media were surrounding Mayor Cabrera as she made a triumphant news conference in front of the office building where the police raid took place. One of the law enforcement officers spotted my car and allowed me to park on a nearby sidewalk. A small crowd of pedestrians, mostly office workers in the financial district, stood by and watched. Within minutes, the news cameras turned when a group of locals and foreigners were led out of the building and placed into the back of a small fleet of police cruisers. One of the first to be led out was Roderik Navarro. He was a short, brown skinned local with bulging, frog-like eyes and crooked teeth. Navarro had a deer in the headlights look as they placed him at the back of one of the police cars along the sidewalk.

One of the police officers walked over to where my car was. I lowered the passenger side window down. He grinned at me, and started to speak with a very think accent. "Sir, which one do you want to interrogate?"

I pointed to the car where Navarro was sitting in. "That's him- over there."

The policeman nodded. "Okay, sir. Do you want to question him at the station or somewhere else?"

"Uh, is it okay if I could talk to him somewhere else? Somewhere private, maybe?"

He nodded. "Yes, sir. I know of a place. Just follow us."

"Okay."

While the main convoy headed towards the nearby station, the police car I was following made a detour towards a side street and started moving along the narrower, one lane avenues. There were street hawkers selling barbecued mystery meats on a stick, and half naked children were darting back and forth across the roads while we slowly made our way alongside a shantytown. In all my years in Southeast Asia, it was moments like this that made me feel lucky to have been born in a first world country like America. I just couldn't imagine living in a wooden shack, surrounded by all this fifth. Just spending a day amongst the barking dogs, the sewage and the noisy, teeming masses of stinking humanity would probably make me blow my own brains out. It amazed me how these locals were able to retain their optimism, much less their sanity, living in this kind of world.

After about forty minutes worth of driving around the public squalor, the police car in front of me turned a street corner and was soon driving along a waterfront. The murky, hopelessly polluted Pasig River was at my left as the police car sped up, now that the street had become wider. We kept going until we reached an abandoned industrial area by the side of the river, a compound of abandoned, rusted steel factories looming over us. There was a rotting billboard on top of one of the factories that boasted of the area's premier location for low cost manufacturing. Apparently, whoever ran this place ultimately found a cheaper location.

The police car stopped beside a deserted warehouse and two police officers got out. One of them took out a pack of cigarettes and started smoking as he leaned on the side of the police cruiser. The other cop gestured over to me as I parked my car a few feet behind them and got out too.

I walked up to the grinning cop as I pulled out a wad of one hundred thousand pesos bundled up with a rubber band, then placed it on his hand. "Here you go, Officer."

The other cop walked over to us and they gave each other high fives as they began to divvy up the cash. The cop that I gave the money too thumbed his hand towards the police car. "You can go ahead and do what you want, sir. Nobody will hear us over here."

I nodded and smiled as I walked over to the back of the police car. Navarro was sitting there in the back seat and he looked like he was going to cry. Good. I opened the door to the front seat and sat down. There was a shocked look on his face the moment he stared up at me. For a brief minute, neither of us said anything.

Finally, I turned my head so we could make eye contact.

"Hello, Roderik. How are you doing?"

I could tell he was trying to recall who I was. "Y-you, you are Sir Dan, right?" he said.

Close enough. Better if he doesn't know my real name. "Yes, it's me."

"W-why were we raided?"

I sighed. Either he was totally stupid or he was just making this harder for himself. "Look Roderik, let's just cut the crap, okay? You stole leads and paid accounts from my office in Bangkok. I know Doc is the one who's financing your operation. Where is he?"

"B-but, you and S-sir Doc work together, right?"

"We did," I said. "But he never told me about this office in Manila, and he never told me you were running it. You need to tell me everything. Right now. Did he tell you to steal my accounts? You need to tell me the truth, because I will find out if you're lying to me."

His mouth was trembling. Roderik sensed he was in bigger trouble than his crew was in since we were in the middle of nowhere and it was just us. When Filipinos want to show signs of respect or just plain brown-nosing they start addressing you as sir, like you were a knight or something. It was something akin to a colonial mentally, since many Filipinos viewed themselves as inherently inferior to white-skinned foreigners. "S-sir Dan, I was told by Sir Doc that it was okay to transfer a few of my accounts to the new office he wanted me to manage. W-when I asked him if I need to tell my manager about this, he told me to ch-change my number and not to contact Sir Bob or you anymore."

I knew it. Doc was doing things behind my back. "So he made you set up a secret office and told you not to speak with my manager anymore?"

"Y-yes, Sir Dan. I-I promise you what I'm t-telling you is the truth. He t-told me I will manage this office on my own s-so I thought he was promoting me."

"You still didn't answer my question, Roderik."

"W-what question is that, s-sir?"

I leaned closer so he could look into my eyes. "Where is Doc?"

"Y-you don't know wh-where he is, Sir Dan?"

"He hasn't answered my calls in the last several days," I said. "When was the last time you spoke with him?"

"O-over a week ago, Sir Dan. He left me money and h-he said he was going to Australia for a business meeting."

Doc was in Australia? What the hell would he be going over there for? "Who was he meeting in Australia?"

Although Roderik's arms were pinned behind his back in handcuffs, he was able to shrug his shoulders. "I-I don't know, Sir Dan. S-sir Doc doesn't tell me anything outside of running the office."

I figured as much. It would explain why I couldn't reach him by phone. But he never returned my email queries to him either. "He never gave you a hint as to what he was doing in Australia?"

"N-no, S-sir Dan."

It looked like he was telling me the truth. Although I now knew where Doc went to the week before, the information I got from his flunky just opened up a whole new set of questions. Something must have happened to him, otherwise he would still be in contact with Roderik. "You're sure you haven't been able to contact him since he went over there?"

"No, Sir Dan. I tried to call him and even sent him many emails, but he never answered."

Whoever took out Panupong might have taken out Doc too. It was the only conclusion I could come up with at this time. But if Doc was in Australia, then there was a low probability that he was dead, since assassinations would be much harder to come by over there. I figured I could maybe convince Crystal to head over to Australia to try and find him. I wasn't aware whether Doc had any properties in the land down under, but it would make sense to check out that lead anyway.

I nodded as I opened the front passenger door. "Okay, I believe you- for now."

He let out a deep breath. "Thank y-you, Sir Dan. What's going to happen to me now, sir?"

I turned around and looked at the front windshield before looking at his reflection in the rearview mirror. If I were any of the other owners I would have him shot. "You tell me- if you were me, what should I do with you?"

He put his head down in shame. "I-I am so sorry, Sir Dan. I thought that S-sir Doc told you about the office here in Manila and I thought it was okay. Please forgive me, Sir Dan. I will do anything to make it up to you. I have a family that I am supporting, sir. Please, have mercy on me."

"Let me think about it," I said. "Did you ever meet with

Doc anywhere other than in the office?"

"Sir Doc never went to the office, Sir Dan," Navarro said. "We usually met in a coffee shop or in a restaurant nearby."

"He never brought you to a house or a condo?"

He seemed to be lost in thought for a brief minute, then he started beaming. "Oh yes, Sir Dan. He had a party once in a condo unit about three weeks ago. It was a unit in the Karnak Towers, sir. I think it was unit five oh three, sir, Tower A. It is along Paseo de Roxas, sir."

So Doc did have another secret pad in the city he had never told me or Jessica about. I should have known. In the end though, not much of a surprise the more I thought about it. "Was there anyone living with him in that condo when you visited him?"

"He introduced me to his girlfriend from Thailand during that party, Sir Dan," Navarro said.

My eyebrows shot up. "Was it Waen?"

"I'm sorry, Sir Dan, I forgot her name," he said sheepishly.

I pulled out my smartphone and opened up the picture gallery that was in it before I thrust it to his face. "Is it this girl?"

Navarro looked at the picture of Waen carefully. "Yes, Sir Dan, I think that's her."

I put the phone back in my shirt pocket as I slid out of the front seat. "Okay."

He started getting nervous again. "W-what's going to happen now, Sir Dan?"

"You'll see," I said as I started walking over to where the

two cops were standing near my car. I could sense Navarro turning his head to look back to see what his fate would be.

One of the smiling cops pulled out a pack of smokes as I stood beside them. "You want a cigarette, sir?"

I smiled. "No, thank you."

The second cop placed his hands on his pistol belt. "So what do you want us to do, Sir Don? We can shoot him here and place his body in the river if you want."

I chuckled while I held up my hands and shook them. "No, there's no need for that. You can let him go. I think he's gotten the message."

The first cop smiled and handed me a worn out business card. "Okay, Sir Don. My cell phone number is at the back. If you need anything done, just send me a text or call me. I am at your disposal. We can do any type of job, and the mayor doesn't even have to know if you prefer it that way."

I nodded as I looked at the number on the back of the card. "Actually, there is something I could ask from you. Can you put a condominium unit under surveillance for me? It's along the main financial district in Paseo de Roxas."

The second cop started laughing. "No problem, sir! We will be off duty in a few hours, we can find out for you. All you have to do is call us later tonight."

I shook their hands after I gave them the address for the Karnak Towers. "I will do that, thank you."

When I got back in my car I started the engine again. I noticed the two cops get inside their police vehicle and drive away. Since the Philippines had the same time as Singapore, I cycled through my contact list until I found Crystal's phone number. I went ahead and dialed it.

Two beeping rings later, she answered the call. "Don, how is my favorite son in law?"

I laughed a little. "I'm your only son in law."

She snickered. "How do you know? Maybe Jessica actually has a sister we never told you about."

I started chuckling. "Knowing you, it wouldn't surprise me at all. How's everything going over there?"

"Well, I'm staying at Paul's lovely house in Sentosa Cove. The weather's perfect and I could see the all the sailboats out from the balcony right now. His Filipino maid is a wonderful cook so I don't even need to eat out anymore. How are you doing?"

"I'm in Manila. I'd like to ask, did Paul ever disclose to you that he owned another condo unit aside from the one he has in the Fort?"

"Nope," she said. "He only gave Jessica and myself the keys to the one near your place. It wouldn't surprise me if he did have another unit though, just like you have one that only you know about."

I sighed. "You seem to think I'm just like my father in law. Why is that?"

"You both have the same attitude, Don. You were exactly like Paul when he was your age," Crystal said.

"I can't tell if you complimented or insulted me, Crystal."

"Maybe it's both."

"Nice," I said softly. This is one scary woman. Sort of like the female version of Doc. "I heard through the grapevine that Paul might be in Australia, but my source couldn't tell me what it was for. Would you know anything about that?"

"He never disclosed his business dealings with me, honey."

"Okay, does he have property in Australia?"

"He never told me, but it's funny you should say that since there was a real estate catalog for rental properties in Melbourne right here in the coffee table in front of me," she said.

I placed my ear closer to the phone receiver. "Can you look through the catalog, did he make any markings on it?"

"Let's see, hold on," she said. There was a short pause as I could hear the shuffling of paper in the background. "There's some properties that were marked with a pen, a couple in Altona Beach and one in Hampton. What's all this about, Don?"

"I'm not sure," I said. "All I know is Paul left for Australia, then no one has heard from him since."

"Hang on," she said. "I remember meeting an acquaintance of his. Paul said he was a lawyer in Melbourne, his name is Nick Katsalides, I think. I have his number on my phone."

"Okay, can you give him a call and try to find out if Paul is down there?"

"I'll do that," she said. "Be honest with me, Don. Is my ex-husband in any sort of trouble?"

"I really don't know. His partner in Thailand was assassinated and he disappeared off the face of the earth at the same time while he was in Australia," I said. "Honestly, I suspected it was Paul who made the hit at first, but now

I'm not so sure."

There was another pause on the line before she said anything further. "Are you saying Paul had his own partner killed and now is on the run?"

"I really don't know, Crystal," I said. "All I can figure out is that this whole mystery will be revealed once I know where Paul is and I can speak with him."

"Do you think Paul was killed too, Don?"

"Unlikely if he was in Australia."

"Okay," she said softly. "I'll give this lawyer guy a call. I won't say anything to Jessica about it, at least for now."

"Thanks, Crystal."

"You know, you can call me mom too, Don."

"Okay, Mom," I said.

"If I get in touch with him and he knows something, I'll call you right back."

"Okay, thanks."

"Bye for now, Don."

"Bye bye, Mom," I said before turning off the phone. The whole conversation felt awkward. I could sense Crystal's concern, but at the same time I felt she was holding something back, maybe it was her worry over Doc, or it might be something else. One thing was apparent though: Jessica's mom was a very hard woman to read. Even though I prided myself on being able to judge people just from hearing their voice inflexions over the phone due to my skills and experiences, my mind seemed to draw a blank when it came to trying to figure out what Crystal.

Not wanting to stay cooped up in the condo, I drove over to Burgos Street, Makati City's red light district and unofficial hangout to most of the players in the industry. We naturally gravitated to the whores and bar girls since we were desperadoes ourselves. Being a college graduate, I was one of the few exceptions while the typical opener usually didn't even finish high school. I remembered a fellow colleague of mine had actually asked me why I even bothered to work on the phones, since I could have conceivably gotten work with an actual, legitimate corporation based on my educational attainment. In the end, I just didn't have an answer for him. This was a kind of job that got me the most success and I sure as hell couldn't stop now, not when I was on the verge of my ultimate triumph.

After parking my car along the sidewalk and giving a few pesos to the security guard watching the vehicles, I walked into Zools, a sports bar frequented by expatriates. The inside of the place was bathed in a bluish violet light. There were no chairs in the bar, just chest high circular tables that jutted out from the concrete floor. Tub thumping house music blared out in the background so conversations tended to be muted whispers, with people leaning over and cupping their ears to hear one another. Flat screen TVs jutted out from just below the ceiling, broadcasting European soccer matches on a satellite feed. Most of the crowd were foreigners, with the occasional local rich man flashing their expensive watches and jewelry. There were a few girls hanging out, most of them near the bar counter near the entrance.

I glanced around and didn't notice anyone familiar, so I

walked up to the bar and ordered a bottle of imported pale ale. The local beers were four times cheaper, but they were also pretty crappy. It wasn't like I was desperate for money these days. Two of the girls glanced in my direction, but I had a feeling that they might not actually be girls, so I looked away. The tough part about being in Asia was that their gay culture tended to be transsexual, so this meant that local homosexuals pretty much would dress and act like women. Since Asians usually don't have a lot of body hair and have slender builds, one can readily mistake one of these lady boys as actual women. There was heavy news coverage last year about a visiting American serviceman who took a girl up to his hotel room and ended up killing her after he found out that she was actually a he. It was even worse in Thailand since sex change operations were pretty cheap over there. One of my buddies told me that the only way you could really tell was to feel up her pussy, if it was too dry like plastic, it was time to bail.

While I stared up at one of the soccer games being shown, I noticed another man looking at me. He was tall and had brown hair neatly combed back. His clothes looked ubiquitous enough, like that of a typical expatriate wearing an office shirt and trousers. He was trying to be discreet about it but I could tell he was sizing me up. I jogged my memory, trying to recall if I knew anyone like him in the business, but he didn't look familiar to me at all. If anything, his appearance looked way too neat and proper to be one of us. I kept sipping at my beer and wondered if he was gay, but he seemed to be ignoring the lady boys across the bar while concentrating instead on the other expatriates like me.

Whatever he was up to, I wasn't going to be a part of it. I downed the last third of the beer and slipped some money over to the acknowledging bartender. Then I walked out of the place and headed towards the Kagera Club across the street. The moment I stepped inside, I noticed that the place was half empty. Since the music in this particular bar was much more low key, I went up to the wooden counter and sat down on an empty barstool. One of the girls approached me, but I waved her off.

I recognized the old bartender as he came over. I think his name was Darry. "What will it be, sir?" he said.

I placed some pesos on the counter. "A triple shot of Jack Daniels, please."

"On the rocks, sir?"

"Yeah," I said as I leaned closer to him. "Where is everybody?"

He just shrugged while he turned away and took out a bottle of bourbon from the rear counter. "I dunno, sir. Last few days it been like this."

I nodded as he placed the glass of whisky in front of me. The whole situation over here seemed pretty strange. Normally when there was turmoil in Thailand, this whole street would be buzzing with guys from my line of work, since the modus operandi was to transfer all the offices out of Bangkok and over to Manila until the heat died down. If there was too much heat over here, it would end up being vice versa. I shook my head as I took a sip of the bourbon in front of me.

"Hello, mate," a voice behind me said. The accent sounded Australian.

I turned around. It was the same guy who was looking at me in Zools. He was smiling, trying to put me at ease. The hairs at the back of my neck started to stand up.

"I'm Mick," he said as he held out his right hand. "You're Don, right?"

I kept my hands to my side. "I'm sorry, but I'm afraid I don't know you. I think you've got the wrong guy."

He started laughing as he withdrew his hand. "Look, I'm sorry for coming up to you like this, but one of my mates told me you're the man to see."

I shook my head. "I'm sorry but I have no idea what you're talking about. You've really mistaken me for someone else."

"Look, I got a friend named Joseph Guccione, mate. He told me that you've got an office here and I really need a job. I'm quite good on the phones, I made a lot of opens in Australia since I'm one of them, if you know what I mean," he said.

I knew a Joe, he worked as an opener for Doc a few years back. But this guy, I didn't know. "Listen dude, I don't want to be impolite, but I don't know who you are, I don't know a Joe and my name isn't Don. Now, will you walk away or do I have to open a can of whoop-ass?"

He smiled while turning around and walking away. "Hey, can't blame a guy for trying to find work, mate. Sorry for bothering you."

I watched him walk over to where the bar girls were

hanging out and he started to joke around with them. This Australian asshole hanging around here and referencing one of Doc's former buddies just couldn't have been a coincidence. Something big was going on. I was beginning to think that going to Burgos was a mistake. With my paranoia spiking up to near uncontrollable levels, I downed the rest of the booze and made my way out.

Instead of heading back to my car, I called for a taxi on the street and got inside. If that Australian was following me, the last thing I wanted to do was to let him know what my car and license registration was. I told the taxi driver to take me to a hotel near the commercial center so I could cover my tracks while being surrounded by other foreigners in a more formal setting.

After the taxi dropped me off in the hotel driveway, a smiling usher led me through the revolving glass doors of the entrance. I sat down on the couch near the lobby and pulled out my phone. I was thinking about using my newly acquired cop friends to arrest this guy, but I had a feeling it would backfire on me. I stared out through the massive glass windows to see if he had tried to follow me, but so far all I saw were tourists being led through towards the reception desk after being dropped off by the airport shuttle.

Better of be on the safe side so I decided to call up Casper instead. After several rings he answered. "Hi, bro. What's up?"

I leaned over and started whispering so that the other people sitting nearby couldn't hear me. "What's going on at Burgos? Why is it so dead?"

There was some laughter on the other line. "Ah, well bro, nobody is going there for now."

"Yeah, no shit," I said. "Did I miss something?"

"The Australians, bro. They are doing some investigative work. A few days ago I heard they arrested someone in Melbourne, somebody big in the industry."

My eyebrows shot up. "What? Are you serious?"

"I'm serious, Don. You remember Molson?"

"Mike Molson? The Canadian office recruiter who hangs out in Burgos? Yeah I know him very well, why?"

"Well a few days back, Mike met up with an Australian guy who was looking for work, so he went ahead and referred him to the Wolinski brothers. The next day the Wolinskis got raided and everyone ran for the hills."

"Holy shit, why didn't I hear about this?"

"You just came back to Manila yesterday, right?"

"Yeah," I said. "I always seem to be late when it comes to news about what's going on. So who are these Australians? Cops?"

"I heard they're from Australian Intelligence. From what my banking sources tell me they arrested someone in Australia and that someone told them who everybody is and where they all hang out over here."

"Burgos," I said softly. Fuck, this was not good.

"You got it, bro. So when the news broke, everybody's staying away from that very area for now."

"Fucking hell," I said. "You know what? I just happened to run into an Aussie over there less than half an hour ago. He also knew who I was."

"Shit! He knew who you were?"

"Yeah," I said. "And I think I know where he got my name and likeness from."

"From who?"

"Doc obviously," I said. "I know for a fact that he left to go to Australia about a week ago and no one's ever seen or heard from him since. If I put two and two together, then it only means that the Australians have him in custody and they haven't leaked it out in the news as of yet."

"Can they do that? What can they get him on?"

"Doc's my father in law. I know for a fact that there's a Federal warrant out for him in America and he's been using his fake passport to go around. It would mean that the Australians might be working with the FBI," I said.

His reply was typical Casper understatement. "Wow, this is bad."

"Alright, thanks for the news," I said. It felt like the whole world was suddenly after me now. "I need to go."

"Okay, bro. Take care. Bye."

I stopped the call and placed my phone back in my shirt pocket. So there was no way that Doc could have engineered the hit on Panupong. My father in law was actually being arrested in Australia at the same time. It would only mean that whoever was behind all of this was still out there, and I didn't have the faintest clue who it was.

14.

I was still in bed the next day when my phone started ringing. I looked at the caller ID and realized it was my mother in law. I quickly pressed the answer button and held the receiver to my ear. "Hello."

"Good morning, Don," Crystal said. "I'm in Melbourne and I just met with that Katsalides lawyer. You were right, they are holding Paul in a jail cell right now. The Australians are waiting on a US Federal prosecuting team that will be coming into the country in a few days. Against the lawyer's advice, Paul has been giving them some information."

"Goddamn it," I said softly. "Why in the hell did he have to do that?"

"Well they actually allowed me to see Paul, believe it or not."

"Wow, okay. And then what happened?"

"He wasn't in the best of spirits," she said. "He seems to think that you're behind his arrest."

I sat up on the bed. "What? Why the fuck would I want to have my own father in law arrested?"

"That's what I asked him," Crystal said. "He told me that you were planning to undercut him and take over his business."

My worst fears were confirmed. So it was my own father in law who gave me up to the fucking Australians. Doc was a paranoid loon who saw enemies everywhere, and now he thought I was the one that did it. "Why would I want to do that? I was partners with him for chrissakes!"

She sighed. "I tried my best to talk to him, Don, but he seems to be dead set on trying to get even with you."

"Get even with me? From his jail cell? He's nuts!"

"I'm not taking his side here, Don. You know I've had issues with him too."

"So what's going to happen now?"

"He's trying to make a plea with the Australians to let him go if he can give enough information to nail you," she said. "Which once again, is against his lawyer's advice. Paul is very afraid of being brought back to US territory, so he's desperate."

"I won't bite. Doc can give them all they want about me but these guys will have to prove it first," I said. "All they got is desperate words from a desperate man."

"I'm going to stay here for a few more days to try and ask for another chance to talk with him," Crystal said. "He's gone completely off the deep end and I'm so sorry he's taking it out on you."

"How can he even suspect that I'm after him? I was nearly shot and killed by a gunman the same time he was arrested in Aussieland!"

There was a short pause. "You were what?"

I shook my head. "Never mind. You don't need to know all of this. All I'm going to say is that while he was being arrested, I was nearly killed by someone. I think whoever is behind this wants both me and Doc out of the way."

"You're saying there's a third man involved in all of this?"

"Yeah," I said. "Look, thanks for the update, Mom. I really appreciate it."

"You're welcome, dear. I'll call you again in the next few days if I can visit him again. Don't worry, I'll keep trying to convince him you're not the one pulling the strings. The one problem with Paul is once he's made up his mind, there's no changing it."

"I appreciate it, Mom. Thanks."

"Bye for now, Don. Take care."

"Bye bye."

I turned off the call and threw the phone near the edge of the bed. It bounced off the comforter and landed into a pile of clothes on the carpeted floor. I threw the blanket aside, got up and walked into the bathroom. This whole situation was now unbelievable. Doc actually thought I was gunning for him and so he sang like a bird to the authorities! I pulled down my boxer shorts, kicked it away and got into the shower. The hot water cascading down my back took the goose bumps out, but there was a nagging feeling I was being set up. As I closed my eyes while letting the shower spray wash my face, my phone started ringing again. I quickly got out of the shower stall. I grabbed a towel and partially dried myself before rushing out into the bedroom. The phone kept on ringing while I started rummaging through the pile of clothes on the floor, hoping to answer the call before it stopped buzzing.

By the tenth ring I finally had it in my hand as I thumbed the accept call button. "Yeah?"

"Sir, it's me," the cop from yesterday said.

"Oh hello," I said. "How are things?"

"Good, sir," he said. "We have been doing surveillance on that condo unit here in Paseo de Roxas all night, sir."

"Okay, did you find anything?"

"Yes, sir. We spotted the subject and made a positive identification, sir. It looks like she went out to go to the grocery store, but if she moves away to another location we will let you know."

"Okay, "I said. If Waen was in the Philippines, what was she up to? "I'm going to pick up my car and then drive over there. Thank you."

It was still early morning, so Burgos was largely a deserted street. The security guard who was watching over my car was still there, so I smiled at him and gave him more cash which he gratefully received. I got in, started the ignition and drove off. The drive to Paseo de Roxas only took about fifteen minutes since it wasn't that far from Burgos. I wondered if there was still a point in even trying to bother Waen since I already knew where Doc was, but since she was also Panupong's mistress, then I figured she might lead me to the culprit that ordered the hit in the hotel.

There were still a number of parking slots available on

the side of the building. I maneuvered my car until it was parked just in front of the condominium complex. I didn't see the two cops anywhere so they must have been using an unmarked car instead of their police cruiser. The grocery store was a short walk away since the mall was nearby, so it meant that she would be coming back soon. As I kept observing the people walking along the sidewalk, my phone started ringing once more.

It was the two cops again. "Hello," I said.

"Sir, the subject has left the grocery and should be there soon. What do you want us to do? Should we arrest her?"

I thought about it for a few seconds. There was no reason to harass Waen. For all I knew, she might not have even known about Doc's arrest and incarceration. Stalking her wouldn't be prudent either since pretty much every luxury condominium in the city had close circuit TV cameras in every corridor. "You can go, thanks for everything," I said. "Let's meet up later so I can give you some more money."

"Okay, sir. We'll see each other then. Bye for now."

I turned off my phone while I opened the car door and stepped out. There was a coffee shop in the ground floor of the condo, so I locked up the car and walked inside. A young server greeted me from the counter. There were glass walls all around the place so if Waen made her way back I would definitely see her. Walking up to the front of the cash register, I ordered a shot of espresso and paid for it using the wad of cash in my pocket. Since there were only two other customers in the place I got my order pretty quickly. I took the small cup and walked up to one of the tall counter tables that lined the sides of the room. From there I could observe the outside street traffic without incurring suspicion from the reception staff of the condominium.

Sure enough, less than five minutes passed when she appeared down the street. Waen was carrying two plastic bags of groceries in each hand as she strode through the main doors of the condo lobby. I turned and walked out through the side exit of the coffee shop which led directly past the receptionist's area. After a couple of brisk steps, I was soon directly behind her as she walked up to the front of the elevators.

"Let me get that for you, Waen," I said as I pushed the up button by the wall.

She instantly turned around but said nothing. I could tell that she recognized me, but I couldn't read her expression. I made the wai greeting and smiled.

The elevator doors opened. An old couple walked out. Waen glanced over to the empty elevator before walking into it. I followed and got inside just as the doors started to close.

I held my hand out, palm forward. "Let me help you with those bags."

Waen was stone faced. "You push button. Floor twenty-eight."

"Okay," I said as I turned and pushed the right button. "I'm sorry, I didn't mean to surprise you like that. I just wanted to ask some questions and to see my father in law's condominium."

She didn't answer. As we made it up to the tenth floor, the elevator stopped and the doors opened. A young Korean couple wearing shorts and flip flops were followed in by their two noisy children and stood in between us. A young girl stared at me while elbowing her equally obnoxious brother before being chastised by the smiling father. Her mother pushed the button for the top floor, they evidently were planning to use the pool and gym. I stole a glance at Waen but she just kept staring straight ahead.

When the elevator chimed as we got to the twenty-eighth floor, I walked out first and kept my hand holding the door panel open. Waen maneuvered her way past the Koreans and got out. The narrow, winding corridor was painted in cream but there were less than half a dozen doors in the entire floor. I followed Waen until she stood in front of a door at the end of the corridor. She placed one bag of groceries down on the floor as she reached into her jeans pocket for the keys to the place. I picked up the plastic bag with my right hand and waited until she inserted the keys into the lock and twisted it open.

I smiled at her as I gestured with my free hand for her to go in first. "After you."

Waen walked inside and I followed her in. There was a narrow anteroom which led into an adobe colored living room. The usual bunch of padded chairs and sofas surrounded by coffee tables furnished the place. As soon as I walked into the living room, Waen slammed the door shut and locked it with an audible click.

I turned to look at her as I placed the bag of groceries on top of a nearby dining table. "I'm not here to cause any trouble, Waen. I just want to find out if you know what happened to Mr. Panupong."

She just stared at me. Then I sensed someone else was in the room as I started to turn around. The stun gun caught me right on my left shoulder, just as I was about to bring my arm up. I was immediately jolted and slid down onto the floor, as several million volts coursed through my body. The pain was intense and I couldn't think about anything else. All I could hear was the powerful crackling of the electricity being generated from its tip. I didn't lose consciousness, but I screamed out loud and kept my eyes closed, hoping that the pain would finally end. The next thing I knew, the stun gun attack had stopped and I felt something very sharp and painful just underneath my chin. I opened my eyes.

Crouching down to face me was the Thai man with the scar. He was holding a knife, with its point touching my chin, his knee was on my chest. His English was crude, but understandable. "What you doing here?"

The knife at my throat felt like a painful pinprick. I didn't dare move my arms. The last thing I wanted was a confrontation against an experienced killer. "Can you please put that knife away? I didn't come here to fight with anyone. I just wanted to ask Waen a few things."

He had an intense stare, like he had mentally hyped himself up into a ball of rage in order to keep on the edge. It felt like he was ready to kill me at a moment's notice. "How you find us?"

"I-I didn't know you were here," I said softly so I wouldn't have to move my chin much. The point of the blade really hurt.

Waen stood over the two of us. Her face remained emotionless. "Doc told me, this place secret. Nobody knows about it."

"I found out from one of the people who worked with him," I said before glancing at Scarface. "Please don't let him kill me."

Waen spoke rapidly in Thai. The man with the scar said a few words in reply. A second later he withdrew the knife from my throat as he stood up. I ran my fingers along the bottom of my chin and noticed a few drops of blood. It was a small cut, nothing serious. Waen took a box of tissues from the top of the dinner table and threw it at me. I caught it with one hand and wiped the blood away.

I sat up and leaned along one of the legs of the dining table. "Thank you."

Waen bit her lip. "Why you come? Where is Doc?"

"He's in Australia," I said. "They have him in custody and he is awaiting extradition back to the United States."

They both spoke rapidly in Thai with each other again. The man with the scar turned to look at me. "What he do?"

I sighed. "They caught him while he was looking for some property over there. He has an outstanding warrant against him. They were waiting for him. Someone tipped off the Australians as to who he was."

For the first time, Waen finally showed some emotion as she made a quizzical look on her face. "Who told police about him?"

I shrugged. "I don't know. I was hoping to find out some information from you. That's why I'm here."

The man with the scar narrowed his eyes. "You not looking for me?"

"Nope," I said. "I was just as shocked meeting you here. I thought you were going to kill me now that we met again. If there's anything I could do to make you reconsider it, please let me know."

He shook his head rapidly from side to side. "I not kill you."

I exhaled deeply. It was like a black huge cloud that was hanging over my head had suddenly dissipated into wisps of smoke. "Thank god for that! If I could ask, why did you try to kill me in the hotel?"

The man with the scar folded his knife and placed it back in his pocket. "You not target, only Panupong."

My eyes became like slits. "What? But you killed my loader, and you tried to follow me into the kitchen. You kept on shooting at me."

"My other partner kill your friend," he said. "He was only suppose to kill guards so I sorry for that. I only shoot at you to make it look like you target too, but I make sure to miss you. If I want to kill you, you dead now."

I let out another deep breath. So Elliot was just unlucky in the end. Goddamn it. "May I ask, who ordered you to shoot Panupong?"

They both spoke rapidly to each other again in Thai. Waen seemed a little upset and it looked like they were arguing for a bit. I just kept quiet and let them finish. The bickering went on for quite awhile. Finally, they both stopped and turned to look at me.

It was Waen who spoke in English. I could see tears forming in her eyes. "Thaksin took my daughter. He won't allow me to see her."

I pointed to the man with the scar but kept my eyes on her. "So you told him to kill Panupong?"

Waen looked away. "Yes. My daughter belong to Doc. He is father."

Oh shit. This just made everything more complicated. No wonder Doc had her living here instead of in Thailand. The whole thing was some weird love triangle between my father in law, Panupong the elder, and Waen. My eyes shifted to Scarface. "So it was Doc who financed the shooting? How did you get away to go here in Manila? You must have had help," I said to him.

"I no tell you who help me," he said tersely.

Waen started shouting at him and they both started quarreling in Thai again. For almost ten minutes they were just going back and forth at it. I couldn't understand all the nuances and their rapid fire, emotional deliveries would sometimes confuse me, but there were little snippets of words that seemed familiar since I had been steadily exposed to the language over the years. By the time the bickering had died down, Waen was crying. I had a sense they were arguing as to whether they thought I could be trusted enough to help them, now that my father in law was being held in Australia.

I got up from the floor and offered the box of tissue napkins to Waen. "Here."

She took the box and a few napkins to dry her tears. "Thank you."

"Don't mention it," I said as I pulled out one of the dining chairs and sat down while facing them. I looked at the man with the scar. "My Thai isn't very good, but from what I gather, you are Waen's father?"

He walked up to me. A feeling of dread gripped my mind and I thought he was going to hit me or something. But he stopped just less than a foot from me and gave me the wai greeting. "I her brother," he said. "My name is Yut."

I stood up and returned the traditional gesture. "I'd like to thank you for sparing my life, last year, Yut. I'm sure you remember that."

He nodded as he went back to leaning on the side of the wall. "Yes, I had orders to protect your wife."

"You were working for Doc and Panupong then," I said. "Is your current boss still supporting you now?"

He didn't answer. I had a sense he still didn't fully trust me so he wasn't going to tell me everything. I needed to know the whole story and there was still plenty of unanswered questions left. Waen seemed to look disappointed as she sat down on the opposite end of the dining table.

After another minute or so, she finally broke the silence. "We need your help," Waen said to me. "Doc told us to wait here until things become normal in Bangkok, then he was going to take me back there. I want to come with him to Australia, but he said to wait here until he come back."

I placed my hands on the dining table. "If you need me to help, I need to know everything. How did your brother get over here after he did the shooting? Who helped him?"

"General Sangsorn. His man at the airport helped me leave Thailand," Yut said.

My fingers tapped on the table. Finally, it seemed that I had to pry it out of him. So the good general was in on the hit after all. "A man wearing a business suit? Is his name Kit?"

Yut nodded. "Yes, he gave me new passport. I contact my sister and she get me from airport here in Manila."

"Mr. Don, we need your help to go back to Bangkok," Waen said softly.

I gently rubbed my chin. The blood underneath had dried and it started to itch a little. "You haven't found your daughter yet, have you?"

Waen let out a single sob, then she pressed her lips tightly. "No. I know Panupong bodyguards still have her somewhere in Thailand."

I looked away for a bit. I had to earn their trust and the only way to do that was to help them out. But bringing Waen's brother Yut back with her to Bangkok would be extremely dangerous. It was a known fact that Panupong's family would be looking for him. There was a distinct possibility that they would be looking for her as well. Doc clearly had her well-being in mind to the point where he was keeping her safe here in Manila. The fact that my father in law had a new daughter might also allow me to gain some leverage with him since he was spilling the beans on me. If there was one thing that could shut Doc up, it would be having something to bargain with, and his family was the only bet I could count on. So it looked like my choices were already made.

My eyes flicked back to Yut. "So you decided to kill your former boss because he took your sister's child, and the father of this child is my father in law, Doc. And then General Sangsorn's men helped you to get out of the country. Can you still count on Kit to help you if you come back?"

Yut shook his head. "No. He told me never come back."

I leaned back on the chair. So there would be no support using General Sangsorn. Fortunately, I still knew a few people over at Bangkok who could help out. "How far will you go to find your sister's daughter?"

"I do anything for my sister," he said. "She is only family left to me."

I leaned forward so he could see my eyes and I could see his. "Will you be willing to kill people to get Waen's daughter back? You might end up dead you know."

His answer came quickly and succinctly. "Yes."

I looked at Waen. "Are you sure you want to go back to Thailand? It will be dangerous for you too."

Her lips trembled but she maintained her composure. "My daughter there and I Thai. I cannot live here without my child. I rather die than be away from her."

I pulled out my phone and cycled through my contacts list until I found the right number. I immediately pressed the button to autodial it. The number rang for a few seconds before somebody answered it.

"Hello," voice on the other line said. "Mr. Don, how nice of you to call. I was just thinking of you."

"I hope you're doing well, Mayor Cabrera," I said. "I

have decided to do some business with you because I will be moving my entire operations here to the Philippines in the next few months or so."

"That is so wonderful, Don! Let's meet up for dinner in the next few days so we can celebrate," she said.

"I'd love to do that, but I'm afraid I need to go back to Bangkok," I said. "Something came up."

"Oh, that's too bad. Next time when you come back then, my treat!"

I laughed. "Thanks, Mayor. Oh, if I could ask for a favor. You see, I have two Thai friends here in Manila but they are stuck. They came into the country illegally and now want to go back to Thailand, but they don't want to go through immigration there either. Could you maybe help them out?"

"Why yes, Don," Mayor Cabrera said. "I am in partnership with a Thai businessman, we have a rice importation business together and his ships unload their rice in Subic. If you want, I could make arrangements so they can travel by ship, if that's okay. It will be safer than going by plane if they are illegals."

"Sounds great, how do we arrange it?"

"Well, Don. These favors don't come cheap. Will you be willing to give me another gift for my reelection campaign?"

"Of course," I said. "Nothing says I love you like money."

She started laughing. "You're so right, Don!"

15.

I took a flight to Bangkok the very next day. After giving the mayor some more cash, I was also able to secure passage for Waen and Yut back to Thailand with brand new Philippine passports. Since they would be going by boat, it would take them several days to get back to the capital. I tried calling the bankers in Malaysia while I waited near the departure gate, but all their numbers suddenly went to a busy tone. A few hours later, I passed through Thai immigration without a hitch. Moving out of the arrival gate, I saw Bob Duffy's car waiting for me. I waved at him as I walked on over and opened the front passenger door.

Bob grinned as he shook my hand. "Sawadee kap, welcome back, Don! How was your flight?"

I leaned over and placed my hand carry bag at the backseat. "Routine."

He raised his eyebrows as he started up the engine. "Oh, you didn't have a good time in Manila, then?"

I closed the car door and snapped on the seatbelt. "It was business and I learned a lot of things. Not all of them good."

"What do you mean?"

"I know who killed Panupong."

Bob's head turned as he looked at me. "Oh? Who?"

"One of his girlfriends," I said. "Her brother was Panupong's main triggerman, so that kind of made it easy to set it up. In the end it was an inside job, but not the kind we were expecting."

Bob let out a deep breath. "Wow, you don't say. So I guess your suspicions about your own father in law was wrong then."

"Well, Doc kept her safe in Manila," I said. "Which means he knew it was going to happen. And he's in jail too, by the way."

Bob's mouth hung open as his hand froze on the gear shift. "Who? Doc?"

"Yup," I said. "He took a trip to Australia and they nabbed him, right at the airport. They are holding him there while a team of Fed prosecutors and Marshals from the US is coming over to meet up with him. Seems he had an outstanding Federal warrant."

"Jesus H Christ! So he got taken out, just like Panupong, but in a different way though."

I nodded. "They both got neutralized, that's for sure. Now the war for the banking in Bangkok is about to start."

Bob shook his head in disbelief as he drove the car out towards the airport highway. "The two biggest players getting taken out like that. Who'd have thought? At least, this means your problems are over now, right? We can get back to business then?"

"Not quite," I said. "When I heard the news about Doc I called up our bankers in Malaysia. Guess what? Now they ain't answering."

"Shit! Does that mean we have to change banking now?"

"We're going to have to," I said. "We've got two choices in Thailand, or we can take the offer in the Philippines. The one in Manila charges a higher rate, but they're more stable compared to here."

"Well at least the only problem left is the banking," Bob said. "You don't have to look over your shoulder anymore since Doc isn't after you."

I pursed my lips. "It's a lot more complicated than that. Somebody set up Doc and could have helped out in Panupong's assassination. Whoever did it is still out there."

"This is one hell of a pickle, Don. Who are you suspecting now?"

"Well, Paunpong's oldest son wasn't his favorite, so he had some motive to lend assistance to his father's killers, but I just can't get over the fact that he's a pussy. On the other hand, maybe his mother ordered him to do it, but I can't imagine Panupong's own wife killing him over a mistress. Everyone who's anyone in Thailand has got one."

Bob nodded as he kept his eyes on the road. "Well, that still leaves the Thai military."

"Yes, the military currently rules the country and they play a huge role in the political scene," I said. "I got a message from General Sangsorn's flunky on my way out a few days back too. But would they really go out of their way to eliminate someone just to get their hands on more money?

They already control the country for chrissakes."

"You know what they say, never underestimate the other guy's greed."

"Yeah, yeah, I know. They lent some support to Panupong's hit man, but I doubt they would have done so without knowing what kind of a man he was," I said. "Panupong never crossed anyone in the military, he was too careful to do that. I have a feeling he even paid a bunch of generals to look the other way. Sangsorn's a neophyte when it comes to banking for the likes of us. He wouldn't be so bold as to order a hit on Panupong unless he had a trusted ally who could immediately give him business."

Bob glanced in my direction. "You're saying one of the owners might have teamed up with General Sangsorn to eliminate Panupong?"

"It's a distinct possibility."

"But who, though? The last thing any of the shop owners want over here is any kind of local turmoil."

"I'm just guessing, maybe the Singaporean? Maybe even Erich Bierly, I know he's desperate for business," I said.

Bob laughed. "You can count Erich out. He's a craven coward. No way would he ever dream about messing with a local. The Singaporean is greedy, but he's too smart and careful to get involved in internal politics here, nobody would be that dumb. It's gotta be a local matter."

"One big thing that bothers me is Doc. He's totally afraid of being brought back to America so he's stooling like a fucking pigeon," I said. "The son of a bitch is ratting me out because he thinks I was the one who told the authorities about him."

"Fucking A," Bob said. "What does he have on you?"

"Nothing concrete, since my bank details are either in Jessica's name or in one of my fake names," I said. "But the fact that the Australians know my identity will probably prevent me from going down under for the foreseeable future."

"So let me get this straight: somebody sets up Doc to get arrested- and he thinks you did it- so he's ratting on you? That is one goddamn convoluted soap opera, man."

"This is just the tip of the iceberg," I hissed. "I'm thinking of just getting the hell out of this fucking business altogether and retire. If I could just bring that whale in, then it will be enough for me to live a good life out here in the third world with Jess. I'll just get a house built by the beach, partner up with a local for a sustained, legit business and live out my life in leisure and luxury."

"That reminds me," Bob said as we pulled into Silom Road. "Is the Hong Kong thing still on?"

"It sure is," I said. "How many people have you got?"

"Most of the openers said yes, so you've got about eight, excluding myself and my family, of course."

"Just make sure you bring the others and they have to be wearing suits," I said.

"I got it," he said. "There's a cheap suit maker in Hong Kong near Nathan Road that could make up a suit in less than two days. Or there's some cheaper ones here in Bangkok."

"Use the cheapest ones," I said. "I'll pay for the suits, but use that Indian guy over at Pahurat Road. He's pretty cheap.

Get their measurements and just text it over to my phone, they won't even need to go over there for a fitting. Just pick up the completed suits once they're done and take them to Hong Kong with you."

"Ten four," Bob said. "Any word on where the office would be?"

"I'm expecting a call from Jessica anytime today," I said. "She told me she was meeting up with her friend, so hopefully I can get a quote for a one day rental very soon. I told her to try for a swanky location, maybe over at Hong Kong Central if she could work it out."

"I'm sure Jessica will work it out, she knows more about this business than you think."

I stared at him. "Oh? What makes you think that?"

Bob just shrugged while keeping his eyes on the road. "She came into the office once, and spent a few hours just observing what everybody was doing. She mentioned to me in passing that Doc would show her the numbers from the banking and all that because she was curious about how everything worked. When she asked questions on how the pitches worked, they weren't just run of the mill questions, she had a good idea on how the whole system ran. From qualifying leads, to closing, then on to banking. She was familiar with the basic concepts already."

"That's interesting. She never told me she was keen on any of this," I said.

"Ah well, maybe it's just curiosity," Bob said. "I once tried to explain to my wife Lamai how everything works and she just couldn't get it. Jessica on the other hand is a Harvard graduate, you know how tough it is to get into that university? They don't just accept anyone with money, you know."

"Yeah, I get it, Bob, thanks. It's just that she never told me she had an interest in it," I said. "Of all the people that could have shown her the ropes, why didn't she just ask me about it?"

"Maybe she was too shy. Or maybe she wants to surprise you when she tells you one day she wants to be an opener in your newest office!"

I scoffed. "Jessica has never had to work a day in her life. She was born with a silver spoon in her mouth for god's sakes. I doubt she would have the drive or the attitude to sit on a desk all day pitching to clients on the phone."

Bob giggled. "Don't underestimate your wife, man. She's the smartest woman I've ever come across. I remember that time we went out on a double date once. The stuff she knew and the way she carried a conversation was astounding. I'm telling you man, she's a natural."

"I know a woman who's smarter than her. Not in sheer brainpower, but overall."

"Who?"

"Her mother," I said.

"Hmm, never met her. Is she hot?"

"She looks just like Jess, except she's a lot older and with silvery blond hair, of course."

"She's hot then," Bob said.

"Oh, I took care of our Filipino friend," I said. "Johnny Real."

"Navarro? You found him?"

"I sure did," I said. "You were right. Brinton and Dukes was Doc's office. He was doing business right under my nose. The Philippine mayor wanted to prove just how connected she was so her cops raided it and shut everything down."

"Serves that asshole right," Bob said as he parked the car along the curb beside my condominium. "So when do we go to Hong Kong?"

I opened the door while grabbing my gym bag from the backseat. "In a couple of days. The whale emailed me his itinerary and I'll forward it to you tonight when Jess confirms the venue."

Bob nodded. "Okay, brother. I'll talk to you soon."

"See you, Bob, thanks for the lift."

"My pleasure, laters, dude."

My phone started ringing as soon as I got out of the elevator. I ran over to the front door of the unit and fumbled with my keys before I finally was able to unlock it and went inside. The caller ID was from Jessica, so I answered it on the ninth ring.

"Hi, Jess. Sorry- I was in the corridor."

"No problem," she said. "I spoke with David Chen and I got a good quote. He suggests its better we rent an entire floor so we can put up our own corporate signs and logos in place right where the elevator opens up."

I placed the gym bag in the middle of the living room before closing the door behind me. "That sounds good, you can probably get the MAM company logo from the website and then make arrangements with some graphic designers over there to build some sort of signage. We could just place it in the receptionist area."

She giggled on the other line. "Way ahead of you. I've already placed an order for that very thing with some designers here. They should have everything ready in a few days."

"Awesome, babe," I said. Maybe I could have her run the office someday. "I never knew you were keen on all of this. You never told me the time you spent a day in Bob's office either."

"Oh, so Bob squealed on me did he?"

"It wasn't like that," I said. "It just came out during a conversation I had with him and he mentioned it in passing. He thought I already knew."

"Okay, well I was just bored that one day and decided to take a look and see how you guys were making all that money."

"You could have just asked me, Jess. I would have given you the grand tour of everything. Now I feel left out," I said. My jealousy meter went up a notch.

She laughed again. "Oh my god! You are so insecure!"

"When a city college boy like me gets in between the two smartest women I know, yes it does make me insecure," I said. "Your mom is just as smart as you are, in different ways."

There was a slight pause. "Speaking of Mom, she told me where Daddy is."

"She told me too," I said softly. "Sorry, Jess."

"Why do you need to apologize, Don? Isn't this what you wanted?"

I made a loud sigh. "Oh come on, I said I just wanted to be independent, that's all! The last thing I ever wanted was your dad to get into any sort of trouble. You're not being fair to me, Jess."

"It's just that, there's some part of me that thinks you did it. You know that's what my daddy thinks too."

I grimaced. "Oh, bullshit! Why in the hell would I want the authorities to arrest him, huh? There's nothing in it for me, especially since your dad is ratting me out this very minute! Can't you just trust me for even one time?"

"I'm sorry I accused you, Don. You're right, the whole thing sounds silly. Please forgive me for even saying that. He's my dad and the moment I heard what happened, I-I just can't think straight."

"It's okay, Jess," I said softly. "We'll find out who set him up. But I need to get this deal first so I can have some money. Right now, I'm burning through my savings with all the expenses I have to shoulder."

"Our expenses, Don. I'm with you on this, remember?"

"Fine, our expenses," I said. "Going back to the task at hand, can you ask your friend if he knows anyone who could act as a receptionist? We're going to need one woman in there wearing proper office attire who could greet him."

"I'll ask. It shouldn't be a problem."

"Thanks, when are you coming back here?"

"In a day or two."

"I miss you," I said. "I feel so goddamn lonely over here—a part of me wants to get back on the plane and meet up with you over there."

"That is so sweet, Don. I miss you too."

"Don't worry about your dad, I'll do my best to help him out even if he thinks I'm the one who set him up. In the end, I am his son in law and I'll make things up with him," I said.

"I appreciate it, Don. This whole affair, it's tearing me inside out. You're my husband and I'm with you all the way, but forcing me to choose between you or him… it's a terrible feeling."

"You don't have to choose," I said. "I promise we will help him out together. I'll prove to your dad that it wasn't me who betrayed him."

"Thank you, Don. What you just said means a lot to me."

"And to me. Let's talk again soon."

"We will. Bye for now. I love you."

"Love you too, babe. Bye bye."

16.

Otis was able to arrange another meeting with Jet Panupong the following day. This time I demanded we meet up in a secure venue, since I didn't want to be moving around with a clay pigeon in public again. To my surprise, Jet agreed and told me to meet him in his father's karaoke club. I parked the car on the sidewalk and proceeded to enter through the padded double doors leading into the main hall. Two bodyguards wearing suits were standing just behind the cloakroom, and they searched me for weapons before allowing me to go inside. The air conditioner had been turned down to a minimum so there was a musty odor hanging in the air.

It had been a year since I stepped inside this place. The interior now had a bluish hue with twinkling colored lights embedded in the ceiling. The large, glittering mirror ball loomed over the central stage but it was not in use. The glowing Chinese dragon motifs were still along the walls, their neon tongues glowing faintly as they tried to imitate an actual breath of fire. The white marbled sunken stage was in the center of the room, all around it were circular leather sofas and coffee tables for the audience that wasn't there. Since it was late morning, the club was closed and everything was eerily quiet. I didn't even see any staff around. The bar was on the far side of the hall and Jet was there, sitting by himself on a barstool. Half a dozen more bodyguards, with obvious bulges beneath their suit coats, were milling about near the entrance. A few of them gave me blank stares while the one in charge pointed over to where Jet was.

I walked along the side of the hall until I got over to the bar counter. As soon as Jet saw me, he stood up and raised a cocktail glass. I walked up to him and gave him the wai greeting. "Sawadee kap, Jet."

He just started laughing as he sipped at his whisky. Jet was wearing a black, long-sleeved shirt and dark slacks. There was an opened bottle of Laphroaig on the bar counter beside him. "Hello, Don. Long time no see!"

"It's only been a few days since we last met actually."

"I guess you're right," he said as he put the glass down on the counter. "Seems I've lost track of time, just came from the funeral of my late father."

I looked down. "Oh, I didn't realize that. I'm sorry."

Jet took the whisky bottle and poured some more into his glass, almost filling it to the brim. "Oh, it's no problem. What's done is done. I'm just glad it was all over. Would you like a drink? This was my father's favorite. A single malt Scotch, he had it imported directly from Scotland."

I smiled and shook my head. "Too early for me, thanks. The last time I was here, we all drank this syrupy green fruit juice. It tasted like flowers."

"Ah, I think you are referring to nam bai bua bok, it's a green herb used to make tea. My father had it mixed with other fruits I'm sure," he said. "Would you like a glass of it?"

"Oh, no, no. That's alright. I'm good, thanks."

"You know, I am drinking to show everyone that I can be like my father. When I was at the funeral earlier, I saw that my brother and my mother crying when we all watched the cremation of my father's body. But for some reason, I could not cry," Jet said wistfully. "All I could think about was my weeping brother standing beside me, and how he tried to have me killed. He didn't even look at me or talk to me during the whole time. It was as if I was a ghost to him."

"And your mother?"

"She didn't acknowledge me either. I could see the look in her eyes. They still think I'm the second son, the one who just spends money and does everything for pleasure. But I will show them who I am," Jet said. "I will show them that I am my father's son and I deserve to be the head of the family."

I just stayed quiet. He was letting it all out. Most Thais wouldn't confide in strangers, much less a foreigner like me. I figured that he seemed to trust me more than most since we were in the car together when he was attacked. Jet must have thought that we were now brothers in arms. I so wanted to have him as an ally, but the thought of him having to deal with both his family and General Sangsorn made me hedge my bets. I needed to see if he was capable first before I could pledge full allegiance.

He sensed my reluctance. "Don, we been through hell together. You were with me when my brother's men tried to kill me. You need to think of that as some sort of baptism ritual. You could see that I was calm, even though men were shooting at us. I can tell you now that if both of us team up together, then the sky's the limit!"

I looked around. We were out in public and the last thing I wanted was to be in another shootout. "How well do you trust your men here?"

Jett gestured at his bodyguards at the other side of the room. "I trust them enough that they won't try to kill me. You see, if any one of them does that, then it would be too obvious and my mother will be forced to have them killed in return, even if she was the one who ordered them to do so in the first place. So in that regards, I am safe. But as I've told you before, if I am going to strike back at my brother, then I would need outside help."

I looked at him straight in the eye. My words were in a low voice even though the bodyguards were too far away to hear anything. "What if I told you that I can get outside help to deal with your problem?"

Jet grinned. "Then you will have my eternal gratitude. Do I know who it is?"

"You might," I said. "He is a man who used to work for your father. He's a professional. A man with a scar on his face." I was hoping that Jet didn't know him. If he knew who Yut was, he might have already suspected him as his father's actual killer.

Jet pursed his lips. "I don't think I know him. My father

did a lot of shady things besides the banking stuff, but he didn't tell me everything yet."

So he didn't know Yut. That was good news to me. "But this man has his own price though."

Jet tilted his head up and laughed. "Ah, that is nothing! I'll give him a million baht, maybe even two million!"

The next part was going to be tricky. I needed to choose my words very carefully. "He wants something else," I said. "It seems that some of your father's bodyguards are keeping his daughter somewhere."

Jet's eyes suddenly narrowed. "What? My family bodyguards kidnapped his daughter?"

I shook my head rapidly from side to side."No, no, no. It was from a gambling debt. He doesn't speak very good English so his story is a little... messed up. But from what I could gather, I think that he knew one of your dad's bodyguards, and ended up owing a lot of money to the said bodyguard. So what happened apparently was that this bodyguard- and I don't know his name, decided to take his daughter for safekeeping."

Jet crossed his arms. "If this man of yours doesn't know the name of my father's bodyguard, then how does he know it was one of the men in my family who took his daughter in the first place?"

Fuck, he had me there. I had to think of something quick. "What I'm saying is he knew the guy's name and he told it to me, but you know how terrible I am with Thai names, I've pretty much forgotten it."

"I can give you a list of all the bodyguards my family

employs," he said. "You can probably pick out the name from memory, right?"

I shook my head again. "I don't think I can remember it at all."

"Then let me talk to your assassin," Jet said. "All he has to do is to tell me the name, and I will have that bodyguard's head on a silver platter."

I raised my hands up to chest level, palms forward. "No, no, no. I think there's an easier way of doing this. If you go after your bodyguard now, the others will not be loyal to you."

Jet scratched the top of his head. "You've totally confused me, Don. So you're telling me that you know a guy who used to work for my father, but one of my bodyguards has his daughter stashed away somewhere? Are you telling me the full story?"

"As far as I know, that's it," I said. "Now I think we can do this quietly. If you could try to find out where his daughter is being kept, then you could just authorize me to take the girl back to her father and all will be good."

"Just like that? You don't want me to punish any of my men?"

"No need," I said. "If you go after your own bodyguards, then they could turn on you. If we do it this way, I can easily bring the girl back to her father and this man will do the job you need for him to do. With this plan, you get what you want in the end, and your bodyguards stay loyal to you. With General Sangsorn looking to take over your business, you need as many loyal men on your side as possible if you want to take him on."

Jet looked away as he was lost in thought for a minute. When he stared back at me again, he was beaming. "You know what, Don? You are a very, very smart guy. I need someone with your kind of experience in order for me to learn the ins and outs of this business. I like this plan of yours. Okay, so what do you need for me to do?"

I had him! My mind was working overtime to come up with something plausible and it looked like he believed me. The only problem was that I would have to be directly involved in this whole affair. I needed leverage against Doc, and having his other daughter with me was the key to shut his yapping to the fucking authorities. "Jet, I just need you to be discreet. All you have to do is to find out where this daughter is being hidden. Do you have like a chief bodyguard or something?"

"That would be Paradorn," Jet said. "He was my father's most trusted bodyguard, but he was with my mother when the shooting in the hotel happened. Para came to us afterwards and begged for forgiveness in front of the whole family. My mother said it wasn't his fault. Para made a vow that day to find my father's killer and make him face death in return."

Oh shit. That was one guy I didn't want to mess with. "Okay, if you could maybe find out through him if any of the bodyguards are hiding anyone, like a child."

"How do I ask him that?"

At this point, I was simply guessing. "Uh, do your bodyguards have a schedule or something? Like, when they are off-duty and all that?"

"Yes, Para has a small office in the house, actually. He has a computer which prints out all the schedules for my family's bodyguards," Jet said.

I nodded. "That's it. If you could find out where maybe one or two of them are being shifted to an unfamiliar location, that might pinpoint where the daughter is at."

"So I have to be like a spy? Can't I just ask him directly?"

"Well, look at it this way," I said. "If Para was loyal to you, then he should have told you about this already, right?"

Jet seemed confused again. "So you think he knows one of the other bodyguards took another man's daughter? Knowing him I don't think he would stand for it."

Damn, I was being boxed in again. I needed to stay logical or else this whole ploy would unravel. "Look, I don't know if he knows it. But maybe he does, and he is under orders by your mother and your older brother not to tell you. If he finds out that you know about this, he might let your brother know and our chance of pulling the job off is gone. Does that make sense to you?"

"But if Para is not loyal to me personally, then he needs to go too, right?"

I gestured at him to calm down. "Let's not get too far ahead, okay? One thing at a time. All you have to do is to make sure Para isn't in his office so you can sneak in there, access his computer and try to get some information from it. It may be there or it may not, but it would be a start."

He nodded. "Okay, that makes sense. I will try to find their schedules and locations for you."

I smiled again. "Good. Now there is another favor I need

to ask. This one is from me."

"Go ahead, Don."

I took a deep breath. Here goes. "I have a client who's flying into Bangkok in a few days time. He is a very big client, and he thinks there is a factory out here that produces pharmaceutical drugs. Since we are blood brothers now, I figure you can help me out with this one."

"This client of yours," Jet said. "He thinks there is a pharmaceutical factory out here, but is there really one?"

I looked up at the darkened ceiling. "Well the website of the company he is investing in says there is a factory out here, but there really isn't any, you see."

Jet giggled. "Ah, so you are swindling this guy, yes?"

"It's a very big swindle," I said. "If I pull this off, I can give you a lot of business, enough for you to take over your father's holdings without a problem. It will also give you enough leverage to negotiate with General Sangsorn."

He gave me a serious look. "Okay, so what do you need for me to do? Build a factory in a few days time?"

Since Jet was keen on getting me on board with him, this was a very good time to try and make him a part of the scheme. "No, I was actually wondering if you know of a factory that produces medicine here. If you know of one, then all we have to do is change a few signs and tell the managers that I will be escorting someone to take a look for less than an hour. After that, they can take all the corporate signs off and resume normally, as if nothing had happened. I could give them some cash to make it worth their while."

Jet laughed a little. "You people sure come up with the

craziest ideas in this business of yours! It must be fun to work like this."

I rubbed my forehead. "It's not all fun and games, let me tell you. Do you think you could help me in this?"

He nodded. "My father has many holdings in the medical field. I will ask around. What kind of medicine would this factory produce?"

"Any kind of pills, even a candy factory might do the trick as long as it looks like the product is some sort of tablet, or a lozenge or something like that. I need this to get arranged as quickly as possible. The client will be in Hong Kong in just two days and I could hold him there for no more than a day or so. After that, he will be here in Bangkok and everything needs to be in place. I'll email you the company logo so you can make some corporate signs with it. You've got to convince the person running the factory to replace all of his corporate signs with the one I'm sending you, it's just for an hour"

Jet took out a phone from his pants pocket and started to punch some virtual buttons. "Leave this with me, Don. I think I know how to handle it."

I felt a sense of relief. Another problem possibly solved. "Thanks, buddy. I know you won't let me down."

"And the bodyguard schedule too, I will look into it for you," he said.

"Good, good, so we're all set, then."

Jet leaned over the counter and grabbed another glass tumbler from behind the bar. "This calls for a celebration then! You need to drink with me, Don- I won't take no for an answer this time."

223

I sighed as he poured me two shots worth of Laphroaig. "Okay, I guess this does deserve a drink."

The day was not yet over as I immediately hopped on the next available flight to Hong Kong. Jessica was supposed to fly back to Bangkok in the evening, but I could no longer bear her absence, so I flew into China anyway. The combined stresses of the past few days felt like a cannonball had crushed my skull—I needed her. As soon as I got through passport control, I activated my smartphone and dialed Jessica's number. She answered almost immediately.

"Hey Don, perfect timing! I'm just about to head to the ticket counter to reserve my seat," she said.

I was grinning ear to ear. "I'm here, Jess. In the same airport as you. Just going through the arrivals terminal right now."

"What? I thought you were going to meet me in Bangkok. Did something happen?"

"Yeah, I missed you, babe." Just talking to Jessica gave me a sense of security. She was great stress relief.

She giggled. "Oh, that's so sweet. You just couldn't even wait a few hours, could you?"

"No, I need you right now, Jess. I could do you in the bathroom stall, I'm that desperate," I said while I moved along the terminal's massive hallways. "Let's meet over at the Midfield Concourse."

Her laughter was audible. "Okay, I'll still have to confirm my ticket then and go through the security checkpoints to get inside. Anywhere in particular?"

"There's a duty-free liquor outlet near the children's play hall area. Meet you there, babe."

"You got it, Don."

Half an hour later, I saw Jessica carrying her small backpack with her handbag as she strolled along the carpeted floor of the gigantic hall. The Midfield Concourse had recently been completed to handle the increased traffic of the airport, which served as a regional hub for all major airlines in Asia. The walls around us were huge glass enclosures and passenger airplanes were parked on the outside. The darkening clouds in the sky signified a thunderstorm was going to start. Jessica sprinted over as soon as she saw me and we collided like two runaway freight trains on a head on collision. We both had our arms around each other as our lips met. For a long minute we did nothing but wiggle each other's tongues.

Once the long kiss was done, Jessica rested her forehead on my chin. "I know we've only been apart for a few days, but it feels like an eternity."

"I know, babe," I said softly. "It feels exactly the same to me."

She looked up at me. "I'm sorry about the outburst from last time."

"There's nothing to forgive. We were both on edge over what happened to your dad."

"If I have to choose," she whispered in my ear. "I'll choose you over my dad anyway. He never did much for me and Mom, except give us money."

I gave her a smile. There was still a chance I could win them both over. "If my plan works out, maybe I can convince him otherwise."

"Well about this plan of yours, everything is already good to go over here," Jessica said.

"Great, I've also put some things in order in Thailand, so there's one little thing still left to do. I was going to do this in the airport in Bangkok, but I think there's a better chance of finding the right person here."

"Oh, what's that?"

I picked up the backpack that she dropped on the terminal floor and hefted it over my shoulders. "We need to find someone who resembles me a little."

Jessica looked confused for a moment. "Huh? What for?"

"I need to take a proper, formal picture of his face."

"Really? What's this about?"

"You'll see."

We spent the next hour or so just wandering the airport, looking for someone who resembled me. I told Jessica on what we had to do and while she rolled her eyes at first, she soon realized the necessity on why it was needed. As we strolled through the transfer gates, I soon saw a family of tourists heading towards our direction.

Jessica saw it too. "Don, the guy in front, he sort of looks like you. Different hair and different build, but if the face is all you're after, then he's it."

"Yeah, he'll do."

"He's got freckles though, are you sure he's the one you want?"

"Freckles, schmeckles. All that can be altered using photo editing software."

"Okay, here goes."

Jessica ran forward and called out to the man as she stood in front of him. "Oscar! How are you?"

The man looked bewildered. Two old women who stood beside the obvious tourist stared blankly at Jessica. "Sorry, are you talking to me?" the man asked her. His accent was clearly European, German maybe.

I ran up to them. "Ally, can't you see, that's not my twin brother. You made a mistake."

Jessica put her hand over her mouth. "Oh my god! I'm so sorry, I thought you were my husband's twin brother coming over to meet us here!"

The man smiled while the women beside him started to giggle. "Oh, it's no problem," he said. "I am from Berlin, ja. And many, many people look like me, ja."

Jessica jumped up and down like a giddy little schoolgirl. "Oh my god, this is soo funny! Can I ask you for a favor, sir? Since you look so much like my husband's brother, can I pose with you for a picture so I can post this on the internet? My husband's brother will find this so funny. Is that okay?"

The man looked shocked for a minute, but then his courtesy won over. "Ja, ja. Is okay."

"Thank you so much," Jessica said as she stood beside him and smiled for a pose.

I took out my smartphone and activated the camera. I focused squarely on the man's face and his face alone. "Okay, one... two... three..." There was an audible click as the phone camera immediately took an image of them.

"Oh thank you, sir!" Jessica said. "By the way, can we take one more picture, but this time, could you give us a serious look, while I put my head on your shoulder?"

The tourist seemed confused. "A serious look? Why?"

"Oh, so it will be funny," Jessica said. "We can make it look like you are angry at first, and then the next picture will show you laughing, is that okay?"

The man still wasn't sure what was going on, but a part of him obviously just wanted to get it over with so they could move on with their vacation. "Ja, okay."

"Okay, here we go," I said as I snapped a few more shots of the man using my phone. "That ought to be enough, hon."

Jessica moved away from him and stood beside me. "Of course, sorry for bothering you again, sir. Enjoy Hong Kong!"

The man smiled and waved at us before turning around and going on his merry way. I took a look at the pictures of him in my phone and one of them looked passable enough for a passport photograph. I immediately sent it as an attachment in an email addressed to Otis.

Jessica looked over my shoulder as I pressed the send button. "Did you get what you needed?"

"Oh yeah, Mr. Rick Marietta is now a real person with a real passport. Now let's get outta here."

17.

"Don, hurry up," Jessica said as she put on her office coat. Our room was a mess. There were clothes lying all around the floor and haphazardly placed on the queen-sized bed. The deep, azure blue waters of Victoria Harbor could be seen out in the distance from the windows of our hotel room. It was late morning in Hong Kong's Central district.

"I'm done, I'm done," I said as I stepped out of the shower stall and started rubbing my body down with a fresh towel. This was the day the whale was coming over to the office, and I needed to get over there before he arrived. The plan was for Jessica to meet him at the airport with a chartered car and escort him to me at the office. The moment I patted myself dry, I threw the towel onto the bathroom floor and immediately grabbed a long-sleeved office shirt that was lying on the bed.

Jessica stood behind me as she placed a tie around my shirt collar, while I pulled up the slacks around my waistline. "The car we rented has been waiting downstairs for half an hour already. I should be going, Leopardi's flight could have landed by now," she said.

"Okay, okay," I said while I buttoned up my shirt. "Go ahead and get going, I'll meet you in the reception area at the seventeenth floor and I'll take it from there."

"Fine," she said as she picked up her black suede handbag and made some last minute adjustments to her office attire. "Are you sure that he won't ask me for a passport or some sort of ID?"

"No, I sent him a copy of my passport by email already so he ought to be good. You have a set of business cards so just show him that if he gets real picky."

"Okay then," she said as she started towards the door. "See you in a bit."

My phone started ringing. I immediately gestured at Jessica to hold on while I picked it up. The caller ID was from Leopardi. My wife turned and stood there while I activated the accept call button.

I made a big grin as I started talking on the phone. I was feeling stressed but I couldn't give that sort of appearance when talking to the client. "Hi, Tony. How are you?"

His laughter was audible from the other end of the line. "Good morning, Rick! I'm good! We've already arrived. I'll just drop off my wife to the hotel, and then I'll just go straight to your office. I can't wait to finally see you in person!"

What the fuck? He was already in Hong Kong? "You're already here, Tony? Oh, I was going to have our company car pick you up," I said. Oh shit, panic time!

"Oh, no need, Rick! The airline had scheduled me a free

limousine service to and from the airport. It's one of the perks of traveling first class, as you well know. I'll just have my wife check in to the hotel, so I can drop our luggage off while I take this ride over to your office. It's not that far anyway since we are both in Central."

I was holding my breath. We needed more time! "Okay, we can do that. Let's just meet in the office then. You know the address, right?"

"Yes, you sent it to me by email. I am curious though, on your website it says the office address is Han Corporate Plaza, but the destination you gave me says you have a suite in the International Finance Center."

Shit. I knew this would happen. "Oh, I'm sorry about that, Tony. You see, we are now in the process of moving into our new offices in the IFC. I guess our IT manager forgot to update the address that's on the website. My sincerest apologies."

"Don't apologize, Rick! Those things happen. Anyway, we are now crossing this spectacular bridge and my wife is remarking that we just passed by Disneyland! I know you're busy, so let's talk again when I am at your office, okay? Goodbye and see you in a bit."

I grimaced while putting the phone back in my pocket. Time was of the essence now. "Motherfucker. He's already on his way."

Jessica stood rooted in the alcove by the door. "He's here? Now what?"

Suddenly my phone started ringing again. I picked it back up and checked who the caller was. It was Bob Duffy.

"Yeah, Bob," I said. "Where are you?"

"I'm at our hotel lobby just waiting for the other guys," Bob said. "Right now, there's only two of us here and the traffic looks bad."

My blood began to boil. "Goddammit, Bob, the client is already here and on his way to the office! You guys are still in the fucking hotel?"

"Sorry, dude. The gang was out all night on a bender, and I think a few of them are still asleep in their rooms."

"For fuck's sake, Bob! Get your openers together and get them all lined up in the lobby in five minutes! I'm sending Jess over in a rented car, she will get you morons in the office. We have to do this now!"

"Okay, dude. Lemme get the others. Sorry about this."

"Just get it done," I said tersely before closing the call.

Jessica gave me a blank look. "Are you serious? Your office workers are still in the hotel?"

I bit my lip. "Yeah, I need you to go pick them up, please. This day is turning into a real clusterfuck."

"Their hotel is in Mong Kok isn't it? I'd have to cross the bridge and into heavy traffic. It's going to be close if we make it there before the client does."

I gave her a serious look. "Jess, I need you to do this, please. I know you won't let me down."

She ran over and gave me a kiss. "I won't," she said before turning back around and going out the door.

At least there was one competent person in this group. I grabbed my suit coat from the hanger in the closet and then took out my leather wingtips from the suitcase. By the time

I was out of the door, Jessica had sent me a text that she was in the car and on the way over to Bob's crew. The office was just a block away so I ran through the crowds of people who were milling about at all hours in the city. Hong Kong was a hive of activity, if an alien hovered above in a spacecraft and looked down on us, it would think we were a swarm of ants. Gawking foreign tourists, streethawkers, young office workers in suits, deliverymen, and Chinese from all walks of life were walking briskly to whatever destination they were headed to. A multitude of cars drove by along narrow roads. The air was hot and muggy from the ocean mists of the nearby harbor. Since everyone seemed to be in a rush, my hurried dashes while wearing an office suit didn't seem that out of the ordinary in this bustling city.

My forehead was drenched in sweat by the time I got to the office building. I ran my hand through my hair to pat it in place while I straightened my tie before going up using the crowded elevator. As the door opened up to the seventeenth floor, I turned right and walked through the glass partition and into the fictional offices of MAM. There was a large plaque right above the reception desk that said Marvel Asset Management. A young, twenty-something Chinese girl in business attire was sitting at the front desk and she smiled at me the moment I walked inside. This was obviously the girl Jessica's friend had hired for us.

I smiled back at her. "Hello, you can call me Rick. If anyone asks, I am the general manager in this office okay?"

She just kept looking up at me and continued her smile. "Yes."

I rubbed my hands in satisfaction. My heartbeat was slowly going back to normal. All that was needed now was for Jessica to get Bob's team over here in a hurry. "Good, and your name is?"

The girl's look didn't change. "Yes."

My eyes narrowed. "Uh, do you speak English?"

She nodded. "Yes."

"Okay then, so I am asking you- what is your name?"

"Yes."

I rolled my eyes. "Holy fuck, so you don't know how to speak English and all you can fucking say is yes?"

She nodded again as she kept up her mystifyingly stupid grin. "Yes."

I shook my head. "Fine, I'll call you Mrs. Yes. May I use the bathroom Mrs. Yes? Oh, wait, you couldn't even tell me where it is because the only thing you can fucking say is yes, right?"

"Yes, yes," the girl said.

"Oh, well that's an improvement! At least you can say two yeses instead of just one this time, you stupid chinky bimbo!"

"Yes."

I turned and walked into the inner corridor of the office. "Oh, fuck it."

By opening every single door, I was able to find the bathroom at the far end of the corridor. To the left side of me was a glass partition and I could see dozens of office desks with phones lying on them. Beside each computer workstation was a yellow note pad and some pens. Beyond the desks were huge glass windows that overlooked the harbor below. I stood in the bathroom and ran the sink. I splashed the water on my face and dried my cheeks with some paper towels. At least there was electrical power and the water supply was working. A few minutes later, I walked into the central room of the office. The whole place was neat and tidy. I sat down on a chair beside one desk and turned on the workstation, but all I got was a blank monitor screen. Crap, I forgot to ask if we could activate the internet, now it was too late.

At that moment, I heard sounds of people coming into the reception area. I got up and quickly made my way over there. If it was Leopardi then the game was over. The moment I made it into the front of the office, I noticed Bob and a few of his opener crew wearing not so spiffy office suits trudging their way inside. The receptionist just continued to stare blankly at them while nodding like a retarded parrot.

Bob ran over to me and shook my hand. "Sorry for being late, Bossman. I hope the party's still going. Jessica is downstairs parking the car."

I nodded. "Just in the nick of time, Bob. Get them inside into the main office area. They can pick whatever desk they want—just tell them to act busy- you know, like writing stuff on their notepads or calling on the phones."

"You got it," Bob said as he pointed towards the corridor to his team. "Okay guys, this way please."

While his team of openers filed past me, a few of them recognized who I was and gave me curt nods of acknowledgement. I winked at a few and kept up a dry smile as they passed through. All of a sudden, Scott Wellman came through the door, ran up to me and gave me a big hug.

My eyes nearly popped out of my sockets. "Scotty, what are you doing here?"

Scott gave me a big, shit-eating grin and burped. "Yo, bro! I haven't seen you in a long, long time, Don! How you been, dude!"

"Jesus H Christ," I said softly while holding his arms. Scott was swaying back and forth and it looked like he was in either in a drugged out or drunken daze. Knowing him it could have been both.

Bob came back out into the reception area. "Hey Don, I'm sorry but I had to bring Scotty with us. Two of the guys who were supposed to be here cancelled at the last minute, and you did say you needed at least eight guys- and he was the only one available on short notice."

"I'm okay, bro," Scott said as he leaned on the reception counter. "Whatever you need me to do, I can do. We went through hell and back and back again!"

I gave Bob a menacing stare. "Were you fucking deaf, Bob? What did I tell you?"

Bob placed a hand on Scott's shoulder to straighten him up. "I'm sorry, dude. I think he was out all night. I thought he went right to bed in the hotel when we all checked in yesterday, but it seems he somehow rounded up the others and they went on bar and club hopping all night. When I knocked on his door this morning I think he just didn't stop drinking."

My phone started ringing again. I put my hand up to

shut them both as I answered it. "Tony, how are things?"

It was Leopardi on the other line. "Hong Kong is wonderful so far, Rick! It's been a long time since I was here and I am astounded by the changes since then! I'm currently at the ground floor of your building. Is it okay for me to come up?"

"Sure," I said. "My personal assistant Ally is down there, I can have her hook up with you and escort you up here, is that okay?"

"Sure, Rick! I'll just be sitting here in a sofa by the lobby. I'm only wearing a blue collared shirt and dark pants."

"No problem, she will get to you shortly. See you in a bit," I said before closing the call and dialing Jessica.

"Don," she answered. "I'm at the lobby and will come on up, but there's a line waiting for the elevator."

"Jess, Leopardi's there. He's sitting on a couch by the lobby. He's wearing a blue button shirt. Can you escort him up here?"

"Wait a minute …yes, I see him. No problem. I'll head over to him now."

"See if you can give me ten minutes, Jess. Oh, and your name is Ally, by the way. You're my PA."

"Got it, bye."

I turned to look at Bob. "Okay, he's on his way, tell your guys to make busy and they get a couple hundred bucks each. Now go!"

As Bob walked into the passageway, Scott twisted his head and smirked at me. "What about me, bro? I could use a couple hundred clams too, you know."

I grabbed him by his elbow and led him into the office corridor. "Scotty, we got a problem, dude. The cops are on their way up here, it's gonna be another raid."

Scott's eyes went blank. "Holy fuck! I can't let them arrest me, bro! I fucking can't! Fuuck!"

"It's okay, Scotty," I said while placing a hand to his chest to calm him down. "I think I can talk my way out of this."

"But it's a raid, man! How can you do that?"

"Take it easy," I said softly. "I didn't have any money back then, but I got a lot of cash nowadays, remember? Money talks, bullshit walks."

He gave me a nervous nod as I led him towards the end of the corridor. "Yeah, man. You're as rich as Doc now!"

"Exactly," I said. "Now what I need is for everybody to stay calm. And I need you to do a special favor for me."

"Anything, bro. You know me. We escaped that last raid together. I remember!"

"Yes, yes we did. Now, what I need for you to do is to go into this place," I said while pointing at the bathroom. "Put the lock on and don't come out no matter what. You've got to stay hidden in there. You can't make any noise. You gotta be as quiet as a mouse. Can you do that for me, Scotty?"

He nodded as he stepped into the bathroom. "Oh yeah, Don. Hell yeah! Are you sure this will work?"

I smirked confidently. "It will work, provided that you keep very, very quiet and don't open the door for anyone, okay?"

"Yeah, I will, bro," he said as he closed the door. Just as I turned around he opened it again. "Don, there's no window in here!"

I pointed up to the ventilation shaft in the ceiling. "If you need to escape, you can go out through there, Scotty."

"Oh, okay. I got it, bro. See you laterz," Scott said as the door closed behind him. I heard an audible click as he engaged the lock on the doorknob.

As I walked back out into the reception area, I gave a hostile glance at the Chinese receptionist. "Now, Mrs. Yes-yes. I want you to shut the fuck up and don't fuck this up. You can bare your tiny little Asian knockers to me later. Okay?"

She smiled at me and nodded. "Yes."

At that moment, the elevator doors opened. In stepped the client as Jessica stood by his side. Tony Leopardi came striding into the reception area, all six foot five inches of him. Tall and rangy, with bronzed skin and a golden receding hairline, Leopardi was dressed casually in a blue polo shirt and dark slacks. Jessica was about to introduce us, but he took one look at me and moved forward as he extended his hand while making a big grin. His teeth were pearly white and perfect.

I met him halfway and shook his hand. "Mr. Leopardi, welcome to Hong Kong and welcome to our humble offices."

He let out a cheerful laugh. "Mr. Rick Marietta! It's a great pleasure to finally see you in the flesh! I must say the passport copy you sent to me through your email doesn't do you justice, you look much, much better in person."

I returned his smile. "Oh, thank you, Tony. Would you like to come into my office for a brief, chat?" I turned to look at Jessica. "Thanks, Ally."

Jessica gave me a wink while Leopardi turned to stare at the people working on the other side of the glass partition. "No problem, Mr. Marietta."

While I ushered Leopardi down the corridor, I glanced over at the smiling Chinese receptionist. "Please hold all my calls, Mrs. Wang."

"Yes, yes," the Chinese girl said.

As we walked slowly along the corridor, Leopardi turned to look at me. "Oh, you know what? I haven't been to the toilet since the airport, can I please use your restroom?"

The thought of this naïve whale sharing a small bathroom with a deranged and hung over Scott Wellman would not be a good idea. I had to think of something fast. "Oops, I'm so sorry Tony, but our bathroom is currently on the blink, I've asked maintenance to have a look at it, but they haven't gotten back to me yet."

Leopardi seemed a little surprised as we stood just outside my bare office. "Oh? So how do your people go to the toilet then?"

I shrugged apologetically. "They have to go downstairs, I'm afraid. The building management has assured me they will fix the problem sometime today. But since you do need to go, why don't we both go down and have some tea at a nice café nearby? It would sure be a lot better than being stuck around in a stuffy office like this."

He was beaming. "An excellent idea! Let's go."

I laughed as I led him back towards the reception area. Glancing quickly at the others, it seemed that Bob's crew were more or less just goofing around and wildly exaggerating; a few of them pretended to call on phones with no visible cables, while others were typing on keyboards in front of blank monitor screens and pretending they were playing the piano. I needed to get him out of here as quickly as possible.

While passing by the door to the bathroom, we both suddenly heard some banging noises coming from the inside of it. The hairs at the back of my neck started to stand up. What in the hell was Scott doing in there?

Leopardi stopped and pointed at the door. "Is there someone in there?"

I moved past him to try and influence him to get to the reception area. "Oh, I think it's the building plumber. He's fixing the toilet now as we speak. This way, please."

He seemed to accept my explanation as he started walking again. "Hmm, alright then. It looks like a new office after all, it must still have teething problems."

When we made it back to the reception area, Jessica was now standing beside the Chinese girl. Leopardi waved and smiled at them as he got to the elevator doors first and pushed the button. I stood beside him while using my body to block his view of the ongoing shenanigans occurring at the other side of the glass partition.

While waiting for the elevator doors to open, I turned and faced the Chinese girl again. "Oh, Mrs. Wang, if anybody calls, please tell them I'm out of the office with a very important client."

"Yes, yes," she said diligently. Jessica did her best to suppress a smile.

When the elevator doors opened, Leopardi stepped inside and I followed. This time, there was nobody else on the lift so I was somewhat relieved. All I had to do now was to make sure he would not come back to this building. Within seconds, the doors had closed and we were on our way down.

He gave a slight nudge to my elbow. "I must say, that office worker you have there is quite beautiful. Her name is Ally, yes?"

I nodded. "That's correct, Tony. Yes, Ally is quite popular in the office."

Leopardi gave me a slight wink. "I would sure like to have her for the night, if you know what I mean."

"I would too," I said. "But her husband is a sniper in the US Marine Corps, and I sure wouldn't want to mess with those guys."

He gave a slight laugh as the elevator doors opened, revealing the ground floor. I quickly led him out of the building and we walked over to a nearby tea house. There were red lanterns suspended up in the ceiling of the café. As he went to the bathroom, I ordered some milk tea for us. So far so good.

When he came back, Leopardi maintained his good mood. "It was indeed a good idea for us to stay down here, Rick. It's more casual and since I am on holiday more or less, I think the fewer office interiors I see for the next couple of days, the better."

I nodded. "I completely agree with you, Tony. I like to come down here for a nice cup of sweet milk tea when the stress gets too much to bear."

He looked down at his steaming cup of coffee, the added condensed milk giving it a thick, syrupy body. "I must confess and be honest with you, Rick. When I came over here, it was indeed at the insistence of my accountant. You see, he had serious misgivings with the share offering for Apgen."

My heart skipped a beat. "Oh, why? He doesn't think the company is going to be profitable enough?"

Leopardi shook his head. His voice had turned soft, like he was apologizing. "No, no, it's not that. He thinks this whole deal is bogus."

My eyebrows furrowed. Don't tell me he's going to back out now? "What gave him that idea?"

Leopardi seemed reluctant to talk, like the truth was being forced out of him. "It's just that he says he's never heard of your brokerage firm before. We have no track record in regards to dealing with this. I hardly know about investing and so I have to put my faith in you and David Johnson. How is his wife doing, by the way?"

"Tony," I said calmly. I needed to close him again. It was now or never. "We do have a track record. You've been dealing with David for many months now. Everything is going well. As for your second question, David had to go on leave because he is with his wife- she's back in their home and is resting."

"Oh my goodness! I hope the tests that were done gave some good news."

"Actually, it's stage four pancreatic cancer. It's

inoperable, and the doctors don't think any additional chemotherapy will help. I believe they gave her six months at the most. I'm sorry for telling you this," I said softly. "David will not be back at work for awhile, he wants to be with her until the very end."

He was stunned. "Oh my god! Please, wish him and his wife well for me."

"I will do that," I said. "He told me to make sure you get the best advice on this deal, he wanted all of his clients to have substantial investments in Apgen because he knows it will be his defining legacy."

Leopardi looked away for a moment, He seemed lost in thought. Then our eyes met. I could see a glimmer in his pupils. "Thank you for being honest with me, Rick. I actually came over because I felt I needed to prove my accountant wrong. Your candor and seeing your office has strengthened my view that this is a very good deal."

For a moment there I thought the deal was lost. I fought the urge to jump up and hug him. Time to reel him back in. There was one final test though, just to make sure he wasn't stroking me. "Well Tony, if you really don't think this deal is for you, and you'd rather go with your accountant's recommendation, then that's fine. I have two other clients ready to take the shares I have allocated for you. At two dollars a share, they are set to make a killing even if it opens at the bare minimum of four during the IPO launch. It's a guaranteed doubling of their money, even on a worst case scenario."

Leopardi slammed his fist on the table. The glass cups of

milk tea rattled, but didn't spill their contents. "No, I have made up my mind! This is an excellent deal. We're going to go with it. You've got the letter of intent, and I will follow through on it. I will not only do this to make some very good profits, but for David's wife as well. You've convinced me."

I grinned as we once again shook hands. All the worries in the world had suddenly evaporated. It felt like I was floating on air. "That's excellent news. I will have to go soon since there's a lot of documents that I need to file on your behalf."

Leopardi was back in feeling the mirth once more. "I understand. I think my wife would want me back at the hotel soon, anyway. She wants to visit Macao before we go to Thailand."

Shit. It's not over yet. "Oh? So you would like to still see Apgen's factory then?"

He giggled. "Well since we're already here, then why not? The flight and hotel is booked. That won't be a problem, would it?"

I smirked. "Oh, no problem at all. I have my tickets scheduled to go too. In fact, I'll meet you at your hotel with a rented car. This time I must insist I'm the one who takes you to the complex. I'll be your personal guide."

His eyebrows shot up. "Oh, you'll be there as well? That's wonderful news, Rick! I thought you were just arranging someone from Apgen to meet me when I go to their factory, but this is even better. I hope this doesn't take time away from your job. I would like to reimburse your travel expenses over there, if I may."

I held up my hand. "No need. The office is paying for this trip as they feel that you are an important client to us."

"This is very, very good. I'm so glad I made this trip. Prior to this I had no confidence in standing up to my accountant," he said. "Now, after talking to you in person and seeing everything with my own eyes, I can tell him to shove off and just send the payment over to your account."

"Oh, don't be too hard on him, Tony," I said. "After all, you know more about this deal than he does."

He nodded. "You're right. As always, you're right. Okay then, I think I will need to head back to my hotel and get those ferry tickets to Macao. My itinerary is to stay here for another day after that and then fly to Bangkok. When will you be going?"

"By tonight actually," I said. "The only bad thing about this is that you won't see me in the office if you decide to visit it again."

Leopardi tilted his head up and laughed. "Oh, I've seen your office already, no need to do it again! I'll come back in a few month's time when the Apgen IPO goes through the roof and sponsor a party for your entire firm. How does that sound?"

"Sounds wonderful, Tony! But let's not get ahead of ourselves, I need to make money for you first, then we can talk about celebrating."

We chatted for a few more minutes, then we shook hands and bade each other goodbye. I stayed in the lobby of the office building as I observed him walking down towards the subway entrance. I didn't want to go back upstairs until I was sure he wasn't going to come back. After an interval of fifteen minutes, I finally made my way back up to the office.

When the elevator doors opened, I noticed Bob Duffy's entire crew were taking turns chasing the Chinese secretary along the corridors. Jessica was sitting in the receptionist's desk while she rolled her eyes and shook her head. I could hear Scott's screaming coming from the closed bathroom. He was ranting and raving about the cops trying to get inside and how scared he was just sitting in the dark.

I walked over to Jessica as I saw the Chinese receptionist trying to climb up on top of a cubicle while on the other side of the glass partition, as two men were trying to grab at her ankles. Bob was gesticulating wildly, trying to get everything under control.

"I think we got him, Jess," I said to my wife. "Though he still wants to see Thailand."

"That's great. Now maybe you might want to tell your kids to behave themselves. Bob doesn't seem to be doing a very good job at it," she said.

"Why is Scotty screaming?"

"He thought it was a real police raid, so he apparently broke the doorknob to prevent anyone from opening the bathroom. Now he's stuck and in the dark since one of the other guys fiddled with the fuse box. The air-conditioning system is out too."

Bob walked into the reception area. He looked to be in a daze. "I think one of the crew got their hands on some ecstasy or cocaine last night. The moment you left, they all took it. Except for Scotty, of course."

I glared at him. "They're your crew, Bob. Fix it or none of you are getting paid."

Jessica took me by the arm and led me towards the elevator. "Let's get out of here."

"Let's do that," I said while pushing the down button.

18.

Jessica and I flew back to Bangkok the next day. I gave Bob's crew only half of what I promised them since they turned the office rental into a complete pigsty. Leopardi sent me an email update, saying he was enjoying Macao and gave me his flight itinerary to schedule a pickup at the hotel for the next day. I was in my condominium when I sent word to Otis I needed another meeting with General Sangsorn's people and within minutes, I got a call from Mr. Kit.

I lifted the phone up to my ear. "Hello."

"Mr. Don, you said you wanted a meeting?"

"Yeah, I wanted to ask if I could get a bulk discount when it comes to sending money to the general's accounts. You see, the amount will be pretty big."

Kit's voice was cold, emotionless. I hated talking to him. "How big, Mr. Don?"

"Around mid eight figures."

"Could you be more specific?"

I sighed. "Say around ten to twenty million."

"Dollars?"

"Of course."

"That will not be a problem," he said. "We can give you a special twenty percent rate. I have your email, and I'll send you the bank details in a few minutes."

"The banking, will it be in Thailand?"

"Yes, do you wish it to be somewhere else?"

"I would prefer Singapore or Hong Kong if that can be helped," I said.

"Okay, give me a few hours to arrange something for you."

"One other thing," I said. "How do I know that the general will give me the amount that's owed to me when the money clears?"

"General Sangsorn is an honorable man. He is not motivated solely by money. A lot of cash that goes through the firm's accounts are much, much higher than the figures you gave me for this transaction," he said.

"Oh? If he isn't motivated by money, then what is making him want to do this?"

"A sense of duty to his country, Mr. Don. The general believes that order must be maintained and if there is a single system in place, there will be less chaos, so to speak. General Sangsorn is very patriotic and he loves the King."

"Okay, I'll wait for your email then," I said, just before I turned the phone off and stuck it back in my pocket.

Jessica came out of the shower. She had a towel wrapped around her body and she held a second one while drying her hair with it. "So which of these bankers are you going to take?"

I slumped back into the soft cushions of the sofa. "That's the million dollar question. Jet is giving me the best rate and he's the one I feel I can trust the most, but I don't know if he's going to prevail in all of this. General Sangsorn is the most powerful, but he could just decide to keep the money and there won't be anything I can do about it. The Philippine mayor sounds okay too, but I have a feeling I'll be constantly paying a fee to keep my operation in her favor for a very long time."

Jessica sat down beside me. She had a freshly scrubbed scent, which I always found sexy. "Tough choices, you can't maybe split the payment so you can hedge your risk against any one of them?"

"That's a good idea," I said. "But the client might get suspicious if I ask him to send parts of the payment to three totally different banks. The other concern is the proportion, even if I could split it up, a third of twenty million- which is about six point six-six-six mill, is still a lot of money to lose."

Her head rested on my shoulder. "Do you really need all that cash, Don? I mean, if you just lose a part of it, it's not going to be the end of the world, is it?"

"No," I said. "But it'll be a big setback. I had plans to be my own boss, babe. We also need as much cash as we can to try and help out your dad."

She turned her head and looked away. "In a way, I think being in jail might be better for my dad."

I gave her a quizzical look. "Are you serious? What kind of good does it do for him to be in prison?"

She sighed. "It'll teach him a lesson."

"What kind of lesson?"

"That crime doesn't pay?"

I placed a hand on her arm as our eyes met. "Seriously? I'm in the same business as your dad. Do you want me to go to jail too?"

Her eyes flickered for a bit, then they refocused on me. "Of course not! I love you, Don. But at the same time, I think you need to move away from all of this. I know I've had talks with you before about what you do and what Daddy does, but it seems you just come up with excuses to keep doing what you're doing."

This again? I was totally exasperated. "If it wasn't for what I do, where would we be now? Back in America, struggling to pay the rent on a two bedroom bungalow in some trashy, gang infested neighborhood? Where the only pleasure in life would be barbequing prepackaged hotdogs on an old grill in the weekends? Is that the kind of life you want to live?"

"You're exaggerating, Don. You and I, we both graduated from college, we can lead normal lives, be part of society again, rather than living like outlaws on the fringe."

I shook my head. "Jess, I can't lead a normal life. Not now, not ever. I spent a week back in California when you were visiting your friends a few months ago, remember? I stayed in a crappy hotel in Beverly Hills and I called you every night while you were in the East Coast. I looked at everyone around me doing their mundane existence and just going about with their work. You know what? That was when I realized I could never get a normal job again. This business that I do right now, it's the only thing I've ever been good at. I just can't do anything else, and I sure as hell don't want to either. This is my calling. I've never had so much success with this game because I'm good at it and I don't want to change that."

"I remember. What were you doing in back in LA?"

I looked down at the coffee table. "I tried to find my mother."

"Did you find her?"

"No," I said. "She must have obviously changed her address and maybe even her name. It's been years since I last knew where she was anyway. Then I met up with some old classmates from college and we had a drink. I spent a few more days just wandering around the places where I used to hang out as a kid. In the end, the whole place looked foreign to me. It was like I was standing on an alien planet. The entire city just felt …empty, it was as if I knew that I no longer belonged to that kind of world. I got back to Bangkok the very next day and waited for you here until you finished up with your friends."

"I'm sorry you didn't find your mother, Don. I bet she would be proud of all the money you've made, just don't tell her how you were able to acquire it when you finally do meet her. We could hire a private detective or something, I bet they could find out where she is."

"I bet she wouldn't care even if I told her I was a criminal," I said. "She never cared about me or my brother Randy. I got away from her the first chance I got. Not that she cared anyway. She didn't even show up during Randy's funeral."

She rubbed my chin. "I'm so sorry about your life, Don. I know it must have been hard growing up like that."

I took her hand and stroked it with my own. "I don't care about her anymore. I just wanted to see if she was still around."

"But you still do care, Don. You may not want to admit it, but the fact that you went back there shows it. Deep inside, you still have an affection, or just even an attachment for her. She's still your mother."

I shrugged. "She could be dead for all I know. Even if she isn't, well... it'll be tough finding her."

Jessica started to get giddy. "Then let's hire a PI then! I bet you we can find out pretty quickly where she is and you can get together again!"

"It doesn't matter to me anymore, Jess. Whether she's still around or not, what difference does it make? I got nothing to talk to her about. That kind of life I once led is gone. I don't owe her anything and I sure as hell won't give her a pension just because she's my mother."

"Do you really hate her that much, Don?"

"No," I said softly. "To be honest, I really don't have any feelings towards her at all."

"I see. You know, this is exactly what Daddy told me about my mom, just a few months ago. Seems to me that this kind of work turns you both into psychopaths."

I rolled my eyes. "Oh, come on! So that's what you think of me now? A psycho?"

"Maybe not a psycho," she said. "There's another term for it. I took a psychology class as one of my electives back in college and it's on the tip of my tongue ... ah, oh yes- the correct word is a sociopath."

"So you think I'm a sociopath? Is that it?"

Jessica pressed her lips together. "Well, you exhibit some of the characteristics."

"Oh, really? Such as?"

"Lack of empathy or remorse. You don't seem to have a conscience for the lives you ruin with your schemes. Total disregard for the law. Living a life of pure impulse. I've seen you manipulate people with the snap of your fingers, Don. There isn't a shred of morality inside of you. You don't care about other people's feelings. It all seems to come naturally to you."

I let out a deep breath. "Wow, I can't believe I'm hearing this from my own wife! The reason I do this kind of work is for the both of us! And now you're saying I don't have any empathy? Bullshit! Every time something bothers you, it bothers me too- doesn't that count for something? When you have a problem, I listen to you and do my best to solve it! I give you everything you want. I busted my ass and nearly got killed to get us this far, and now you're saying I'm just manipulating people?"

She held my hand tightly. "Please don't be so defensive, Don. I'm just being honest. You definitely care about me, I know that. But when it comes to everybody else, I see this twinkle in your eye when you talk to the others. It's like you view everyone but me as expendable or something. If somebody isn't either yourself or me, then it seems you just think of them as not really people, but as either obstacles or temporary allies that you can easily throw away when they aren't useful anymore. My daddy is exactly the same way, the one person he cares about is me, I think."

"You're wrong," I said. "I do care about others. I care about Bob, and Scotty and a whole bunch of people that I work with. I even care about your mom, believe it or not."

"What about my daddy? You care about him?"

"I do. Since he's your dad."

"That's what I mean," she said. "If someone isn't in your inner circle, you don't give a shit. This is why I think you're trying your best to get this deal with that South African guy. You waited until you had the right opportunity and you planned on jettisoning my dad once you got it. You even admitted that to me."

I angrily took my hand away from her grip. "You're wrong, Jess! I'm doing this load because I know your dad was going to betray me the first chance he got, so all I did was beat him to it! If you look at what he's doing right now, while he's being held in Australia, you can see what kind of a man he really is. The moment they caught him, he started telling them everything about me!"

Her lips started to tremble. "Why couldn't you two just get along?"

I stood up. "I don't know! Why don't you ask him? He was the one who set up a secret office in the Philippines right under my nose. If his stupid ass manager didn't steal leads, then I would have never found out about it. I tried to be loyal to him, and this is what I get for it!"

A tear slid down her cheek. "See, this is what I mean! You

and him are so alike, looking at you is like seeing a younger version of Daddy. He left Mom as soon as he started making money and the only reason he kept sending us cash was because I was his daughter. I can't help but think you might do this to me someday."

I sat back down again and held her head in my arms. "I'll never do that to you, Jess. I am not your dad. I'll always stay with you. Till death do us part, remember?"

She wiped way her tears using the towel. "I trust you, Don. But promise me, that this final deal will be it for you. I want you to retire from the business after this."

I leaned back on the couch and sighed. "Come on, Jess, What am I gonna do after this? We still need to earn money. Even if I get the full twenty million, it's not going to last forever. I'm sorry, but I can't give you that kind of guarantee."

Jessica got up with a huff and walked into the bedroom, slamming the door shut behind her. I took the remote control from the coffee table and turned on the flat screen TV that was on the wall. A documentary about some wild animals in Africa started blaring in the living room. Did she expect me to lie to her? I gave her an honest answer. There was no way I could ever work a nine-to-five job ever again. Being in the whole business had changed me. I felt it was for the better. We had a good opportunity and I was going to milk it for as long as I could. If she was so adamant about me leaving what I was doing behind, then maybe she ought to have volunteered to go find a job herself then. She was just being unrealistic and selfish. A feeling came over me that since we were only married for a year, it would still take her some time to adjust to the harsh realities of a dog eat dog world. Perhaps in time she would be more like her mother Crystal and accept the status quo. I was hoping it would be sooner rather than later, so I wouldn't have to keep putting up with this shit lecture about morality every time she had an attack of conscience. If Jessica only knew what the real world was really about, then maybe she wouldn't be such a whiner about it.

19.

It was almost noontime and there were swarms of butterflies churning in my stomach. I had parked the car in front of the hotel driveway as I waited for Leopardi to step through the glass doors. I had spent the entire morning I trying to call Jet to confirm his arrangements were all set but I hadn't received a reply. The night before, he had sent me a text message saying everything was in place and gave me the address on where to take my client to. It was the first time I was doing something this elaborate, and in person, no less. I had a deathly fear that everything was going to fall apart, just when I was so close.

Sweat began to pour down my forehead even though the SUV's air-conditioning system was at full blast. I had already gotten a text message from the client saying he was on his way down to see me. Due to the last minute timing of this scheme, I was not able to check the location in order to confirm it was an actual drug manufacturing plant, or at least, something resembling it. All I had done so far was give general guidelines to Jet on how his people would go ahead and set up the place. The sweat ran down my wrist as I cradled my smartphone on one hand, while glancing nervously at the hotel lobby for any signs of Leopardi. When my phone suddenly began to ring, my sweaty hand was so slippery that I dropped it. The beeping phone fell onto the floor in between my feet.

"Goddamn it!" I twisted sideways while trying to reach down for it. The steering wheel was in my way, but my wet fingers finally felt the plastic top of the phone as I grimaced and finally scooped it up. I immediately answered on the seventh ring. "Hello."

Jet Panupong's reassuring voice was on the other line. "Hey, how is my buddy Don! Sorry I couldn't return your calls earlier, but I was in a golf tournament."

"You made me awfully nervous, Jet. I'm picking up the client now. Is everything all set?"

"Of course, my good friend! Just head over to the gate and the guards will let you through. I gave them the plate number of your car so it won't be a problem."

I tremendous sense of relief washed over me. The nervous heat wave in my body began to subside. "Oh, thank god. Who is the contact person that will show us around once we're in there?"

"The person who will meet you at the entrance is a man named Udom. I have instructed him to help you out in any way possible, there is one small problem though."

Right after he said those words, I heard a tapping noise on the passenger side window. As I snapped my head around, I noticed that Leopardi was just outside of the car, smiling into the tinted glass and waiting for me to unlock the doors.

"The client is here, I gotta go," I said as I punched the button to unlock the doors. "What's the small problem?"

"He doesn't speak English," Jet said. "Anyway, good luck and I'll update you on the child later. Bye for now."

The front passenger door opened and a smiling Leopardi stepped inside. As he slipped into the seat, he turned and held out his hand. "Good morning, Rick! How are you doing today?"

I wiped the sweat off my palm using my pants before I shook his hand. "I'm doing well, thank you. Are you ready to see Apgen's new factory, Tony?"

Leopardi kept on grinning as he closed the car door. "I am very excited to see it! It's such a pity I'm only here for one day, I would love to see more of this country. It seems so exotic!"

I returned his smile as I put the car into drive. "Oh I'm sure we can plan a more elaborate holiday for you the next time you drop by."

He nodded enthusiastically while putting on his seatbelt. "Yes, let's plan it a few weeks after the share offering. I'll have plenty of loose cash afterwards!"

I drove out of the hotel driveway and headed north. The dashboard GPS was already programmed in so all I had to do was to follow the directional prompts. "The drive should take about half an hour. Have you had breakfast?"

"Oh yes," he said. "My wife is still somewhat sleepy from the jet lag, so I ordered room service for the both of us. I don't think she will be going out today, which is a pity since Thailand looks very interesting and it's our first time ever to come here. I will probably go back to bed once this factory tour is over as well, it seems all the traveling and the sightseeing is finally starting to get to me."

"Oh, no problem," I said while the car made it to the highway. "I'll drop you back at the hotel when we're done, unless of course you'd be interested in some lunch."

"Thank you, but that won't be necessary," he said as he glanced in my direction. "You seem to be sweating, Rick-even though the interior of this vehicle is quite cold. Is everything alright?"

"Oh, I was having trouble with the aircon system before you got inside, that's why. But don't worry, it's all good now," I said. Nosy bastard.

"Ah yes, I tried to take a stroll yesterday evening and I had to come back inside the hotel lobby. This place is extremely humid!"

"That it is."

We continued the small talk as we passed through Chatuchak district along the toll road. The GPS was telling me to keep on going northwards as we started driving through the outskirts of the city. Since there was less urbanization at this point, the gridlock had lessened and we were soon moving along light traffic. From the chitchat I soon learned that Leopardi was an Italian national. He had been living in South Africa for almost twenty years, being he was one of the company directors in charge of mining the diamonds from their numerous digs all across the continent.

I didn't like having to be so friendly to him since I preferred not to know anything about the client at all. The less I knew of him as a person, the easier it would be for me to get over the scam I was about to pull on him. I figured that any guilt I felt now would be assuaged later once I saw the cash lying at my feet. When I started thinking about what I would do with all that money, my remorse rapidly began to fade away.

The dashboard positioning system instructed me to turn left into a side road and so I did. Within minutes we were passing through a series of industrial compounds. Empty lots and white painted warehouses cordoned off by chain link fences were on both sides of the road. After a few minutes, I drove up in front of a rusty iron gate. A dark-skinned local wearing casual clothes but clearly carrying a pistol on his hip noticed us and he began to open the gate.

Leopardi had a quizzical look on his face. "Is that man carrying a gun?"

I drove into the compound as the man waved us through. "Oh, don't worry about that. It's standard operating procedure in this country to have armed security guards around."

He nodded. "Oh, I see. We have similar arrangements in South Africa too. Plenty of black troublemakers back in my country."

The guard gestured at me to drive up the far building. I slowly brought the car over to the front of what looked like a clothing factory. The main entrance was open and I could see dozens of people milling about, all locals. Another man soon came out of the opening. He was wearing a sky blue buttoned shirt and he had a white lab smock over it. He smiled and gestured at the empty parking space just to the side. I maneuvered the SUV until I was just inside the yellow lines and turned off the engine. After getting out first I walked over to the man wearing the lab coat.

The man smiled and gave me the wai greeting. "Sawadee kap, Mr. Don?"

I nodded as I returned the wai. "Are you Udom?"

"Chai," he said. That meant yes.

"Okay," I said as I noticed Leopardi getting out of the car. "Where is the drug factory?"

Udom just kept smiling. "Mai khao jai."

It basically meant that he didn't understand. Wonderful. I started gesturing to him. "In there?"

"Chai, chai," he said just as Leopardi walked up to the both of us.

I turned and looked at Leopardi. "Mr. Leopardi, this is Mr. Udom, he is the general manager for Apgen's Thailand manufacturing division."

Leopardi held out his hand. "Please to meet you, Mr. Udom. Sorry for the unexpected field trip, but I truly wanted to see what Apgen's capabilities would be."

I made the wai greeting as an example. "Tony, in Thailand, this is the way they greet people, they don't shake hands."

Leopardi laughed as he copied what I did. "Oh I see, sorry about that."

"Kun poot paa-saa ang-grit bpen mai?" Udom said. From my limited vocabulary, it seemed that he was telling us that he didn't understand any English and was asking if we knew any Thai. Leopardi looked in my direction to see if I would translate for him.

"What Mr. Udom has said is that he welcomes you to Apgen's manufacturing plant. It is still in the startup phase, so you may not be too impressed by it at this stage. But he says don't worry, the manufacturing division will be moving into a larger building the moment the IPO happens," I said.

Leopardi's eyebrows furrowed. "He said all of that? Seems to me he spoke in less than half a dozen words and he formed it as a question too."

I smiled. "Oh, that is the way they speak in Thai. One word has multiple meanings."

Leopardi nodded in amazement. "What an excellent language."

I gestured at Udom to lead us to the manufacturing area. "Shall we proceed?"

Leopardi started moving towards the entrance as he walked side by side with Udom. As I walked behind them I noticed that the price tag was sticking out behind the neck of Udom's collar. I quickened my pace as I wrapped my thumb and forefinger around the tag and pulled it off. Udom suddenly stopped as he turned around with a surprised look on his face. I winked at him while pocketing the tag. With a shrug, he continued on.

The three of us entered the factory floor as Udom began to lead us towards a set of doors at the far end. There were uniformed local women sitting on tables with sewing machines as they busily stitched endless reams of multicolored silk. A large sign along the wall said APGEN PHARMACEUTICALS in bright crimson. I grimaced as we passed through. The logo was correct but the color for the letter fonts should have been blue, not red.

Leopardi slowed his pace until he was walking beside me, his face was now a mask of concern. "Why is the lettering of the sign different than what was on Apgen's website?"

Shit. He did notice it. "Oh it's just that the locals here insisted on making it red. You see, red is considered good luck here."

Leopardi nodded as he pointed to the people working on the factory floor. "I see. Also, are these people here- the ones who are sewing those clothes- are they part of Apgen as well?"

"Oh not really... well sort of," I said. At this point, I was making things up on the fly. "They are part of Apgen's outreach program, you see. They have partnered with a local clothing firm in order to help out disadvantaged women. All the girls you see working out here were abused by either their husbands or parents. It's Apgen's way of giving back to the local community."

Leopardi seemed taken aback at first, but then he looked impressed. "Oh, that is a worthwhile cause, then."

The both of us made it to the far end of the factory as a smiling Udom stood by a set of steel doors. Our guide made a fist and he banged on the door three times. A few seconds later the doors swung open. Just beyond the doors were two men wearing lab smocks; one of them had a pistol holstered around his waist. Leopardi seemed to notice it, but he proceeded inside anyway. I quickly followed.

We ended up inside a narrow corridor as we kept on moving. Another set of doors was at the far end. Udom spoke to the two men by the door for a brief minute before sprinting forward to catch up with us. So Jet must have called up one of his friends and had apparently another factory behind the silk manufacturers. I had been expecting a candy factory but it didn't seem to fit. Why would there be armed men guarding a set of doors at the end of a manufacturing hall? My questions were soon answered as Udom used a pair of keys he had in his pocket to unlock the door at the end of the passageway and we walked through it.

As we stepped into a large room, we could see large, stainless steel vats looming over us. There was a glass partition that separated us from the main area. Leopardi stopped and took a look. From the other side of us were about a dozen men wearing industrial coveralls and respirators. They had thick rubber gloves and galoshes on as they were moving drums and placing liquid chemicals onto steel sheets. There were plenty of plastic pails and hoses on the floor.

Leopardi seemed fascinated as he observed the men moving about their work. "Those pharmaceutical workers seem to be wearing protective clothing for industrial chemicals. I thought when it came to manufacturing medicines, all one had to wear were light clothing like those plastic shower caps or something like that."

I shrugged while standing beside him. "In this country, heavy protective clothing is a government requirement.

They are paranoid about safety here. That's why Apgen chose Thailand."

He seemed satisfied with my answer. "Okay, let's get moving then. I don't want to hold the staff up any longer."

Udom then led us past another door and into the second part of the plant. The room at the other side of us was slightly smaller than the last one. Two workers wearing the same heavy protection gear were scooping out white powder from a stainless steel vat and placing it into a press mold. A third worker was taking out the pressed pills from a second molding unit and placing them into what looked like a stainless steel washing machine with plastic tubes sticking out of it. Leopardi watched in amazement as the powdered pills were being coated with the now familiar pinkish red color. Standing behind him, I did my best to suppress a grimace. That idiot Jet had us touring a yaba factory. The powdered pills were actually methamphetamine, and the coating was a caffeine mix. No wonder this place was situated behind a nondescript clothing factory with armed guards, it was used to hide an illegal drug manufacturing plant in plain sight.

Leopardi smiled. "So that's the Ophemerol pills, is it? Seems to be quite simply made, even though it's a drug that's set to do wonders for the medical establishment."

I nodded. "The secret is in the formula."

Udom then opened the door to the other side. I tapped my client on the shoulder and he turned and followed us to the third room. As we stepped through the door, the three of us could now see that this place was the largest of the three compartmentalized areas of the whole place. This time there was no glass partition. All around us were narrow conveyor belts that sent millions of yaba pills into a large pile at the end of the line. Over a dozen people in casual wear but wearing brand new lab smocks were packaging the pills into plastic packs and placing them into boxes. At the far end of the room were delivery vans being loaded full of pills.

Leopardi placed his hands on his hips as he looked around. "Well, this is definitely a very large operation for a drug that has yet to be officially approved by the American FDA."

Once more I stood beside him. "Well, Apgen wants to make sure that there will be enough supplies of Ophemerol the moment the approval goes public. When Pfizer first announced Viagra way back when, there was an immediate shortage for about six months because of demand. Apgen Pharmaceuticals wants to make sure there will be enough supply since an anti AIDS drug will be a medical necessity."

Leopardi nodded in assent. "Quite right, quite right."

Udom grinned as he ran over to the large pile at the end of the conveyor, grabbed a few pills and ran over to us. He showed the reddish pink pills to us. "Yaba! Yaba!"

Leopardi's eyes widened. "Does he want to give us a sample? I could bring this back to South Africa and show my friends, perhaps they might want to make a last minute investment too if they see the finished product."

The mental image of him being arrested at the airport for a yaba pill and telling the authorities how he got it was too much for me to even think about. I quickly moved forward until I was in front of Leopardi just as he was about to take a couple of pills. "Our host is being too generous and I think you'd better not take one, Tony. Please remember the drug hasn't been officially approved as of yet and the last thing you want to do is to get questioned about pills at the airport," I said while rapidly gesturing at Udom to take the drugs away.

As the idiotic local walked back towards the pile of drugs to return what he took, Leopardi scratched his head. "He said something called yaba. What does yaba mean in English, Rick?"

"It means good luck," I said as I pointed to a door marked EXIT. I needed to get him out of here as quickly as possible. "Shall we head back to the car?"

"Of course," he said as we walked towards the door. "I must say I wasn't expecting the factory to be laid out like this, but it does make sense to manufacture these life saving drugs in great quantities before the big announcement. It seems to be very sound strategy on the part of Apgen."

I got him! "You're absolutely right, Tony."

The walk back to the parked SUV took five minutes. As Leopardi got inside the car, Udom came running up to me. The local started gesturing frantically at me. I sort of figured out what he was trying to convey so I took him just behind the car so Leopardi wouldn't see us. Taking out a wad of cash from my pocket, I counted around fifty thousand baht and gave it to him. Udom made the wai gesture in thanks after he pocketed the cash and started walking back inside.

When I got back in and restarted the car, Leopardi

extended his hand out to me. "Rick, you have gone above and beyond your job in showing me what an excellent investment opportunity this is. I appreciate it. Thank you."

"You're welcome," I said while shaking his hand. "I hope everything was to your satisfaction."

"It was indeed," he said as I drove the car out of the compound. "I knew I could count on your firm even before we started this tour. To be honest with you, I had already given my banker the instructions to send the funds to your corporate account. All you have to do is to confirm the details to me by email since you gave me three banks to choose from."

I tried to suppress my feelings, but I couldn't help grinning from ear to ear. "Welcome aboard, Mr. Leopardi! You will have the email with the banking confirmation by this evening."

Leopardi could see that I was in a very jolly mood and he laughed. "You're most welcome, Rick. It is a pleasure to work with you on this."

We spent the rest of the trip swapping jokes and stories. When we got back to the hotel driveway, it was early afternoon, and I quickly got out of the car. By the time Leopardi made it out of the passenger side, I stood with him near the lobby entrance.

I had my phone out and was fiddling with it. "Tony, does your phone have an internet link right now? My phone seems to be on the blink, it's not getting a wi-fi signal."

Leopardi grinned as he took out his own phone and handed it to me. "Yes, mine does have one, go ahead and use it."

I inputted a few things on his phone using his internet before giving it back to him. It took less than five minutes. "Thanks, that should do the trick. Just sent out an email to my wife, telling her that I'll be back in Hong Kong by this evening."

Leopardi placed the phone back in his pocket. "No problem, Rick. Since you are quite busy, this is where we temporarily say goodbye. I will meet you in Hong Kong in a few month's time. Once again, it was a pleasure to be with you these past few days. Thank you."

I eagerly shook his hand for the third time that day. "No problem, Tony. Welcome aboard. Don't forget to forward me the transfer confirmation once your funds are sent, okay?"

"Of course, once I get that email the funds will be released. Take care, Rick."

"You too. Bye for now."

20.

Night had fallen over the city as I parked the car in front of a slum area near the Klong Toey district. I received a call from Jet not long after the field trip to the yaba factory, and he told me where his father's bodyguard was keeping Waen's daughter. When I got back to the condominium after dropping off Leopardi, Jessica was gone. She left a note saying she would be joining her mother at Doc's house in Singapore. I double checked the GPS console to make sure I would be going to the slums next when I heard a tap on the driver's side window. I lowered the glass panel down, and I was soon staring into Yut's intense black pupils. I nodded and unlocked the passenger doors.

The front passenger door opened and Yut climbed aboard. "You find Waen's daughter?"

I nodded as I locked all the doors of the car. "Yes, Jet told me she is in an apartment complex near the edge of the city. We'll go over there and I'll pick her up alone. Jet already told the guards to expect me, and they are under orders to give the child over to me. So you can just stay in the car."

Yut said nothing as I restarted the engine and drove off towards Bang Khun Thian, west of the river. From what Jet had told me, there was an old apartment complex that was built back in the sixties and was facing a mangrove swamp. Apparently one of the old units in the area was rented by the Panupong family's chief bodyguard, and Jet believed that the young child was being held there. Since Jet had already called ahead, this would be an easy run, more like an errand than anything else. Once I got the child back, I would just head back to Waen and then Yut could go ahead and plan the hit on Jet's older brother and mother.

The drive took about half an hour. I maneuvered the car into a number of side roads, but since this was a less heavily congested area, I didn't have much of a problem. The car's tires crunched over bits of concrete and gravel as I parked the car in a demolished lot that faced the four story apartment complex. There were few functioning streetlights nearby so there were plenty of shadows around us. I could see the distant lights in the water, across the skeletal mangrove forest and the darkened sea beyond.

I turned on the car dome light above us and looked at Yut. "Just stay here, okay? I'm going to get the child and come right back."

Yut didn't answer. He kept looking down towards the floor of the vehicle interior as he took out a Glock pistol from behind his back and checked to see if there was a round in the chamber.

I was taken aback. "Whoa, hey! Put that gun away."

He looked at me. There was a palpable rage in his eyes

that he was barely keeping in check. "I give you five minutes. If you do not come back with girl, I go up there and kill everyone."

I held my palms up in an effort to calm him down. "Look, there's no need for this. Just wait here for ten minutes and I'll be back, okay?"

He looked away but the gun was still in his hands. Thankfully, the weapon was pointing downwards, away from me. "I wait. But not long."

Sensing that I wasn't going to win this argument, I turned, opened the door and got out. My shoes slid a little as I walked along the bits of demolished concrete. After a minute, I walked past the wide open doorway of the building and moved into the dimly lit entrance. A large, undecipherable wooden sign in the Thai language had been attached to the side of the wall by the entryway. There wasn't even a reception area, just two corridors going to the left and to the right. I could see a number of doors had fallen off their rusted hinges, it looked like a number of units in the ground floor had been abandoned a long time ago. The old painted concrete walls had faded to a dim, dusty grey color. In front of me was a landing leading up to a wide staircase. There were no elevators, so I just started trudging up the worn steps. I heard stories about local Thais abandoning old dwellings like this because they were haunted by malevolent ghosts.

When I got up to the second floor landing, I noticed a local man just sitting on the floor in the middle of the corridor. Curiosity getting the better of me, I moved closer to get a better look. The man looked to be between fifty to sixty years old, hairless and full of wrinkles, his bald scalp was polished clean like a mocha colored bowling ball. He wore nothing but a pair of shorts and a dirty, sleeveless t-shirt. His arms and legs were like matchsticks as loose folds of flesh hung limply over the bones. Even though I had come close enough to be noticed, the old man's eyes were glassy and he just stared off into emptiness, it looked like he was completely out of it. Looking around, I noticed a small, flickering candle was set on the floor beside him. A dirty, heavily used syringe and a burnt spoon indicated he was using heroin. Not wanting to get distracted any further, I turned and walked back up the stairs to the third floor of the place.

The corridor which led to the apartment in question had a single, flickering bulb that cast a dim, yellowish light along the dirty passageway. I contemplated pulling out my smartphone and using the flashlight application to get a better view of the door numbers, since all of them had nothing but Thai numberings on the side. I remembered enough to note which one was the right apartment as I finally stood in front of the door in question and knocked a few times. A long minute passed before I heard the sound of a lock being unbolted, and then the door swinging open to reveal a room of white light.

I stepped inside. The living room interior had no furnishings other than an old wooden chair and a small TV by the window. Two local men were in the room with me. They were both wearing t-shirts and jeans. Each one of them had a pistol tucked in their waistbands. One of the men closed the door behind me as soon as I was inside. The TV set had been turned on, but the reception wasn't good as it showed an intermittent local soap opera which was frequently interrupted by a storm of static white snow. This place, just like the rest of the building, was filthy.

"I'm here for the little girl. Dek?" I said, referring to the Thai word for child.

Both men said nothing. After what seemed like an eternity, the second man turned and walked over to where the bedroom was located, knocked twice on the door, then opened it. The other man just kept staring at me. I wasn't sure whether he was thinking about killing me, or just feeling a sense of pity. A few more precious seconds passed, then a light-skinned Thai woman came out of the bedroom carrying a small, sleeping child in her arms. She looked to be middle aged and wore a loose blouse and shorts. The child had pasty white skin, it was obvious the baby was part foreigner. Just as I was about to take the child from her arms, she turned away with a snort and one of the men drew his pistol and pushed me back.

I held my hands up in the air. "What the hell is going on?"

There was a knock on the door. The second man opened it while the first one pointed his gun in my direction. As soon as the door swung open, Jet Panupong stepped inside and surveyed the room with a smile. The way he casually walked into the apartment made it seem like a big joke was being pulled on someone, and I was guessing it was me.

But there was a slight feeling that this could really be something else so I kept my hands up in the air while letting out a big grin. "Jet, so glad to see you! Your man over here pulled his gun on me, could you tell him to put it away? A farang like me is no threat to anyone."

Jet had his hair spiked and the tops were dyed purple. I couldn't tell if the look on his smiling face was that of menacing contempt or if this was just a sort of prank. "Don, how did you like my friend's factory?"

"Well it was a little unexpected, but it turned out okay," I said. "Can I put my hands down now?"

"Not yet," Jet said before turning to the woman and speaking to her in rapid Thai. As the woman took the child back into the bedroom and closed the door, I heard a commotion just beyond the front door of the apartment. It sounded like someone was struggling and in pain out in the corridor. The screaming and shouting out in the passageway soon intensified.

I laughed a little. "Okay, Jet, this was a good joke, but can we get back to business now? I would just like to take the child with me and be on my merry way if that's alright with you."

Jet's demeanor suddenly changed as he walked right up to me and bared his teeth in a menacing grimace. "You're the one playing a joke on me, Don. I thought you were my brother!"

I kept on chuckling to try and ease the tension. "Jet, of course we're brothers, wasn't I in your car when those assassins tried to gun you down? We're partners aren't we?"

He suddenly became calm again as he backed away near the door. "That's what I thought, and then I found out you betrayed me."

I frowned. Oh shit. "What are you talking about, Jet? Why would I betray you?"

"Don't play coy with me, Don," he said. "I found out about the person who you suggested would be doing the killing of my brother and my mother. It seems my chief bodyguard Paradorn knows him very well."

I shook my head. Goddamn it. "I have no idea what you're talking about, Jet."

"Really?" Jet said as he turned and started barking out orders in Thai. Then he gestured at me to follow him outside. As I walked out into the adjoining corridor with him, I noticed four other men out there with us. Paradorn and three of his men all wore tactical vests as they alternately punched and kicked at another man who was lying on the dirty floor of the passageway. Since all three bodyguards had surrounded their victim, I couldn't see who it was so I took a few steps closer. As soon as Paradorn kicked his victim in the face, the wounded man fell forward and I finally saw who it was beneath the dim light. I nearly gasped out loud, but I was able to suppress it at the last minute.

It was Yut. His mangled hands were tied with chicken wire behind his back and his face was a bloody, pulpy mess. Yut's arms had cigarette burns on them and his blood stained shirt was torn in places. He was alternately groaning and gasping for air. As Paradorn kicked him in the back of his spine, Yut moaned as lay on the floor, his one functioning eye starting up at me, as if he was either begging to be saved or asking to be put out of his misery.

Jet stood beside me while the other two guards from the apartment were behind me with guns drawn. "Yut here, he used to work for us," Jet said casually as he paced back and forth in front of his victim who was just lying there, groaning with pain. "I had wondered about who had the knowledge of how to get past my father's bodyguards, who would be good enough to know when to strike. So I put two and two together, Don. It could only have been Yut. And when my bodyguards noticed him sitting in your car, the truth finally revealed itself. Paradorn here told me about the incident with you and another farang named Finny. You see, when Yut executed that other man, Paradorn was with him- I guess you just never noticed. So it seems to me that either you had a hand in my father's murder, or you knew that it was Yut and you lied to my family when they asked you about the shooting."

"Okay, I admit lying to your mother and brother when they asked me if I knew who the suspect in the hotel shooting was," I said. "But I did that because I thought my own life was in danger. I figured it was an inside job so I might have been killed if I told anyone. That's the truth, Jet. I nearly got killed in that shooting too."

He turned to look at me. "But I thought we trusted each other, Don! There's no way a man like Yut here could have missed a kill on you."

"My own loader was killed too," I said. "You know that. If he didn't want to kill me then it was for his own reasons.

I had nothing to do with that shooting."

Jet nodded. "Maybe I believe you on that last part. Yet, the fact that you tried to pass him off as an asset to use against my family without telling me who he really was is inexcusable, Don."

"I made a mistake on that, I admit it. But he was the only one I knew who was capable of doing what you wanted."

Jet shook his head and made a sarcastic laugh. "This must have been one heck of a joke to you, Don. You lied to me in order to make me hire my father's killer- so he could kill the rest of my family. It was a good thing that I went to Paradorn and told him what had happened when I asked him about this little girl they've been keeping here. And you also never told me that the baby belonged to one of my father's concubines. Now I know the whole story."

"The baby isn't your father's though," I said. "The child is—"

"Is Doc's, yes, I know," Jet said. "So this whole mess started because your father in law decided to help out his girlfriend, who also happens to be my father's girlfriend. So what happened then? My father got angry and took the child away and so that bitch told her brother, who happens to be Yut here, my father's top enforcer. Ah, Don, why is our families so fucked up like this? Why can't it just be simple so we can all be happy and make money together?"

"I don't know," I said softly. "I guess it's what happens when you have people like them in your family. I didn't know about the whole story until just recently. I would have told you soon enough, but I needed to get Doc's daughter first."

"Why?"

"I need some sort of leverage against him," I said. "Doc's has been detained in Australia and he thinks I put him in there."

"Did you?"

"No, I think it's somebody else."

"So that's another mystery you need to figure out, Don. Though it's a pity you've run out of time," Jet said as he pulled out a small pistol from behind his waist and fired at the back of Yut's head. The sound of the gunshot reverberated across the corridor. I cried out and jumped up in the air the moment I saw him shoot Yut, but the two men behind me pressed their own guns to the back of my spine to keep me steady.

As Jet put the gun back in his waistband, he shouted orders in Thai once more before switching back to English. "Okay, let's go," he said while pointing to me. "Put him in the back of his own car. Bring the child with us."

One of the men took out a handkerchief and used it to tie my hands behind my back before leading me down the stairs. The last thing I remembered about that old haunted building was the pool of blood that formed around Yut's body, the dim yellow light in the corridor gave it an orange hue.

I sat in the backseat of my car, in between two men who had their guns pointed at me. The woman who held Doc's baby daughter was in the front seat. The little one looked to be around a year old and was sleeping like a log—the gunshot hadn't even awoken her. A third bodyguard was in the driver's seat as he followed Jet's car up ahead of us. I had thought that they were bringing me to a place somewhere in the city but I was again surprised when the two car convoy traveled northwards. The moment we passed by Chatuchak, I already had an inkling as to where we were going. By the time we were waved through the security gate I knew we were back in the same factory compound that I had visited with Leopardi that very morning.

My déjà vu had come full circle as the bodyguard parked my car at the exact same spot that I had placed in just a few hours ago. The two men in between me immediately got out and for a brief moment I was pulled first to the left and then to the right, as both men tried to drag me in their respective directions. One of them finally had the intelligence to allow the other one to do it as I was violently pulled out through the right side of the car. I nearly stumbled onto the concrete pavement and was mere inches away from doing a face plant, but I was able to right myself in the nick of time. The driver spoke to the woman carrying the baby and for some reason she stayed in the front seat. My two handlers formed up behind my back and started pushing me towards the open rear entrance of the factory that was located across the empty lot. Other than the guard at the front gate, the rest of the compound looked deserted. Only a few street lights were functioning as I was prodded to keep on moving until we got to the rear, right where the yaba pill factory was.

There were two nondescript vans being loaded full of boxes at the opening by about half a dozen men. From my vantage point, it looked like an open aircraft hanger, only instead of airplanes being stored in it, the great hall had stainless steel vats and conveyor belts for the yaba pills they were manufacturing on an industrial scale. The dual thugs at my rear kept me going until I was facing Jet and Paradorn, a few feet near the open entryway. Just as I stood less than ten feet away from them, I noticed that I was standing on a thin sheet of blue plastic tarp, it must have measured thirty feet across from all four sides. Not far from the nearby vans were two 100-liter industrial plastic drums, and their tops were open, revealing their emptiness.

So that was it then. This was where I was going to be killed. My knees began to tremble. "Jet, why did you bring me here?"

"Killing a local like Yut was easy in that old building," Jet said. "Since my family knows most of the police, they can just write it off as another lowlife cocksucker getting robbed and killed in an abandoned slum. Maybe the media will even say it was the ghosts who did it. You on the other hand are a farang, a white foreigner. We can't just kill you anywhere and leave your body where people would find it. Your American embassy will send their specialists over and it could make things hot for us. I can't afford any disruptions or suspicions at this time, especially when everyone is talking about my father and how he died."

I was breathing so rapidly I felt like I was hyperventilating. "Jet, please reconsider. You need me! Yut couldn't have pulled that hit off by himself- he must have had support coming from somewhere! Let me help you find out who it was that set up your father and Doc, he's still out there!"

Jet started to giggle. "Don, you underestimate me. I may be young and all that, but I found out about your little trick with Yut. I'm sure with my resources, I will find out who was behind everything in due time—I won't need your help for that. Anyway, there is a part of me that thinks you set it all up, Don. I have a feeling that you were even going to use Yut against me too. You've proven to me that you are a dangerous man and therefore cannot be trusted. It's better for all of us this way if we say goodbye to each other."

My fear gave way to defiance as my temper shot up. "Well, if that's how you feel about me, then fuck you, Jet. You're just another rich boy who grew up on your daddy's money and I'm rooting for whoever set him up because you're gonna be next."

Jet was momentarily taken aback by the insult. Paradorn pulled his pistol out and was just about to shoot me, but Jet pushed him away as he pulled out his own handgun and pointed the barrel to my face. "Goodbye, Don."

The terror gripped me again as I closed my eyes. I hoped that it would be quick because the last thing I wanted to happen was to survive as a quadriplegic or in a brain dead coma, now that would be a fate truly worse than death.

When the shot rang out, I immediately flinched. For a brief second, I thought I was dead, but suddenly more gunfire erupted and I realized that I wasn't hit at all. As I opened my eyes, I saw Jet lying on the plastic tarp. He had been shot through the back of the head and his blood was oozing all over the ground. I quickly dove onto the pavement, bruising my right shoulder as it hit the hard concrete first. People were running all over the place. I saw Paradorn screaming at the top of his lungs while returning fire at a group of black clad men hiding behind the numerous pill making machinery near the back of the factory.

The closest thing to some cover was one of the delivery vans, so I started rolling sideways on the ground like a river log. My hands were bound fast as the loud popping noises of firearms were all around me. After what seemed like an eternity, I had somehow made it beside one of the delivery vans. I crouched up behind the right front wheel as I took a look around. One of the thugs who had been pushing me around tried to make a run back towards where my car was, but he took two bullets in his back and he lay sprawled out on the ground in the middle of the driveway. He twitched for a few seconds and then was still.

Paradorn had made it to the van on the opposite side of me. He knelt down behind the vehicle's engine block, while placing a fresh new magazine into his pistol. Just as he was about to stand up and return fire, he looked in my direction and our eyes briefly met. For a short moment I thought he was going to aim in my direction and finish me off, but instead he gave me a wry smile as he turned and stood up while shooting at the assailants making their way from the interior of the factory. Paradorn managed to fire about a dozen rounds from his handgun before he took a shot in the leg, Then he looked at the wound for a bit before pulling himself back up and using the hood of the van as his support. He kept on firing until his handgun was empty, then he just threw it at them. A split-second later, his head was torn open as multiple shots converged on him and he fell backwards into the concrete floor. The remaining people in Jet's crew soon had their hands up as they were quickly surrounded by helmeted commandos in black body armor.

Hearing footsteps behind me, I stood up and turned around. Standing just a few feet away was Kit and two black clad troopers. Kit was wearing his usual suit, while the two masked commandos beside him pointed their sub-machineguns at me.

"I'd love to raise my hands, but they're tied behind my back," I said.

Kit said something to them in Thai. One of the troopers moved behind me and used a knife to cut my restraints away. As I rubbed my sore wrists, the two troopers moved away towards where the dead bodies were. One of them bent down and started to strip Jet's body for his valuables.

I tried to smile, but the most I could come up with was a grimace. "Thanks, looks like I owe you one."

Kit smiled as he adjusted his glasses. "Oh, it's not me you owe, Mr. Don. It's General Sangsorn. And you owe him considerably more than just one."

I looked around. The commandos were moving about their work briskly as they started to lay out some plastic body bags for Jet and his bodyguards. At the far side of the compound I noticed two more commandos escorting the woman carrying Doc's baby as they headed slowly in our direction. "Looks like you arrived in the nick of time, or maybe you were already here. I'm guessing it's the latter."

"You've been under military surveillance ever since you arrived back in Bangkok, Mr. Don," Kit said. "We also have placed key logging programs in your server and your mobile phone was tapped. We had a tracking device attached to your car as well."

I sighed. "So you've been behind my back the whole time. Figures. What was the general's plan? Was it to save me at the last minute or was that your decision?"

"When our forward observers noticed that Jet Panupong executed one of our assets, we decided to act," he said.

"So the good general did help out Yut when he made the hit on Panupong the elder, then."

"We only provided material assistance, and the second man with him was an off-duty special forces soldier who wanted to earn some extra money," Kit said. "The actual planning and motive was purely Yut's idea. The general saw a possible opportunity and he helped out a little. As far as Jet Panupong goes, he was out of control and needed to be stopped. The fact that he had a stake in an illegal drug manufacturing plant will only strengthen General Sangsorn's conviction to safeguard the country from evil men like him."

I pointed to the vats and pill making materials near the entrance. "And it looks like you've shut down a major competitor in the yaba business too."

Kit let out a wry smile. "Oh, the factory will continue to operate. Under new management, of course."

"So the general takes it all," I said wistfully. "Well good luck to him. Can I bring the baby back to Waen now?"

"There is one last thing you need to do for us," Kit said as he signaled for two commandos to head over to where we were. "I understand that your client is waiting for an email from you in regards to sending him your bank details."

I shook my head in disbelief. "Boy, you guys really are good. You had my car bugged and you were listening to our conversation."

The two commandos stood beside Kit, their weapons on the ready. "Yes, an audio microphone just underneath your vehicle dashboard. Since the general saved your life, he would request that you use his banking. I believe you already have the transfer details in your email."

I took my smartphone out of my pocket and activated it. "I do. You sent it to me a few days ago. It's in my inbox."

"Good," Kit said as he walked over until he stood beside me. "You have two choices. Either you email the client our bank details, or you will be arrested and sentenced as being the partner of a drug manufacturing lab. I can guarantee that your sentence will be life in prison and there is a distinct possibility you will get the death penalty if you choose the latter option. We have very strict laws about illegal drugs here in Thailand, you know."

"Is the good general going to take all of the money that gets sent over?"

Kit blinked a few times. "General Sangsorn will probably let you keep a million, or maybe even more. If you can guarantee him a steady flow of business, then he might just take half and give you back the rest. Please remember that you are alive because of him, so even though the penalty is steep, it's monetary worth is about as much as what your life is, right now."

"Good point," I said as I engaged the internet link on my phone and logged into my email server.

Kit took a step sideways until he was peering just behind my shoulder. "I will of course, personally witness that you do send the email to the client, so as to make sure that you will do as you say."

I let out a deep breath as I copy and pasted the general's banking details into the email and pushed the send button. Less than a second later, the server indicated that the email was sent to Leopardi's inbox. "There you go," I said softly.

Kit then walked around until he faced me again while he pointed to the woman carrying the child. "Good. Now you may go. Take the baby girl with you and enjoy the rest of the evening."

The woman looked scared as I took the sleeping baby from her arms. I turned to look at Kit. "What about this lady, are you going to kill her too?"

Kit just smiled as he signaled the commandos to take the woman away. "Oh no, she was merely an innocent bystander, that is what the news will say. We do not kill them, only the bad people. We are not barbarians."

21.

The last time I stayed over at Doc's house in Singapore was during my honeymoon with Jessica. We stayed in the best hotels and in every one of Doc's hideaways for weeks, just partying and making love from one part of the continent to the other. All that had happened a year ago, but I still remembered it all as if it was yesterday. Those times were the happiest days of my life. For a brief moment, I had forgotten about the crimes, the betrayals and all the pain that life threw at me. The world always had a habit of coming full circle, and now the cycle was about to be completed once more.

I parked the rental car in front of the house and got out, the early afternoon sun at my back. The posh residences of Sentosa Cove was mostly made out of reclaimed land, so the landscape was quite orderly, even the trees were laid out in a uniform line as they hugged the outskirts of the luxury golf course at the opposite side of the street. Doc's house was a modern, two-story glass box with its own private pier at the other end. I had heard that he bought a speedboat a few months back, I guess it was time to see if he really did. After walking up the front steps, I rang the bell of the main door. Seconds later, the entryway was opened by the same old Filipino maid that ushered me in the first time I had been here. She knew who I was, so she merely bowed a little and stepped aside as I walked in.

The walls facing the bay were made of tempered glass and I could see a cruiser speedboat tied up in the adjoining pier, just past the infinity pool that wrapped around the exterior of the house. It looked like a forty-footer, with a cabin that allowed people to rest inside the closed head. The boat's hull was pearly white, with gold and blue racing stripes along its sides. So the greedy bastard did buy it after all.

As the maid closed the door and went back to the kitchen area, I saw the sliding door by the infinity pool open up. Jessica stepped inside the living room and smiled at me as she ran over. Her skin was a little reddish from staying out in the sun all day, and she wore a one piece blue bikini underneath her beige robes. There was nothing to be said as we hugged and kissed each other for several long minutes. The sparkling waters from the bay reflected the sunlight around us with shimmers of mirrored intensity, it was as if we were bathed in the star's golden radiance. The feeling of bliss temporarily overcame my cynicism and for a brief moment, I thought everything was going to be alright, even though my mind was telling me otherwise.

After a while, the kisses and the coddling ended. Jessica's hazel green eyes met mine as our foreheads touched. "I'm sorry, Don," she said softly.

I blinked twice. I thought I was going to cry but my tear

ducts were dry. When it came to betrayal, I had a heart of stone. "I know."

For a brief moment her eyes suddenly lost focus as she realized that I already knew. The rapid movement of her pupils indicated that she wanted to back away, but something held her back and made her stay still. My arms were still around her waist and I felt her body shudder for a second. At least we would be skipping the part about the accused and the denials. I didn't want to stay here any longer than I had to.

There was another long silence as neither of us had anything else to say. It was as if we were waiting for the other to speak first. A long minute passed, and I soon heard the sound of footsteps coming down the stairs. Jessica and I each took a step back as our hands finally let go of each other. I turned to see her mother standing on the landing beside the stairs.

Crystal Bull smiled at me as she walked over to the white leather sofa and sat down. She wore faded denim shorts and a loose white blouse. The filtered sunlight in the living room gave her hair a silver radiance. "Welcome, Don. Would you like to sit down?"

My face was a blank slate. "I'm not sure if I'll stay."

"Sit down anyway," she said. "Beats having to strain my neck looking up at you."

I sat on the opposite sofa as Jessica seated herself on a nearby chair. "It's nice to see you two again," I said. It was time to get it over with.

Jessica wanted to say something, but it looked like there

was a lump in her throat. She let out a brief sob before jumping back up and hurried up the stairs and out of sight.

Crystal crooked an eyebrow while crossing her legs. "She told you?"

I shook my head. "No, I figured it out myself."

Her mother gave me a wrinkled smile. "That's very good, Don. I always knew you were smart. If I could ask, when did you find out?"

I sank back into the cushions and sighed. "The last time I talked with her, when Jess told me her feelings about her dad and me. That was when everything suddenly came together. Very few people knew the fake name on Doc's passport. I thought it was Otis at first since he does everyone's documents, but I soon realized he was happily retired. He wasn't a greedy guy and he had his boys to occupy his mind. After I accepted that fact, the unthinkable suddenly became the improbable. And when General Sangsorn started exerting his influence, the improbable soon morphed into the most likely."

Crystal nodded. "Very good, Don."

"I remembered that party bash with the mayor last year. I was with Jessica the whole night and Doc was with his friends. But he brought you along too. Now that I think about it, you spent the whole time with the general, just sitting by his side and talking to him. Was that when it all started?"

"That's why Paul brought me along," she said. "He wanted me to hang with Kla, because he knew the general had an interest in blond farangs. I wasn't beholden to Paul and he did offer me a lot of money, so I went along with it. Kla took me in a storeroom that night. He was rough at first, but I soon realized he was just a big pussycat. He speaks very good English, by the way."

"Kla?"

"Sangsorn's nickname," Crystal said. "Come on, Don. You've lived in Thailand long enough to know that when a Thai gives you his nickname, it means that you become a close, trusted friend. What Paul didn't know was that I cultivated Sangsorn's attraction for myself, not for him."

I leaned forward. "So you used your influence with the general to help out on the murder of Panupong senior. Tell me, did you plan to have me killed along with him as well?"

"No," she said tersely. "They fucked up on that. I don't think they knew you were even meeting with Panupong that day. It was just a case of bad luck on your part."

"So why did you do it, Crystal? You really hated Doc that much?"

"As soon as Paul started making money in this business, he stopped caring about me. The only reason he kept sending me money was because of Jessica," she said. "He was a piece of shit and he never had any affection for anyone. Even my daughter knew it, he only saw her six times in her entire life before she graduated from Harvard. Six times!"

"But he made it up to you, didn't he? You're here now, right?"

Crystal snorted. "Please. You were the one who spent money to make sure I was having a good time here, not Paul. He only grudgingly gave me the keys to some of his houses on the condition that I stay away from him. It's one thing I appreciate about you, Don. You were always good to me and Jessica. That's the reason why you're not in prison, unlike him."

While we talked, Jessica came back down the stairs. She walked up behind the couch where her mother sat and placed her hands on Crystal's shoulders. "My daddy had to go, Don," she said. "I was trying to convince you to stop what you do, but you just wouldn't listen to me."

I exhaled deeply and looked into my wife's eyes. "You wanted me to stop, yet you conspired with your mom to steal my money. You had all my passwords and you had full access to my emails and servers. I find that very hypocritical, Jess."

Jessica bit her lip. "You had to be taught a lesson, Don. Just like my daddy had to be taught one. I knew my words couldn't convince you to stop your scams, so I did the next logical thing."

I looked down at the marbled flooring. Of all the people who could screw me over, why did it have to be her? "So you betrayed me. Your own husband."

Crystal placed a reassuring hand over her daughter's own. "We did it for your own good, Don. The money is now with General Sangsorn since he sent me a message saying you sent the bank details to your client. I can talk to him, maybe give back some of the money to you."

I shook my head slowly. "Just like that, huh? So what's the deal then?"

"You work for me now," Crystal said. "With that money,

I can help finance your offices. Sangsorn will take care of the banking. All will proceed as before. Don't worry, you'll still be in charge."

"Only this time, instead of Doc, I have you as a boss," I said. Then nothing would change and I wasn't about to let that happen.

"Obviously," Crystal said. "Paul was already doing things behind your back anyway. I can promise you it will be different this time. You and I, we make a wonderful team."

I looked out into the bay. "And if I say no?"

"You don't get the money. It's as simple as that," Crystal said. "I know you've got some emergency cash stashed away somewhere, but how long will that last you? Anyway, you love this game too much to be away from it. Of course, you could always start from the bottom all over again, but why make it hard on yourself when you can take my generous offer?"

I looked up at Jessica. "I thought you said you wanted me to stop? How is this any different?"

My wife glared back at me. "You don't want to stop anyway. So at least this time we have a leash around you. Now I can squeeze you dry if you ever decide to see your stupid Thai girlfriend again!"

My eyes widened as I said nothing while I stared at her mother.

Crystal made a short laugh. "Don't look at me. I didn't tell her. She found out by herself."

"I've known about it for a long time, Don," Jessica said. "I'm not stupid. That's the other reason why I became a part of this."

"Come now, Don," Crystal said. "Everything will be fine. Take a few weeks off, hell- take a month or two off if you need to cool down. I know guys like you. Once the resentment stops, it's back to business again. The last thing Paul did was to give me power of attorney over all of his properties and bank accounts, so I'm working with my own lawyers to take it all. I can even give you that speedboat sitting out there. It's a man's toy and I wouldn't know what to do with it."

I stood up. "How do I know you won't betray me again?"

"You'll just have to trust us," Crystal said. "As long as you behave, I don't foresee any problems at all."

"I still love you, Don," Jessica said. "But I need you to stop your freewheeling ways and listen to me from now on. I know we can work this out. I'm really sorry, but I had to do this to you."

I turned around and headed towards the door.

Jessica's voice started to tremble. "Don, I still love you, you know that don't you?"

I placed my hand on the door knob and turned it. As I got the door open, I twisted my head and looked back at my wife. "And I love you, Jess."

Jessica's voice cracked. She was crying. "Don, come back! Please!"

Crystal's calm voice tried to sooth her daughter. "Let him go. All men need some time to themselves. Don't worry, he'll be back. We've got his money."

I moved past the entryway and closed the front door behind me. As I walked down the marbled landing, I took out a new smartphone from my pants pocket. I activated the internet application and checked my backup email server. The first thing on my inbox was a notification. It confirmed the money had hit the designated bank. What they didn't know was I already sent the bank details to Leopardi that very day we toured the yaba factory when I used my client's own phone just outside of the car while we said goodbye to each other. I also disabled my email server so the whale never got the email with Sangsorn's bank details. This meant that the twenty million was now in the Philippines, in a bank account only I had access to.

As I walked up to the driver's side of the car I rented, I checked the local time on my phone. It was just after two in the afternoon. It meant that Waen had already crossed the border into Cambodia with Doc's baby. I had Otis issue her with a fake Thai passport so she could get out of the country through the land crossing. All I had to do now was to get her to the Philippines and find a way to contact my father in law. With his other daughter in my hands and the truth about who really betrayed him, Doc would have no choice but to ask me for help.

In the end, I still wasn't sure about Jessica. Whether we would get back together would be a decision that would be made some time in the future. Right now there was too much hurt in me to even think about it. The basic questions began to tumble in my mind. Could I ever trust her again? What's the point of being with someone you can't trust? Would I ever be able to get her away from her mother's influence? When it came down to it, it really wasn't about the money, it was about loyalty and being true to one another. I still loved her, but the trust part had been shattered, and that was the most important part of all.

I got into the car and drove off towards downtown Singapore. I needed a drink.

J Triptych Publishing

Spellbinding literary entertainment
at an affordable price!

Crime Thrillers:

The Expatriate Underworld Series: John Triptych's gritty, no-holds barred exploration of South East Asia's expatriate underworld, a sordid society in which one man is determined to succeed at any cost. Recommended for mature readers.

The Opener (Book 1)
The Loader (Book 2)

The Amoralist Series: John Triptych returns to the thriller genre with a new series that focuses on a highly unique assassin who travels the world for all manner of whims and murder.

A Man of Leisure (Book 1)
Savage Wanderings (Book 2)

Science Fiction and Mythology:

Wrath of the Old Gods Series: The entire world is thrown into turmoil as the ancient gods of myth and legend return. An epic, post-apocalyptic series with multiple characters, mythical beings, and world spanning adventures.

The Glooming (Book 1)
Canticum Tenebris (Book 2)
A World Darkly (Book 3)
And more to come!

Wrath of the Old Gods Young Adult Series: A complete and standalone series for young adults that ties in with the main Wrath of the Old Gods series. This trilogy centers on a young British boy and of his quest to save his country from supernatural forces.

Pagan Apocalypse (Book 1.5)
The Fomorians (Book 2.5)
Eye of Balor (Book 3.5)

Look for these books in e-book and paperback formats via the internet or by request at your local bookstore!